MAGGIE'S WAY

Montana Bound Series Book 1

LINDA BRADLEY

SOUL MATE PUBLISHING

New York

MAGGIE'S WAY

Copyright©2015

LINDA BRADLEY

Cover Design by Syneca Featherstone

This book is a work of fiction. The names, characters, places, and incidents are the products of the author's imagination or are used fictitiously. Any resemblance to actual events, business establishments, locales, or persons, living or dead, is entirely coincidental.

Published in the United States of America by
Soul Mate Publishing
P.O. Box 24
Macedon, New York, 14502

ISBN: 978-1-61935-956-7

ebook ISBN: 978-1-61935-836-2

www.SoulMatePublishing.com

The publisher does not have any control over and does not assume any responsibility for author or third-party websites or their content.

For my mom, Marjorie Jean,

and in loving memory of my dad,

Byron Thomas.

Acknowledgements

When Maggie and Chloe came to life, so did I. It was the year I found my voice, determined to share their story. It was the year I battled cancer, began a new marriage, and discovered that with a little faith dreams can come true. Thank you to my excellent team at the Van Eslander Cancer Center in Grosse Pointe Woods, Michigan. Your care and dedication gave me the gift of time thus allowing me to pursue this endeavor that called to me.

Thank you to Debby Gilbert for connecting with my pitch and recognizing that Maggie's Way would speak to readers. I am grateful for your support and guidance in this new adventure.

Thank you to Jane Porter and Lori Nelson Spielman for reading the unedited version of this story. You are true inspirations. Jane, I've followed you since The Frog Prince and knew then you'd be a driving force not only in my world, but the literary world, too. Lori, when dear friend, Annette Shauver told me about The Life List, who knew that our paths would cross that very day. You are both such dedicated and talented women with big hearts and open arms. Thank you for embracing me.

Thank you to the Greater Detroit Chapter of RWA for inspiring me to work hard, write often, and hone my craft. I will forever miss our beloved Patti Shenberger, as she was a strong voice in my head telling me to just write the damn book.

Thank you to my LOFT ladies and my colleagues at school. Your encouragement and friendship means the world. Liz Parthum, thank you for telling me that I could take something so vanilla, turn it into a sundae with whipped cream, and a cherry on top. Pam McCarthy, I love you for reading every word, discussing story lines, encouraging me to write the next book, and the next, and cheering me on every step of the way. Kimberly Pachy, your love for reading and gentle nudging pushed me to believe in myself. Kristie O'Callaghan, your bright eyes and excitement for the next book let me know I was on the right track.

And last, but not least, thank you to my family. To my husband, Scott Hammond, thank you for being by my side, having my back, supporting my dreams, and understanding the need to live life creatively. To my sons, Trevor and Griffin, you keep me on my toes, make me laugh, love me unconditionally, and inspire me. For that, I am forever thankful. To my mom, Jean Bradley, thank you for reading all my work. Mommas are sacred, and your love has been constant and strong. You're the first person I share good news with and the last person on my mind before I close my eyes under the silvery moon, no matter where I am.

I love you all!

Linda

Chapter 1

Time burrowed its way into the tiny cracks of my existence, wedging into the nooks and crannies like sand between my toes on a hot summer day at the beach. Taunted by the past, I knew I would have married Beckett Littleton anyway. Being middle-aged brought unexpected changes, but in my book, middle-aged didn't mean middle of the road even if I did feel like a confused squirrel darting across four lanes of oncoming traffic.

A lock of strawberry-blond hair grazed my cheek as I sighed with exasperation. I twirled and slid my wedding band over my bony knuckle to finger the metal as if it could turn back time, back to the day when I gazed into Beckett's eyes, when we vowed to stay by each other's side, for better, for worse, for richer or poorer.

I snickered at the thought of irreconcilable differences. My ring clanked against the tempered glass tabletop next to my chaise lounge. It was time to give up the charade. We hadn't been together for months. I quit counting the days since my diagnosis of breast cancer.

Ribbons of sunlight washed over the backyard. Glad for summer, I relished the school break and time alone to heal, even if I had been instructed to stay in the shade per doctor's orders. Gentle breezes tickled my nose with the scent of fresh-clipped grass. My mind wandered, mulling over our division, to relive Beckett's truth. Why didn't I see it? How? When? Maybe this was Beckett's weird, midlife crisis. If not, it was surely the beginning of my own.

Supported by the pillow on my patio chaise lounge, the cool fabric against my neck in the midday Michigan heat brought relief. I breathed deeply, contemplating the future.

Time morphed my life even if I didn't drag my feet. Ticking hands beat steady, keeping a calm pace even on hectic days. My grandmother's grandfather clock reminded me of this on sleepless nights now that I slept alone. Time pushed me forward like that impatient person behind me in grocery store checkout, their cart nipping at my heels. I didn't have the energy for *forward*. I opened my eyes, took my wedding ring from the table, thought about putting it back on, but then decided not to.

Purple petunias cascaded over the edges of oversized clay pots lining my patio. Hanging baskets of red geraniums reminded me of last spring when Beckett and I spent hours landscaping after purchasing an abundance of flowers at Eastern Market, so many, the hatch to my Equinox barely shut. Thankful for the privacy fence that hides me, I am captivated by the little garden of tomatoes, parsley, beans, and strawberries. The tall fence keeps out cats that hunt in the vacant yard next door along with nosy neighbors.

When the Murphy family lost their home a year ago, I thanked God for our two incomes. Worry scraped the bottom of my stomach now that I was living on a teacher's salary in an upscale neighborhood, thanks to Beckett. He assured me I wouldn't lose the house, but without him or Bradley it didn't seem much like home anymore.

The gate to the privacy fence creaked.

Sitting up, I glanced around to see who was there. The quick movement tugged at my left breast. "Hello?" I wasn't expecting anyone today. Rays of sun peeked out from behind the clouds and I shaded my eyes trying to recognize the visitor. "Who's there?"

"Can you play? Anybody here that can play?" a youthful voice rang out.

I leaned closer to see the girl's face. She was short and resembled one of the students from my classroom. My eye twitched. "Excuse me?"

"Hi! I'm Chloe McIntyre. I live next door. Do you live here, lady?"

Chloe shoved her hands into her pockets. She squinted to see me better. The corner of my mouth twitched at the sight of her tussled pixie haircut and freckled face. "Yes, I do." Perplexed, I twiddled my thumbs. Again, I'd missed something. When was there a SOLD sign in front of the Murphy house? I didn't see anyone move in, but then again, I'd been so self-centered lately, I probably would have missed a parade of elephants parading down the street.

"Nice to meet you, Chloe. My name is Maggie Littleton," I heard myself say and decided I should go back to my maiden name, Abernathy. "Maggie Abernathy," I mumbled, liking the way it sounded. I focused my attention back to the little girl standing before me. She chewed at her thumb.

"You got any kids here?" she asked as she ripped off a hangnail on her left hand. "Ouch, that kind of hurt."

My smile grew as Chloe peeked around the stone column at the edge of my patio. She waltzed by and my gaze followed her. I repositioned myself in my chaise lounge as she made herself comfortable next to me. She touched the cover of my Jane Porter novel.

"Personally, I think reading's overrated."

Quietly I watched Chloe pick up the book while I secretly wished the author would write me into one of her stories with a happy ending. Cowboy or surfer, I fantasized. Maybe both. Again, middle-aged didn't signify middle of the road and my state-of-mind needed an overhaul.

"There aren't any pictures," Chloe noted, sounding disappointed.

The skin on the bridge of her nose wrinkled, and I smiled. "No, no there aren't."

"I prefer books with lots of pictures. The less words, the better. You don't need a whole lot of hard words to get your point across. A few easy words will do just fine." Chloe exhaled and crossed her dangling feet.

I grinned at the knots in the shoelaces of her Converse pink high-tops. Bradley'd had black high-tops at that age.

"You got any kids here?" she chirped as she wiggled in the chair, picking at her knee.

I shifted my chaise so I could see her better. "I have a son, but he's not here right now." I wondered who cut her choppy dirty-blond hair, evidently someone with an unsteady hand or a drinking problem.

"What's your son's name?" she asked, crossing her legs.

"Bradley. He's twenty-two." As the words left my mouth, the corners of her lips drooped. "Sorry, no one your age." I leaned back in my chair, closed my eyes to the sun peeking over the umbrella's edge, and took a deep breath knowing that my chest was fully covered, doctor's orders. Bradley was our miracle. Beckett and I were told we couldn't conceive, but by some phenomenon, Bradley was our gift, the one thing that'd held us together.

The scraping of chair legs across the cement pierced my ears.

"Where's he at?" Chloe continued.

I turned my head in her direction, scrutinizing her proximity to me, her breath now warm on my cheek.

"My dad makes that face, too." Chloe paused. "Dad says, I shouldn't use a preposition at the end of a sentence." She smiled. "Not sure what that is, but whatever."

I closed my eyes and leaned my head back. "He's right, you shouldn't," I mumbled. "Smart man."

"How old are you?" she asked.

My toes curled at the question. I sat quietly thinking she just might go away if I ignored her. Another warm breath brushed my earlobe. I opened one eye and peered in her direction then jerked away from the back of the chaise lounge cushion. "Jesus," I yelped. I was nose-to-nose with my uninvited guest, so close I could count her freckles, the number of missing teeth, and see her blue tongue as she cackled with glee. I caught my breath then leaned back, keeping both eyes open. "Did your dad also tell you it's not polite to ask a person their age?"

"Yeah, but I like to know. It lets me know what I am up against." Chloe shifted her weight and leaned on one elbow. "This is a nice backyard. I like the flowers and the garden." She sighed. "I'm seven. It's different when you're a kid. Kids are proud of their age. Grown-ups don't think that way."

"You got that right." I smiled at her. Chloe was on to something. With her front tooth gone, her smile reminded me of a jack-o-lantern. The only thing missing was the glowing candle. How I missed the days of playing Tooth Fairy and carving pumpkins with Bradley.

Chloe stood, whirled around, and plopped down at the end of my chair. "Come on," she begged. "Just tell me."

I swung my legs off the chaise lounge. The cement was hot against the soles of my feet. "Maybe another day." I secretly scolded myself for opening the door to another visit. This was summer and I was supposed to be home recuperating from a year of seven-year-olds and breast cancer. I did not sign up for summer school. The regular school year was taxing enough after twenty-six years. "I think I hear your dad calling you."

"He's not home," she chirped.

"Listen again." I pointed toward the Murphy home. "You live over there, right?" I raised an eyebrow.

"Yup."

"Maybe it's your mom calling your name," I said.

"Not possible," she purred with a shake of her head.

"Why not?" I asked as I slid my feet into my flip-flops.

Chloe crossed her legs then her arms. "Because I don't have a mom."

A strand of hair fell over my cheekbone and stuck to my lip. I blew it away then inspected the scowl on Chloe's face. "Oh," I mouthed as her eyes flickered with disgust.

"My mom lives in California," she informed me.

"That's tough," I said, thinking that I wasn't the only one with problems. I should remember that. I glanced toward the gate. There was no sign of Charlie Brown's friend Lucy sitting behind a stand saying that the psychologist was in. After calculating inflation, I considered asking Chloe for a dollar. I heard Lucy's gruff voice in my head. It was hard to distinguish who had the more sarcastic attitude.

Chloe picked at her ear and sighed.

"Sure, you don't have any kids my age?" she inquired with doubting eyes.

"Nope."

"Know any?"

"Not around here," I answered in a short breath.

"Too bad for me," she mumbled. "This is gonna be a long summer!"

"You're telling me," I added.

Chloe's shoulders slumped forward and she proceeded to tell me knock-knock jokes.

Chapter 2

With my hands pressed against the massive door, gawking, I stood on my tiptoes spying through the peephole. Beckett twiddled his fingers with nervous expression as he waited on the porch for me. He seemed slimmer in his tennis clothes. His hair cut shorter than normal, I wondered if it was because there was someone special he was trying to impress. I knew it wasn't me. I was the wrong gender. My heart tore open just a little bit knowing he struggled, too, in many ways I didn't understand.

I turned the brass knob, the shining surface cool against my clammy palm. The door stuck, and I yanked hard to jar it loose.

"Hey there," I said, trying to act cool and collected.

Beckett opened the creaky wooden screen door and took three steps over the threshold then kissed me on the cheek. The overly kind gesture made me uncomfortable. My chest tightened and I stuttered at the simplest of greetings. I hoped he wasn't in the mood for probing into my personal life, in his usual way. Part of me wanted to yell at him, be dramatic tell him that my heart was shattered into a million pieces, although the pain had lessened to a dull throb quite some time ago. What lingered between us was a truth we both were getting used to.

"I packed your books. They're right there." I pointed to a cardboard box at the bottom of the stairs. "I can do a lot with all the shelf room now that you're taking them to your place," I stammered not caring one way or another. I had bigger questions on my mind. My stomach flipped as I held the doorknob to steady myself. "Why did you tell me in a restaurant that you were leaving me?" This inquiry probably too late, but I had been too chicken to ask before. It wasn't his style. "That wasn't fair."

His eyes filled with remorse, and I wondered how the hell he could pull this off without making me want to kill him. He reached to hold my hands.

"It wasn't fair. I know. Nothing about this is fair to you or Bradley," Beckett explained. "It's taken me a long time just to figure it out myself. I was a coward. I thought if we were in public, it might go better. Bad choice, I know," he added as he fidgeted.

I slid my hands away from his as he tried to console me. That was Beckett, always trying to make things right. "Nothing is going to make this better." I swallowed hard and noted that his temples had grayed since I last saw him.

Beckett lowered his head. "I'm sorry," he muttered, "I will make it up to you."

Stepping back, I crossed my arms, knowing he could not perform such a miracle. I found it hard to breathe.

"You look pretty today. You should wear your hair down all the time." Beckett picked up his box, pivoted, and kicked open the screen door. "I know I hurt you. I'm sorry, Maggie, so sorry. I'll be in touch."

My throat tightened. I didn't know I even had any tears left. "Sure," I answered, trying to match his graciousness. He couldn't help being that way. That was Beckett. Being angry with him was difficult even if he did end our marriage. It was easier to blame myself for ignoring my instincts and playing the game. Beckett had finally understood who he was, now I was left to my own devices to figure out who I was going to be.

Beckett meandered down the driveway while I stood in the doorway watching the only man I had ever loved leave and pack the last box of his belongings into his Sea Glass

Pearl Toyota Prius. "I should have known," I muttered to myself in disgust with a snicker. "Shit, this is like a bad episode of *Will and Grace*."

My gay ex-husband drove away, calm and poised, while I wondered how he managed being married to me for twenty-three years.

"You shouldn't swear. It's a bad habit."

I stepped onto the porch, curious to see where Chloe's voice came from and how much she had overheard. I leaned onto the thick railing and peeked into the bushes.

Chloe smiled up at me, and the hair on my neck prickled.

"My dad says girls shouldn't swear. If you really want to make someone mad, end a sentence with a preposition," she chirped as she collected a tiny mound of rocks in the palm of her hand and dropped them into a purple plastic pouch, one-by-one.

"Be careful of the impatiens," I said as she dragged her purple-stuffed cat on a leash through my immaculate garden. I sucked in as much air possible, hoping it would stifle harsh words. "That's some stuffed animal." When Chloe took her last step out of my bed of flowers, I cringed at the matted down ground cover.

"Don't worry, they'll pop right back up. That's what my dad says."

"Of course," I muttered as I rolled my eyes in disbelief that she even had a father. It had been two days and I hadn't seen him yet, but then again I wasn't looking either. I sat on the porch swing, then checked the chains to make sure they were still securely anchored to the porch ceiling.

Chloe joined me. "Is Bradley here?"

"That was nice of you to remember his name, but like I said, he's in Boston. Remember? He won't be coming home for a long time."

Chloe tapped the side of her head. "I may not remember facts very easily, but I am good at names." She yanked on the cord attached to her stuffed cat. "Oops. Didn't mean for him to land there."

I stopped the sway of the swing as she scooted over to pluck the dirty critter from my lap. I swallowed. "It's okay," I said as I wiped away fresh soil that belonged in the flowerbed, not on me.

"Dad says I can't have a pet." Chloe stroked the stuffed cat's head. "That's why I have Voodoo."

My eyebrow lifted toward the heavens at the sound of the name. Chloe's purple matted one-eyed cat stared at me.

"He goes everywhere with me." Chloe hugged him hard. "He's my best friend. Who was that guy and why was he trying so hard to be nice to you?" Chloe dug some rocks out of her pocket and tossed them back into the bushes. "What wasn't *fair*? My dad says life's not fair. I hate that," she sputtered.

"Of course he says that." I rubbed my right temple trying to stop the pulsating. I reminded myself I didn't have to explain anything to anybody, especially a seven-year-old girl. I studied her from head-to-toe. Chloe appeared unscathed by my stare. "Where is your dad, anyway?" I asked.

"Work. He works a lot. He's a doctor. A pediatrician. He takes care of kids. That's how come he knows so much."

Chloe crossed her ankles. "My mom left my dad. They got a divorce. She said she needed to find herself. She moved to Hollywood to be a model and we moved here, next to you."

"So, who watches you when he's not home?" I glanced over my shoulder expecting to see some caring adult come check on her.

"Nanny Nora. She's new. The last one quit." Chloe shrugged.

"Hmmm. Wonder why?" I jested.

"Guess it just didn't work out," Chloe said, picking at her thumb. "Kind of like that thing with you and that guy. Sorry."

She patted my knee. Her touch felt warm beneath the smudges of dirt. "You want some ice cream?" I asked.

Chloe jumped up, dragging Voodoo behind her. "Yeah."

"Maybe you should wait here while I go inside," I suggested.

Chloe sat back down on the swing. The chains jerked as she bounced. "How do you make this thing go?"

I held the screen door open. "On second thought, maybe you should just come in."

"Can Voodoo come, too?"

"Yes, Voodoo can come, too." The corners of my mouth curled up as Chloe's eyes beamed. That purple mangy creature was a lifeline. "So, your mom had to find herself, huh?"

"Yup. She says she'll let me visit, but I don't know when. She hasn't called in a long time. She must be busy making commercials or something." Chloe's eyes widened as she entered the foyer. "Wow, this is a nice house. You need more furniture though."

She was right. I needed more furniture. I needed more than that. "Come this way, Inspector Clouseau," I said in a French accent as I motioned for her to follow me. "Are you sure it's okay that you're here?"

"I can call Nanny Nora if it will make you feel better," Chloe said.

I handed her the cordless phone. She didn't take it.

"Nobody has a landline anymore. Don't you have a cell?" she scoffed.

I poked the phone in her direction. "Just dial," I ordered, listening to her conversation as I organized the vanilla ice cream, chocolate, and bananas on the counter. I peered over my shoulder as Chloe paced back and forth answering yes and no. With her head down and methodic steps, Voodoo followed her every movement.

When she was done speaking, she handed the phone back to me. "It's all good. Nanny Nora just said don't eat too much."

"Doesn't she want to come over and meet me?" I questioned.

"Guess not."

"Nice." I shook my head with disapproval. When Bradley was young I had fifty million questions and he never went anywhere without me meeting his friends' parents. I'm sure I embarrassed him with my over-protective demeanor.

Chloe smiled as she put Voodoo on one of the stools at the kitchen counter. "You sit here. Be good, or Maggie might not ask you back."

I smirked as she waggled her finger at her matted, purple pet. "I'm having a banana split. How does that sound?"

"Great. Do you have peanuts?"

"I almost forgot," I said, winking at her. "If my head wasn't attached, I just might lose it." Opening the cupboard, I rummaged in the cans until I found a half-eaten container of Spanish Peanuts. "Thank goodness my mom went shopping," I said with my head buried in the refrigerator searching for the can of whipped cream I knew was in there. All the sundae ingredients were lined up on the counter. "Are you allergic to any of this stuff?" If Nanny Nora wasn't going to investigate, I was.

Chloe settled into the seat next to Voodoo. She crossed her arms on the counter, licked her lips, and said, "Nope!"

"Me neither." I narrowed my eyes as my stare met hers begging the unspoken affirmation.

"I'm sure, I'm not allergic. Why would I eat something that could send me to the hospital or kill me? I'm sure. Trust me."

I took a deep breath then said, "I can think of a lot of reasons, actually." I picked up the scoop and got to work after deciding to trust the rug rat.

"Hey, Maggie."

"Yeah," I answered, licking ice cream from my fingers.

"You need some pictures to go on all these nails you have in the wall."

I added extra chocolate to my bowl. I could use the calories today. Finally, I felt like pigging out. "Yup." Yet again, I reminded myself that I didn't need to explain to a meddling seven-year-old that my husband moved out and took just a little less than half of *our* things with him.

I sat bundled in my cotton throw on the back patio reading my book. The sun was going down and my eyelids were heavy. I hadn't expected to have so much fun with Chloe. Confined within my compound, I was content. Bradley was settled in Boston for his summer internship. Beckett had settled in a trendy condo in downtown Detroit near Wayne State, while I managed an empty house that was too big for one person.

Voices from Chloe's yard caught my attention. Wanting to hear more, I carefully put my book down, then tiptoed to the fence pretending I needed to check the tomatoes, making sure my gate was closed. I heard Chloe's reasoning voice. "Dad, it was just a little ice cream. It's not like we spent the day ending our sentences with prepositions or swearing. She's not like that. She was just being nice. Nanny Nora said it was all right."

"She—" her father started in a deep voice.

"Her name is Maggie," Chloe interrupted.

There was a pause. I froze, afraid they might hear me as I eavesdropped like a seven-year-old myself. It was hard not to, especially after I heard my name.

"Ever since Mom left, you are nothing but a pooh-pooh head!" Chloe shouted.

Chloe's words teetered on the cusp of belligerent. Drawing the throw around my shoulders tighter, I plucked a medium-sized ripe tomato from the vine, then another one, and then another one. I hadn't noticed the tomatoes ripen. I scolded myself for not paying attention, which seemed like a reoccurring problem. I watered, even fertilized, but didn't realize early plump, red tomatoes were ready to harvest. *I have got to start paying attention.*

I used the bottom of my shirt to make a basket. There were enough tomatoes to make spaghetti sauce. *Bradley loves my spaghetti sauce.* I beamed when Bradley's face filled in my mind.

"I wish you were here," I said to the sky, wishing he would hear my words in the wind.

With my bounty nestled in my homemade pouch, I got up from my knees. Out of nowhere, something landed on my head. I swatted it away. "Shit, shit, shit," I shouted, hopping around. "I hate flying things." The fireflies were my friends, but this thing was huge. When I realized it wasn't a bug, bird or even a bat, I eyed my gorgeous, scattered tomatoes upon the ground. Voodoo was smack dab in the middle of the chaos.

The fence gate flew open. "Voodoo, Voodoo, are you okay?"

Chloe's face fell when she noticed his twisted body amongst the mess. Behind her stood a tall, broad-shouldered man that I assumed was her elusive father. I tried to keep the corners of my mouth from tugging downward.

"This is that lady, Dad." Chloe's disgruntled words rolled off her tongue with ease. "Her name is Maggie," she added as she ran to Voodoo's aide.

I peered in disgust at the mess before me. Chloe's sad face met my stare.

"My dad says girls shouldn't swear."

I frowned at her. "So, you said." I looked her father square in the eyes. His steely glare didn't startle me. I had seen it all too many times on the face of an upset parent across the conference table. He stepped closer then took Chloe's hand and hauled her up from the ground.

"Guess you heard our conversation," he mumbled, giving Chloe the stink eye.

"Pretty clearly," I quickly replied, tucking my hair back into place.

"I'm John McIntyre. We moved in last week."

I nodded, trying to shake off the anger, wondering when he

planned on apologizing. "Yup. And as you know I'm Maggie, Maggie Littleton, I mean Abernathy, the ice-cream lady."

Chloe carefully placed Voodoo down in the grass and petted his head. "Now be good, Voodoo, no more flying for you today. Although that wouldn't have happened if my daddy wouldn't have picked me up so fast."

I inspected Chloe's father as he watched her console Voodoo. What was behind his stern emerald eyes? They were cold and distant. I used my shirt to make a basket for my tomatoes. I picked them up one-by-one, until I felt his eyes upon me.

Chloe yanked on Voodoo's string and Voodoo followed as she walked away. He bumped along the ground like a true soldier.

"I don't want my daughter over here all the time. She has a nanny," he said quietly.

My back stiffened at his abrupt tone. Maybe it was the pent-up anger toward Beckett or a late response to the phone call I received from the doctor's office two days ago. "I didn't invite her over." I peered over his left shoulder to make sure Chloe was out of earshot. He was tall. I had to stand on my tippy toes to see past him. "Your daughter just shows up, and as far as your nanny goes, what nanny in their right mind doesn't meet the adult that your child is hanging out with?" My eyes narrowed as the harsh words left my lips.

Chloe's father turned his back, started to leave, but stopped, then he faced me. He shook his head in only what I can imagine was a gesture of pure repulsion.

My shoulders slumped forward when I realized he was not coming back. With a shirt full of tomatoes I walked back to the patio, straight inside through the French doors and into *my* kitchen, alone, no thanks to Beckett. I kicked the door shut behind me.

"Who was that guy? What a jerk? Maybe he should find a day care." I let the tomatoes roll across the counter as I made a ramp with my shirt. One spun off the counter. I fumbled for it. "Shit," I grumbled. The tomato split open as it hit the floor.

"Maybe you should give people the benefit of the doubt?"

I glanced up to see my mother with a cup of coffee in her hand standing over me. "Couldn't you at least warn me when you are coming over?" I said hastily. The muscles in my chest tightened. My breast ached. "That guy *is* a jerk."

"I saw the whole thing. Quite entertaining," Mom said with a smirk. "What's going on here? I go away for six weeks with my travel companions and your furniture goes missing. Apparently, someone has stolen half of the pictures and artwork from the walls."

My stomach fell as I saw Mom's arched eyebrow. It was time to confess to at least one of my secrets.

"Shit, shit, shit," I continued to sputter as I cleaned up tomato guts from the cold white tile Beckett had chosen. His interior decorating skills were impeccable, but his ability to find function and flare this time had failed. "Damn you, Beckett." I said through clenched my teeth.

"I'll just make myself comfortable while you get yourself together." My mother pulled out the same stool Chloe had sat on just hours earlier. "Oh! Better wipe this off before I sit down. Sticky!"

I handed her the sponge. "Go for it." I scrambled for a pot and the ingredients I needed to make spaghetti sauce. "Better do this now before I lose the ambition." I fake-smiled at my mother. I knew I had to keep my hands busy if we were going to have this conversation. I could tell by the look in her eye she wasn't leaving until we did.

"Marjorie Jean, what is this all about? What are you hiding?" She sprinkled sugar in her cup, and I noticed that a few granules dotted the black granite countertop. She stirred her coffee and sipped.

The hair pricked at the nape of my neck as I felt her stare bore holes into the back of my head. I focused on catching my breath and ignoring my stinging eyes as I chopped sweet onion into neat little cubes. When I dropped them into the pan, the pieces sizzled in the hot oil. Hot steam masked my anguish. I turned the heat down as I stirred in salt, a pinch of sugar, and minced garlic. "What's there to tell? We are redecorating."

"Ha," she scoffed. "Beckett would never let this place look like this even if that were true. He's a neat freak. Furnishings are missing everywhere. You can tell me you're selling off things to support a drug habit or you can tell me the truth."

"How long have you been here, *Glad Abernathy*?" I stopped stirring long enough to peer over my shoulder at her, knowing I should have told her months ago that Beckett and I were divorcing.

"Now, now. No need to take a tone." She snickered. "Long enough to have a good look around."

I reached over, picked up three tomatoes from the counter, and tossed them in the pot. Then I added the rest and smashed them down with my potato masher. "Got any good ideas?"

"You're thinner, what's the mystery? You need to put some meat on your bones."

"You're not any bigger than I am. I ate a sundae today." I added a pinch of sugar, basil, and oregano before putting the lid on to simmer the sauce, knowing half my ice cream went down the disposal before facing my mother. "Beckett is having a midlife crisis. He's moved out." My chest tightened. I couldn't bear to tell her why. "He's decided he wants a new life and that doesn't include living with me anymore." I stayed steady, realizing my wedding band was still outside on the table. "He'll be back," I said with certainty, knowing it was a lie.

"Where's he gone?" Mom asked.

"He's got a place downtown. He says it's near work and will save wear and tear." I peeked into the pot. Little red bubbles percolated so I reduced the heat, put the lid on, and set the timer on the microwave. Tomorrow the married flavors would be perfect.

I uncorked the red wine then opened the dishwasher to retrieve a wineglass. Who was I going to feed all that sauce to? Not the new neighbors.

"Excuse me, Beckett moved out? He wouldn't do that."

Our eyes met through narrowed gazes. She was going to take his side. She always did. "No, I'm pretty sure when he stopped by for the rest of his things today, he said he would call me in a few days from his place." The swig of red wine danced over my taste buds washing away true words that I didn't want to repeat. I savored the dark, earthy flavor before swallowing. I held up my naked ring finger.

"Maybe he'll be back." Her words faded as she finished the sentence. "New life? That doesn't make sense." She shrugged as she peered over the rim of her glasses at me.

My gaze stayed riveted on her as I watched her think silently dissecting my news of Beckett's choice to leave. My marriage had been over for some time. We'd been successful at going through the motions. "Nothing makes sense anymore. It's more than irreconcilable differences." My eyes narrowed. Was she going to acknowledge my hurt? Did my mom understand what I was telling her? I waited. Her insensitivity sparred with the hole in my heart left by Beckett. I finished my wine then refilled the glass. "You don't have anything to say?"

She put her cup down on the counter. "I am stunned."

"Yeah, me too," I mumbled.

Mom got out of the chair and came to me. She smoothed hair away from my face like she had done so many times when I was younger and needed comforting. I relished her cool touch as waves of heat consumed my body all too much lately. I blinked back the hurt and tried to swallow away the burning lump in my throat.

"You poor girl. I am so sorry," she whispered and held me close.

Mom smelled like summer peaches and vanilla. She was soft and comforting. For the first time since Beckett told me his news, I cried with someone other than myself. I had a better chance surviving my diagnosis of breast cancer than my broken heart. The fact that Beckett, husband, father, and life-long companion was gay suffocated me. The fact that I couldn't tell my mother hurt even more. I held my breath, denying my own secret.

Chapter 3

The ringing doorbell echoed through my quiet house. I shoved all the information back into the pink tote before scurrying to the door. When I peeked through the peephole, I saw a tall gentleman standing on my porch. His highlighted, short, dishwater-blond hair complemented his tanned skin. I watched him examine the house numbers then knock at the door. His stunning brown eyes gleamed as the sun washed over him. It'd been Beckett's idea to hire a designer. I wondered how well they knew each other and I questioned why I went along with it.

I cleared my throat and checked myself out in my grandmother's mirror hanging in the foyer. I turned sideways just to see if my mother was right. I didn't appear to be that much thinner. She should talk. "She's the one that needs to eat some cake," I mumbled.

I turned the handle, opened the door, and tried to seem natural. "Hi there, you must be Paul Mitchell." I pushed open the screen door. His cologne tickled my nose as I inspected him further. I waited for goose bumps or the hair to bristle at the nape of my neck, but there was no response to his handsome nature.

"Lovely home you have here," he said.

I took his hand as he reached out to shake mine. His nails were manicured and his touch was warm, friendly. I wondered why Chloe's father hadn't displayed such manners. Too bad he wasn't as pleasant as his appearance. "Please, won't you come in?"

"I love the porch swing. The landscaping is perfect.

The boxwoods accent your stone house beautifully. Love the impatiens."

I focused on the houses across the street. Much of the landscaping included impatiens, maybe not the same color, but the same flowers. It was not an original idea. It was a way of life in my quaint little town of Grosse Pointe. Every year, I chose the same flowers, the same color, and the choice always pleased me. I smiled as I inspected his gray, sleek trousers when he walked past. He was tall and lean.

I walked to the edge of the porch to take a peek in the bushes. No one lurked today. My toes barely touched the floor as I leaned over a tad more. Being bothered by the neighborhood snoop almost seemed like a fanciful alternative to what I had planned. No part of me even believed that redecorating constituted a new beginning, but it was worth a shot. Paint colors and furnishings may change, but the circumstances remained the same. Beckett was gay, and I was alone.

I wasn't sure how much Chloe had already overheard, but I had been successful at keeping the intimate details of my life private for years and I wasn't going to let a seven-year-old air my secrets. My heart pounded at the thought of her meeting my mother behind my back. Now *that* made me bristle.

"Problem?" Mr. Mitchell asked cautiously.

I regained my composure. "No, just checking for critters, thought I heard something." We went inside as he held the door. Beckett used to hold the door for me, too. I always liked that about him.

"This is a fabulous space," he remarked.

I stood in the archway as he entered the living room, smiling. "Thank you, Mr. Mitchell. I hope you can help me spruce things up a little bit." I fidgeted then reminded myself I didn't have to explain my circumstances to him. "New paint, some new furniture, I don't want to reinvent the wheel, but I need to get things back to normal." Whatever *normal* was. Maybe he knew. I felt a twinge of guilt, knowing I was spending Beckett's money. His offer to help me get the house fixed up was all too generous and a bit abnormal when I compared divorces. A part of me cringed knowing I probably wouldn't have been so giving. I was being supported by Beckett's guilt-driven compassion.

"Call me Paul."

Paul sauntered through the great room. The beamed ceiling that ran over to the stone fireplace drew me in. The memory of making love on lazy Sunday afternoons with Beckett tormented me. I felt the creases of bewilderment line my forehead. He'd been so good at making me believe I was what he wanted.

"Damn it, Beckett, you are making this all too hard." I seethed, loathing his very existence, hating him like any normal jilted wife would do. He was making it all too damn hard. What man wanted to make sure his ex-wife was taken care of? One filled with guilt, one more loyal to his family than a Golden Retriever, one with more sense of responsibility than I had ever known, besides my dad. Tears rested at the corners of my eyes.

Paul turned in my direction.

I swallowed, forced a smile, then flipped on the light switch so he could see the room better. "Glad you like it, I do." I more than liked my house. I loved it. It had been my home for twenty-two years. It was the place where Beckett and I brought Bradley home for the first time. Paul ran his fingers over fabric, paint, and leftover furniture in the grand room like Beckett used to caress me. On good days, I wandered through my house, and if I breathed deep enough, I could still smell the scent of the baby we created, Bradley.

Goosebumps covered my arms. Would Beckett haunt me forever? Was it something I did to turn him off?

Paul poked his head around the corner, his eyes curious about the adjacent room. I showed him into the dining room, home to my grandmother's antique dining set, buffet, silver, and antique china. I ignored the dust, as did he. "This room is okay. I won't have to do anything here."

"Beautiful," he replied with a smile as he ran his fingers over the carved seatbacks.

"Thank you." I led him into the kitchen not feeling the energy to tell the story of the grand furniture passed down from generation to generation. "I need to focus on the living room, the library, and my bedroom." I should have insisted on a female designer, someone I chose. "I've been looking for pieces to incorporate."

Paul stopped.

There was something familiar in the way he moved and smiled at me. I'd seen it before in Beckett. My mind reeled. Now I wondered how Beckett really found Paul. My gut twisted. I pushed away the thoughts racing through my brain. "So, how do you know Beckett?"

Beckett had said a co-worker recommended Paul, but I wondered about the intimacy of their connection. Were they lovers? A bolt of hot energy surged through me. Beckett wouldn't have cheated, would he? My knees felt weak. Allowing myself to stumble into the depths of my over-active imagination didn't bode well for Paul or myself. I leaned back trying to support myself on the kitchen island. *I need help, serious help.* My cheeks grew hotter with the intensity of my imagination, or maybe the possibility that I had discovered a hidden affair.

"Beckett called me. I decorated a co-worker's home not too far from here."

"Oh, would that be Dr. Hilton, on Lewiston Road?" I threw out a fictitious name and address. I felt like a schmuck and bit my lip.

"No, Lois Bennett's home." Paul paused. "She's over on Ridge Road."

Damn. Now I really felt like a schmuck. "Yes, now that I think about it, I have seen your handiwork. We went to a gathering there last year. She mentioned she had a fabulous designer, and now I know it was you. Lovely home," I spewed through a toothy smile. My jaw ached as I tired of my own game. My breast hurt. I really just wanted to lie down. I sighed.

"Are you all right?" he asked.

"Actually, I'm not feeling very well. You are more than welcome to see the library before you go. We can talk about the bedroom next time." I pointed through the kitchen. "The library is opposite the great room. Follow me." My lips formed a thin smile. I hoped my fantasies were getting the best of me. Beckett would never hire a lover then send him to the house. Not his style. Or so I hoped. Of course, I would ask him later.

I opened the French doors to the dark room.

"Oh," escaped Paul's lips as he stepped over the threshold. "Wow."

"Yeah, it's pretty empty now." Too exhausted to investigate further, I said, "Beckett took everything. This was his study. It needs an overhaul." *I need an overhaul.* I watched as Paul moved through the room, running his fingers over the dark oak paneling. *What was that?*

Beckett's ghost sat behind an invisible vintage desk scrawling in a tiny book as he peered through his tortoise-shell-rimmed cheaters.

"We can do a lot in here," Paul said. "Or a little. It's up to you."

"I have always loved the oak panels." I trailed my fingers over the thick chair rail. I could smell Beckett's Polo cologne in the still air. I'd have to exorcise his spirit before I could make it my own. I sat in the striped wing-backed chair next to the window.

"Here's my card."

I took Paul's business card. "Thanks. I'll put this with the other one." I pushed myself out of the chair.

"I know this is hard," he said.

A bomb ticked within me. *How the hell do you know?*

Paul headed for the front door then turned to face me. I envisioned myself delivering a flying scissor kick to his head, leaving him sprawled on the front lawn. I stayed quiet, like I always did. It was good to be seen and not heard.

"When you feel up to it, why don't you email me your budget and some expectations then we can go from there. If you have pictures of furniture, you can forward them as well." He smiled politely and held out his hand.

I shook it, because *that's* what people with manners do, not because I wanted to. For all I knew, Paul and Beckett were friends on a whole other level, a level to which I had no insight. I closed the door behind him. My heart ripped open just a little bit more. After twenty-three years of marriage Beckett knew everything about me and I understood nothing about him.

Agreeing to have Paul Mitchell as my decorator may have not been the smartest decision, but I'd get through it just like everything other dilemma I was facing. Keeping the transition to a minimum would insure the least amount of invasion.

I went back into the library, where I sat cross-legged on the floor in the middle of the room. Tiny flecks of dust danced in the rays of light streaming through the leaded-glass windows. There were a few books scattered on the shelves, books Bradley wanted to keep. I pulled out Maurice Sendak's *Where the Wild Things Are* and flipped through the pages, imagining Bradley's face in the wolf suit. It had been Bradley's favorite bedtime story. I returned the book to its respective place trying not to disturb the dusty outline of novels. A small leather notebook caught my eye. Beckett must have forgotten it when he packed and I hadn't noticed it before now. I slid it across the shelf. On the front, there was a word written in fancy gold letters, *Journal.* I glanced over to where Beckett's desk once was and this time I saw him staring over the rim of his scholarly cheaters, a thin smile on his face, and his voice nearly audible. *I didn't forget my journal. I left it for you.*

Chapter 4

The idle revolving door swung into motion as I neared the cancer center entrance. I didn't have a walker. I didn't need one. I wasn't being pushed in a wheelchair. I didn't need one of those either. I was not an invalid. And I wasn't going to be one. The only thing that paralyzed me was Beckett's decision to leave our marriage, and the burden of fighting cancer.

Pretending to admire the gift shop display neatly arranged in the built-in glass case of the moving circular entry, my impatient footsteps were hindered by its lagging tempo. Instead of heading to the elevator and up to the Mammogram Center, I took an immediate right, and followed the hallway toward Radiation. My breast ached. I pushed away dread as I inspected the paintings displayed on the cloth walls. I wondered if all the artists were diagnosed with breast cancer, like myself. And if so, were they all still alive?

My chest felt heavy as I wondered if the doctor mistakenly read the films. Maybe the clusters she saw were residue from my broken heart. Maybe they were chocolate cake crumbs from the technician's lunch. Maybe it was just a misreading. Big, fat mistakes happen all the time.

I rounded the corner, dug my identification card out of my bag, and swiped the barcode through the infrared light underneath the computer wand on the receptionist's counter. I surveyed the empty waiting room. Was I the only one with cancer today? I remembered the social worker's words as she tried to comfort me during the initial appointment. She reassured me I'd make many friends at the cancer center by the time the radiation treatment was completed. This time I whispered into the air, "I'm not really sure this is the place I want to make new friends." I put my card away and followed the signs to the changing room where my faded, blue hospital gown awaited me.

The hallway was empty.

I felt thinner. I promised myself I would eat something when I got home.

The doors opened, and I saw the offices were empty. The place felt vacant, abandon. If I left, would anyone come get me? I coerced myself further down the hallway and pushed the big, metal square button on the wall. Another door opened and I navigated my way back to the dressing room. Today, I was scheduled for tattoos. Dr. Akin, my surgeon, assured me it was no big deal, but it was to me. The soon to be permanent speckles, the color of schmutz would always remind me I was a victim of cancer. I grimaced at the thought of having six black dots mar my freckled Scottish skin that I adored.

The changing room was abandoned, too. As I followed the instructions given to me by the perky young nurse from the previous visit, I studied the overflowing hamper of used gowns and wondered about the women who'd worn them. I changed, hung my things in a locker, and waited outside the room in *my* unflattering, drab gown that hung like a rag. And right on cue, Nurse Rita came around the corner smiling and ready for me. *This must be my first friend.* I silently told myself to shut up. I smiled back.

"Hello there. Nice to see you again."

I couldn't think of anything nice about it, but I complied with a nod as I followed Rita to the room where my radiation oncologist, Dr. Masterson, would do the CAT scan, take pictures, and give me those foreboding tattoos.

Somewhere between the directions to lay still and the flash of the camera, I drifted off to a place that everyone knows when they're afraid. It was dark and doubtful. I thought about my choices. I thought about my mother. I thought about my decision to keep my diagnosis to myself. I figured Mom couldn't handle two blows at one time. I questioned my very existence. Surely, God was sending me a cryptic message. The message blurred, the translation fuzzy, unclear. The camera flashed and I blinked. The hard board beneath my back was cold and unforgiving, the band around my feet tight and suffocating.

"We have to keep you still. The pictures ensure proper placement while having the radiation. Now we're going to take another set of pictures to make sure your heart is not in the path of the radiation."

With a click of a button my hard bed slid into the machine. Whirring roared all around. My heart. My heart? It was already scarred. No one had mentioned this before. I hadn't even thought about it. *Please, God, get me through this. I should have brought somebody, damn it.* My eyes welled. My throat burned. The board slid out of the large tumbler. I felt helpless.

"When the doctor reads this, she will decide if you have to curl up on your side or hold your breath during radiation."

Panic filled me. "What?" I stiffened as the ache in my back felt like my spine was snapping in half.

"Depending on where your heart is in the picture, you may have to lie on your side or hold your breath for the treatment."

I hadn't held my breath since I was twelve and we would pass a cemetery. "For how long?"

"For about a minute and a half. If you can't, we have a breathing mechanism that we'll teach you to use."

What was about to happen to me became clearer. It was bigger than I intended and I wasn't in control. All I could do was lay still and pray like hell that everything would be fine.

"Everything looks good," Dr. Masterson said as she entered the room. "You are the perfect size for this treatment. Your heart is in the clear."

I sighed. *Lucky me. I am the perfect size and shape. I'll have to tell my mother that I'm perfect for something.*

"The radiation will catch the corner of your lung."

I held my breath. *My lung, now my lung?*

"It'll look like spider veins in the future and when a doctor tells you that you have scarring you need to let them know you had radiation so they don't go any further with biopsies or tell you that you have something suspicious that they need to investigate."

"What about breathing?" I muttered.

"Your lungs are big enough. The small portion being affected will not impede your breathing or lung function."

I looked over to her from the corner of my eye. My left arm began to throb.

"I'm very sorry for the delay. I know you've been on that board for longer than usual, but we're almost finished."

"Tattoos." I grimaced.

"Six little pokes and you'll be done." She took her Sharpie and darkened the spots she had placed on my torso at the beginning of our session, making sure the one between my breasts was low enough not to be seen in the event I wanted to wear a low-cut top. Fat chance of that happening, especially now.

"Okay, let's get this over with." I held my breath as I watched the nurses prepare the needles. My eyes watered from the first injection. By the time the sixth tattoo was in place, a few tears escaped the corner of my eyes. I blinked, trying to swallow away the pain. Each stinging jab hit a bony area, leaving me to curse my thin frame.

"Okay, now let's get your arm down and get you up."

Relief washed over me. Too stiff to move, I let the nurse's arms hoist me up.

"Now when you come tomorrow, we'll have a dry run in the radiation room to make sure the tattoos are in the correct spots. The day after that, we will begin your treatment," Dr. Masterson said.

The tattoo sites burned. Worry trickled down to my toes as I made my way back to the changing room. Getting out of there couldn't happen too soon.

"You look horrible."

I opened my eyes. There she was, the newest addition to the neighborhood, and my new best friend, Chloe McIntyre. I moaned then rested my arm over my eyes thinking if I blocked her from my vision she'd disappear. "Shouldn't you be home? Won't the nanny be looking for you?" I didn't want a visit from her father. I turned my head to peek out from behind my arm. She was still there.

"Probably not. Is there something wrong with you?" she questioned.

"Nope. Just tired," I answered with a sigh.

"You look too skinny. You need to eat more."

I scowled. She sounded like my mother.

"Thought you'd be done with your book by now," Chloe said, inspecting the dog-eared page near the end.

"Nope. Almost." I sat up on the edge of my lounge chair. My legs and feet bathed in the summer sun as the rest of me hid in the shade. Both Dr. Akin and Dr. Masterson made it clear that being in the sun should be avoided, especially during radiation.

"Maybe if you put your whole body in the sun, that will help," Chloe suggested.

She tugged on my chair, but her efforts didn't outweigh me. "I think I'll stay put. It's okay, really." I examined her determined expression and bright orange nail polish.

"I'll lay with you. We can talk." She plopped down in the chair beside me. "Don't worry, I left Voodoo at home."

"Good call," I said.

Chloe scooted her chair into the sun then leaned back. The thin strings of blue jean fringe jutted over her skinny thighs. I hadn't worn cutoffs since college. Her plain white tank top screamed minimalist.

"I think I'll just kick off my sandals. Don't want tan lines," she said.

Shit. I closed my eyes and shifted my weight trying to ease my wrenched back. My backyard, supposedly my haven, evidently was now a pest magnet.

"I asked my dad for a puppy. He said no."

"You can get one when you're older." I hadn't used that line since Bradley was fourteen.

"Maybe you should get a dog. It might make you happy." Chloe cleared her throat and rested her head back as she closed her eyes.

"I'm fine," I grunted. I couldn't remember the last time I was truly happy, but I knew barking and dog poop were not a sure remedy.

"You don't act fine. Every time I come over here you get this weird look on your face. You didn't seem so happy when that guy was leaving your house yesterday, you know, the blondish model-looking guy. He was cute. If a guy showed up at my house looking like that, I'd be smiling from ear-to-ear. Our pool guy, at our old house, used to look like that. My mom never frowned when he was around. My dad didn't like him. Go figure. I miss my old house," Chloe rambled.

I thought I'd give her a taste of her own medicine even if I did want all the details on her mom and the pool guy. "That's the pot calling the kettle black."

Chloe winced. "What does that mean?"

"You don't seem so happy either," I grunted in her direction.

"I miss my best friend, Bella."

"Sorry."

"Oh, I almost forgot, your mom stopped by when you were gone this morning. She's a hoot. I told her I'd call her when you got back, but she wouldn't give me her phone number."

"Intuitive," I whispered.

"What's that mean?" she questioned.

"Nothing. Really, you should tell Nanny Nora where you are. She'll worry," I said.

"No, I really don't' think she will. She's taking a nap." Chloe held out her arm and pointed to her watch. "When the big hand gets on the three, that's when I should go get her up."

I rolled my eyes.

"Got any ice cream left?" she asked.

"Nope. Ate it."

"Bradley home yet? I'd like to meet him."

My head began to pulsate and my temples tightened. "Sorry. You know, we could just rest here without talking."

"I'm not a baby. I don't need a nap," Chloe snapped.

I sat up then slid my feet into my sandals. "It's time for me to wash the cat."

"You have a cat?" Chloe yelped in excitement.

She stood in front of me as I tried to make my way into the house. "If you'll excuse me, I have things to attend to."

"It's not nice to lie. That's what my dad says."

I mimicked Chloe as she put her hand on her hip then I picked up my novel and Beckett's little leather journal I didn't have the courage to open. "Seriously, I have to redo the towel closet and reorganize the canned goods in the pantry."

Chloe closed one eye and peered up into my face. Her sandy straight hair fluttered in the breeze. "Need help?"

I breathed deeply, squelching any unkind words. "Nope. Not today." *And if I do, I won't be calling you.* "I'm really sorry, Chloe. Show me your watch." I drew her arm closer so I could see the minute hand. "Look, you've got five minutes 'til it's time to get Nanny Nora up. That's just enough time to sneak back into the house and grab a snack without her knowing." Flashbacks of sneaking around with my best friend Lily Anderson prickled at my heart. How I missed her.

Chloe hurried to slip on her sandals. "Thanks for the idea, sister. So long, I'll be back."

I watched her trot out of the yard. "Remind me to put a lock on that fence," I mumbled to myself.

Chapter 5

Plucking deadheads from the flowerbed seemed like a mindless task as I mulled over the last two days. My nose twitched at the smell of lake water. Its sweet aroma beckoned me to come play, but I ignored it, tugged my gardening hat down, and continued to work. It seemed as if I was always working. I thrived on being busy. I did my best work when I was on overload.

Shooing away the ladybug bound and determined to keep me company took too much energy so I decided to let her stay, besides there was something comforting in her red and black polka-dotted design.

Chloe's footprints matted down the impeccable Pachysandra bedding my shrubs. I leaned through the crevices trying to fluff up the trampled areas. I wondered how much time Chloe really spent down there. Lots, by the shape it was in. I blinked trying to push away the urge to teeter over. I scorned myself for not eating more lunch. Lightheadedness stomped out the ambition to make my bushes look perfect again. My hat got stuck on a twig. I fumbled trying to catch myself. Doing a face plant was not my intention. With my nose in the plants and the strange suspicion of being watched, I carefully pushed myself up with the palms of my hands and backed out of the bushes. When I saw the size of the shadow I considered crawling back into the plant bed. My cheeks boiled with embarrassment.

"Interesting," he said.

I snagged my hat stuck in the thin branches. When he offered me his hand, I took it. With a quick jerk, I was back on my feet.

"Hi there. I'm John McIntyre, I believe we met the other day."

Like I could forget. I glanced over his shoulder to see if Chloe and Voodoo shadowed him. "Maggie Abernathy," I replied in a quiet voice.

"Do you have a minute?" he asked.

Alarms clanged in my head. In the professional world of teaching, bad news usually follows that phrase. "I—"

John gestured for me to come over to the stairs leading up to my porch. Hoping like hell he wasn't going to invite himself inside, I sat on the top stair trying to regain my composure. My stomach dropped as he stood in front of me. I thought about telling him to let me have it, but I chose to sit quietly after assessing his rigid body language. I hadn't noticed his muscular arms until now.

I ventured a bet with myself that his laugh lines made him more handsome, but he'd have to smile for me to actually find out. I was pretty sure that wasn't in the cards. Consumed with his pleasing build, I ignored his frowning mouth. I slumped forward, resting my elbows on my knees and my chin in my hands. I shrugged off the notion I probably looked like a seven-year-old ready for the lecture. I scrutinized his bald head wondering if he was naturally bald or if he shaved his head trying to avoid the conspicuous comb-over. My stomach tumbled at the thought of losing my hair. For him, it was a good look. I knew he was a professional with that white starched shirt and tie and I wondered if his patients were afraid of him. He was kind of burly.

I leaned back trying to look nonchalant as I eyed the neighborhood, mostly for witnesses, credible witnesses, not seven-year-olds dragging a cat around on a noose, related to the assailant.

John crossed his arms over his chest. "I think we need to set some rules."

I held his gaze. My spine prickled.

"I think we have a problem," he said.

The muscles in my neck tensed. *More like you have the problem and her name is Chloe.* "I'm not sure what you're getting at."

John's eyes were emerald-green. He was very handsome. Too bad he was a jerk. I felt as if there should have been a table and a report card between us, shielding me from insanity.

"Well it seems that you told my daughter to come home while Nora was napping and sneak treats. She's lying in bed with a bellyache moaning and groaning. I was hoping that wasn't the case. After all, we didn't exactly get off to a great start the other evening."

My palms went clammy and my mind reeled with excuses. I pressed my lips together then decided not to pussyfoot around. "Unfortunately, I was being sarcastic and while Chloe does understand what it means to end a sentence with a preposition, she does not understand sarcasm." I swallowed, trying to squelch the words percolating in my mind as well as the nerves in my belly. "I am very sorry she isn't feeling well." Just as pride filled my chest, I gazed up to see a flash of disdain in his gleaming eyes.

He cleared his throat. "Excuse me."

My breath caught in my chest. I had no words.

He shoved his hands in his pant pockets. The jangle of his keys even sounded irritated.

I held his stare, unwilling to budge.

"Well, Maggie Abernathy, I am thinking you are not a very good influence on my daughter. She is seven, you are—"

I didn't like the way his eyes inspected my face. I glared at him, warning him not to finish that thought.

"She's very impressionable. We have a nanny. There is no reason for her to be over here so much."

I rolled my eyes. Poor form, I knew, but really? "It's not like I invited her. She just shows up and won't leave." I stifled my rising tone and my body stiffened. "Look, I teach children her age all year long, and when June hits, it's my time for rejuvenation, and entertaining your daughter unexpectedly doesn't fit into that plan. I'm going to be honest with you." I stood, then took a step down, trying to even the playing field. "I've asked her politely to leave. She won't. She hides in my bushes."

I pointed to my flattened plants. "She listens to my conversations. Maybe you should set the rules for her, I'll be glad to follow them, too." I crossed my arms in front of me.

A shadow rolled over his green eyes like cloud cover. I watched him turn in his tracks and walk back home. How was I ever going to live next door to this family? *Shit*. First, my husband tells me he's gay and we divorce. Then I am diagnosed with breast cancer, have to go through surgery and radiation, on my summer break, no less, then this guy comes over to tell me it's *my* fault his daughter is at home not feeling well. I went inside and let the screen door slam on the year from hell.

Turning around halfway up the stairs, I trotted back down in a huff, out the front door, picked up my mess, retrieved my hat then went back inside, and yet again, let the screen door slam behind me. This time I walked through the foyer, to the kitchen, poured myself a glass of wine, and took a deep breath. With one big swig, it was gone. I flicked on the television mounted on the counter, something Beckett had insisted on when he started taking cooking seriously. He said the Food Channel was a necessity. I knew he was full of it, but compromise is what marriage is all about, right? Funny, how that worked out.

A cool breeze flooded the kitchen, and a shiver ran up my spine. I put on my summer cardigan then closed the patio doors.

My face dropped at the sight.

Chloe's wrinkly chin quivered. The instant we made eye contact, she ran away.

I hurried to the front door and stepped out onto the porch. I drew my sweater tight and waited for John to reappear on my doorstep. Looking west, the sun filled the sky with streaks the color of summer sherbet. Looking east, I peered through the hundred-year-old oak trees waiting for the breeze to move the branches in just the right direction so I could catch a glimpse of the cool lake, just blocks away, twinkling in the day's last light. I waited for round two.

When John didn't show, I went back inside. To my left, the orange and red hues from the sunset flooded Beckett's library. It was just as beautiful inside. The library was mine now, and I wasn't sure what to do with it. Stifled emptiness took my breath away. I took Beckett's journal off the shelf and sat in the middle of the room with my legs crossed waiting for Beckett's ghost to call to me. Tonight, I missed his touch. I missed his sense of humor. I missed the man he was to me. I put the leather book in front of me and traced over the golden script reading *Journal*. I opened it up to page one.

I read the date then the first few sentences. *Damn him.* He tugged at my heartstrings through words written twenty-two years ago. "Oh Beckett," I whimpered, trying to catch my breath. Sorrow filled my chest. I spoke soft words to myself, feeling compassion for the man that'd left me. "This is all so unfair. How could you have done this to me, to yourself?" I pushed away the wet tresses of hair from my eyes. I wanted to hate him, but I couldn't. It would be easier if I despised him.

I took my wedding ring out of my pocket and set it on the floor next to me as I reread those first sentences trying to give myself time to decide to read further or shut the book. My eyes blurred, but the words were etched in my brain. *Bradley is one year old today. Bradley is a beautiful boy. I hope he takes after his mother. When I see how happy she is, I don't have the heart to tell her.*

My hand jerked the book shut as the doorbell rang. I caressed the soft, worn covering. The journal fit perfectly into my cardigan pocket. When the bell rang again, I scrambled to my feet and searched the other pocket for tissue. I wiped at the corners of my moist eyes and sniffled.

I switched on the foyer light, peered through the screen door, and swallowed my grief trying to prepare myself. Anguish scraped slowly over the lump in my throat. Maybe I shouldn't have been so short with Chloe.

I didn't open the door, for the steely mesh screen was my veil. I waited for John to speak. This time he was wearing faded blue jeans, a faded T-shirt, and black Teva sandals. He almost looked human.

"I just came over to say, I think, it would be best if we stayed to ourselves. I can't change the fact that we are neighbors, but—" He dug in his pocket. "Here, take this."

I opened the screen door a crack. He slid the paper into my hand. His warm touch melted my cold fingertips. I read the names and numbers, however when I looked up into his green eyes, they were unreadable.

"Call, and we will come get her," he said.

I stood silent.

"Really, she shouldn't be over here bothering you all the time," John mumbled.

His Adam's apple bobbed. His words were soft, restrained, and firm. The deep tone of his voice sent a chill up my spine. His affect gave no clue to his true feelings. He turned to walk away, but before taking that first step down from the porch, he peered back at me, shooting me a steely glance, something I've seen before.

I tucked the paper in my pocket and watched him leave. I contemplated his scowl of pity. I caressed the cold wedding band hidden in my pocket.

Chapter 6

I poured my second cup of coffee. In exactly six hours, I would be lying in a room padded with lead executing *the dry run*. The nurse's words sounded like a military exercise. The angst settled in the pit of my stomach and I wondered why I took the last appointment of the day. I shook my head in disbelief. If I couldn't tell my family and friends about the diagnosis, how could I admit it to myself? I flipped through my stack of business cards for my physician, the oncologist, the radiation oncologist, the surgeon, the dietician, the nurse, the physician's assistant, the case manager, the social worker, and the wellness center that offered classes and massages to all cancer patients. I decided against making another appointment with the social worker.

I shuffled back upstairs to the bathroom, untied my robe, and let the terrycloth fall to the floor. The quick rush of water from the tap drowned that little voice inside of me I couldn't turn off.

I leaned against the counter inspecting myself in the mirror. My bruised flesh was starting to heal. Yesterday, Dr. Masterson, the radiation oncologist, mentioned what a beautiful job Dr. Akin had done with the incisions. When I looked, I saw something different, a permanent scar I'd take with me for the rest of my life. My reminder that I have cancer. I touched the black oblong tattoo on my right collarbone that glared at me. I hated it. I touched the one between my breasts, turned sideways, and inspected the two on the left side of my torso. My throat tightened. Stepping into the shower, I let the warm water rain down over me. I covered my face with my hands trying to stop the tremors, but my shoulders quaked and I slid down into the bottom of the tub to sob.

The lawn was mowed, edged, and the bushes freshly trimmed. Confused by the mystery workers, I stopped the car to investigate the premises. A team of men appeared from the backyard. They were tanned, shirtless, and ripped. I stared as they packed up their equipment. Bandana man loaded the edger and the electric trimmer while a bald man in Ray Bans approached me.

"Everything look okay?" he asked, mopping his brow.

I got out of my car and nodded. "Yes. Who are you? I didn't order your service."

With a straight face, the sweaty worker answered, "I know. It's all paid for. You just have to approve the work."

"Who paid for it?" I asked, stepping close enough to know he smelled of fresh grass clippings and Old Spice. Too tired from the day's appointment, I stifled the part of me trying to picture him naked. Judging by his sculpted chest, I was sure his photograph was on a calendar somewhere.

"Your husband. Have a nice day." He strode to his truck. As he slammed the door, his partner revved the engine, and gave a polite wave as they drove away.

A slow burn ignited within me. "Damn you, Beckett," I hissed. I scanned the yard for the little ears with big eyes. The house was beautiful, I admitted, but how was this divorce thing ever going to work if he made sure every 'T' was crossed for me. I scrolled through my list of contacts on my phone. His line rang once then went straight to voicemail. I hung up without saying a word.

Taken aback by the Coppertone worker boys, I stomped inside without concern. Halfway to the kitchen it dawned on me that I just entered a house I did not leave open.

"Maggie, is that you?" a voice called out.

I stopped in my tracks, not startled by the intruder, and I shook my head at the familiar voice then kicked off my shoes. Mom sat at the kitchen counter playing Solitaire with the cards Beckett and I had brought home from Las Vegas. Thinking back, I remembered how I'd fawned over Cirque du Soleil and he'd loved Cher at the Colosseum. I rolled my eyes as I had the same old epiphany. Again. "I wish you would stop letting yourself in, Mom, or at least tell me when you're coming over."

My mother peered over the rim of her blue reading glasses that matched her denim shirt. "Relax, you're so on edge."

"Geez," I muttered, "I come home and there are strange men in the yard, the door's wide open, who knows what I'll find in here. Rapist, thief, seven-year-old." I smirked then searched the refrigerator for a cold bottle of water.

I ignored my mother as she watched me chug it down.

"You're going to have to have more than that if you want your shorts to stop drooping."

I glared at her. I was allowed. *That's* what daughters do when baited. "Don't worry, I'll have cake for dinner."

She narrowed her gaze and frowned. "I've already been through the cupboards, not much in there. And I'm not seeing any triple-layer chocolate cake anywhere."

I took a deep breath. "I'll get take-out."

She grunted, flipped over three more cards, then peeked under the hidden cards.

"Cheater," I whispered.

"I heard that." Her words and eyes darted in my direction. "Don't be sassy to your momma."

She sounded like an extra in *Gunsmoke*. I walked over to where she was sitting, kissed her on the cheek, then stroked her hair as she finished her game.

"Ah, I finally won," she proclaimed before shuffling the

Vegas cards, tapping the deck on the table like a dealer, then returning them to the box. "So, I was thinking-"

"No, no, and no." I waggled my pointer finger in her direction.

"Oh, I almost forgot, this was taped to the patio door." She handed me a piece of rumpled notebook paper.

I took it from her and inspected the handwriting. "Thanks." I put it on the counter where Chloe sat telling jokes while enjoying her ice cream before John got upset.

"What's it say?" Mom got up and took the note back after I unfolded it. She lowered her gaze, her green eyes silently questioned my actions. "Is that from the little girl that lives next door?"

I nodded, picked up my water bottle, and drained the rest hoping the last trickle would wash away any guilty thoughts I harbored about keeping my illness a secret. I tossed the empty bottle into the recycle bin.

Mom started reading aloud. I swear her flare for the dramatic was a tactic of jest. "'Dear Maggie, I am sorry I got you in trouble.' I love the way Chloe spelled trouble." Mom snickered. "'He's just being my dad.'" Mom held out the paper in my direction and pointed to the picture.

"That's her and her cat, Voodoo," I said.

"Interesting name for a feline." Mom put the paper back on the counter. "Trouble? What did you do?"

"What did I do? I didn't do anything, but try and mind my own business." The way my mom's skin wrinkled at the bridge of her nose irritated me. "Here we go. Really, it's nothing."

"Must not be nothing if she's writing you a letter. Is her father the man I saw over here the other night?"

"Yeah," I huffed. Just the thought of him annoyed me.

"Seems you need to make amends with your neighbors," she suggested. "But then again, not everyone is neighbor material."

"Thanks a lot," I grumbled.

"I didn't mean you. Remember Old Man Johnson?" She pointed her finger in my direction. "That old fart would keep your balls if they went over the fence and call me at the drop of a hat if you rode your bike on his lawn."

I smiled. "Yeah, I forgot about him. He was mean."

Mom opened the drawer to retrieve a paper and pencil.

"I'm not writing an apology letter," I stated.

"Relax, *Marjorie Jean*."

I cringed. "Please don't call me that, *Glad*," I said, emphasizing her given name.

The corner of her mouth curled upward as her eyes smiled.

"I'm making a shopping list. Whatever I buy, you eat. All this worry is making you lose your girlie figure. You're too thin."

"Fine," I caved. "Put cake on the list. Chocolate."

"You got it. And Chloe's dad, he's pretty handsome." Mom stopped writing to catch my eye.

I covered my ears and pretended not to hear her. "Not gonna happen, woman, not gonna happen."

Mom ripped the paper from the tablet. "It's time to get out there. You can't go on living life in a shell. Even turtles and snails poke their heads out once in a while."

I meandered into the living room, plopped down on the oversized leather sofa, and curled up under the Chenille throw. A flash of heat scorched my body, so I kicked off the throw before closing my eyes.

"You're gonna have to tell me sooner or later why Beckett left," Mom called from the foyer. "You can't keep everything to yourself forever," she sang as she let the door slam.

"Oh, yes, I can," I sang back, mimicking her tone. I opened my eyes trying to decipher the mumbling voices on the porch then I blew out a breath of air in exasperation. Craning my neck to get a glimpse, I caught sight of the screen door slamming, yet again. "Seriously?" I whined.

There stood Chloe in a wet bathing suit. In one hand she held a dripping Popsicle and in the other she held the rope to Voodoo who was sitting by her wet feet sprinkled with grass clippings.

"Don't worry, Maggie. I'm not staying. I just wanted to make sure you got my note. Hope there's no hard feelings. I feel better now." She continued licking her cherry treat.

"No worries," I answered as I sat up. It was going to take more than a manipulative seven-year-old to take me out of the game. Twenty-six years of teaching and raising Bradley gave me more than my share of practice.

"Hey, was that your mom?"

"Yup." I cringed when I saw a hunk of red Popsicle hit the floor. I got up, grabbed a tissue, and hurried in her direction.

"You guys look alike except she's got a little bit of gray hair, not very much though, and she's more smiley."

Chloe's green eyes resembled her daddy's. I waited for her to move her foot before I started wiping the floor. She crouched next to me, her soft breaths in my ear.

"I don't want to be a bother. I'll throw this away at home." Chloe swung around then headed out the front door. "I won't slam the door this time either. This door is really old. Maybe you should get a new one."

I was left holding the goopy tissue. "Good idea," I responded.

Chloe stopped on the porch staring at the stick in her hand.

I opened the door to see what the problem was. "Something wrong?" I smiled as she faced me. The wrinkles at the bridge of her nose reminded me of my mother's. They were better than the permanent frown line I had in my forehead from giving students *the look* in the classroom.

Chloe held out the stick. "Can you read this to me? I'm not so good at words. I think we already *'cussed* that."

Instinctively, I took it. The wet wood made me cringe. "Why don't seagulls fly by the bay?"

"Don't know." Chloe shrugged. "Voodoo, do you know?" she asked, staring him in the eyes.

We both waited for Voodoo to answer. Nothing.

"Go on, tell us," Chloe prodded.

"Cause then they'd be called *bay*-gulls? Bagels." I raised my eyebrows as she processed the riddle. The unexpected breeze whisked away the humor and carried off the rules about calling her dad if she came over. "Get it?"

She wrinkled her nose and crouched next to Voodoo. "Yeah. That was dumb. Maybe the next one will be better." She patted Voodoo's head. "Let's try grape this time."

Chloe turned, then trotted down the stairs dragging her best friend behind her while I was left holding her slobbery Popsicle stick.

I spun on my heel, went back inside, then tossed the sticky tissue and the sticky stick in the wicker trash basket in *my* library. This time when I surveyed the room, I had a vision of how to make it mine.

Chapter 7

With Beckett's journal in my lap and a million questions in my mind about its content, I waited. I wasn't sure why, but I knew there was a good chance that if I read the journal my heart would break all over again. My heart bumped against my chest walls begging me to open the cover. I was afraid, afraid of facing the truth, not just his truth, but my own truth. I had one of my own buried deep within me that I didn't want to admit. Somehow, I was an equal part in this failed union.

Sure, it hurt when Beckett told me he was gay and that he wanted to leave, but at least he was being honest, with both of us. The pangs gnawing at the edges of my soul weren't necessarily one hundred percent for the death of our marriage.

Bradley's been grown for some time now. His independence and maturity secretly stole the kernel of mystery that connected Beckett and me. Without Bradley, our household was not intact, our marriage unmistakably out of sync.

I supposed keeping up with the Jones' meant more than impeccable landscaping, current clothing, and new cars. It was *good* to attend PTA meetings and conferences with a united front. It was *normal* to meet other couples for drinks at the trendiest bar with your husband. It was *expected* to have a sparkling diamond-encrusted wedding band, a functional whole family with two *traditional* parents. I snickered when I realized I'd let society dictate my life.

My mother prefaced all great disappointments with, *some things just aren't meant to be.* I opened Beckett's journal and scanned his first words. *Bradley is a beautiful boy. I hope he takes after his mother. When I see how happy she is, I don't have the heart to tell her.* My chest ached. The tears didn't come. Beckett had known all along.

I turned the page. I read each word with purpose and shook my head. We were victims of our own expectations. I closed the book, tucked it under the cushion of the chaise lounge, and turned to see my mother hauling in groceries.

"Hey, I'm not as young as I once was," she huffed.

I got up, made sure Beckett's journal was out of sight, like so many things had been for years, and continued to be. A ladybug landed on my forearm. I marveled at its spots dreaming of a time when everything seemed so innocent, unscathed. And in that time period of discovering life, I went from wading on the shores of youth to having the foresight to run from raging waves ready to knock me down in the big blue sea of contentment, where I chose to ignore life changing experiences so I could float along with my nose pressed to the sky, not seeing the shark fins that circled around me. I closed my eyes, made a wish, then blew the ladybug from my arm. I watched the insect flutter in the sunshine before landing on my perch in the chaise lounge.

"There's lots of good stuff in here, darling," Mom crooned.

I scuffled through the French doors more eager to eat than I had been since the whole cancer thing began.

"Hold your horses," I muttered, "I'm coming."

"I'll get the other two bags, you start putting stuff away." She touched my shoulder, kissed my cheek, and whispered in my ear, "We'll fatten you up and get you back to normal. Mark my words."

Her thread of tenderness soothed me. I shut my eyes and thought how unfair it was to keep so many secrets. When I opened them, Mom was still there.

She pushed my messy strawberry-blond curls away from my face exposing my flushed cheeks. "You're a lot like your father. There's nothing to be ashamed of, you know. He was a proud man, that's a quality many great stubborn souls burden."

My voice barely audible, I replied, "I miss him." The knot in my stomach tightened. "I wish he was here." I knew he would hold me tight, making life bearable.

Mom smiled then touched my chin. "Me, too, darling, me, too, but we don't get to choose when we go." She paused. "We can choose where, but not when, my darling." She closed her eyes, made the sign of the cross on her chest, then pointed to the heavens. "But there is no doubt we will be together once again, when it's meant to be."

Inhaling sharply, I acknowledged that his absence still burned. The day my father's heart stopped beating, so did mine. Beckett was the one who'd revived me and he's gone now, too. I took the cracker box off the counter, and Mom unexpectedly smacked my bottom lightly.

"We've had our moment of sappiness, now let's snap out of it." She clapped her hands. "Lord knows, your father wouldn't want us moping around. Now, I'm going to get the rest of the groceries while you unload."

I leaned against the counter conjuring up his face. I saw his smile, dark eyes, and thick eyebrows. I stared at the ceiling, begging to see him hovering over me. "Come on, show yourself. I won't be scared. I promise. I need you." I scanned the room looking for signs until the screen door slammed, breaking the silence.

I hurried to unpack the bags. When I saw the midget, I stopped. "Oh, it's just you."

Chloe put her hand on her hip. "That's not a very nice welcome."

I was glad to see she wasn't dripping wet. Her flip-flops matched her blue bathing suit.

"Sorry, I suppose not." The Triscuit box slipped out of my hand. "Geez," I huffed. Just as I bent over to retrieve it, Chloe darted in from the doorway, and we smacked heads.

The thud stunned both of us. I slowly stood up trying to keep my balance. Blood trickled down my forehead. I grabbed the kitchen towel and held it on the gash, then blinked away the tears to see if Chloe was okay. She sat on the kitchen floor frantically rubbing her head creating a knotted mess of hair. She rebounded to her feet then moved closer to me.

"Hey," she barked, "you have one hard head. Good Golly, Miss Molly, that stung!"

I pulled the towel away from my head to assess the bleeding. A trickle of blood crept toward my eye. I wiped it away before it dripped into my eye.

"You better sit down. You don't look so good," Chloe stated.

God, she was nonstop. I sat at the counter after she pulled out the chair.

"Let me see your head," I said. My left temple pulsated as I inspected her for damage.

With both hands, she pointed to herself. "I'm good." Chloe shook the knotted mess of hair into place as if nothing happened. She crawled up onto the stool next to mine. It teetered sending unnerving panic through my veins. I lurched to steady the chair. She peeked under the towel pressed to my head then hopped down, and ran out the front door.

"What's going on in here?" Mom yelped when she saw the blood-soaked towel.

I rolled my eyes to the ceiling as she scurried to evaluate my injury. "It's nothing." But it was something. "I just hope John doesn't come over here accusing me of hurting his daughter."

Mom stood back and put her hand on her hip just like Chloe. "Now why would he do that? Accidents happen, you know." She inspected my injury then pressed the towel against my skull. "You just hold that there and don't go anywhere. I'll get some ice."

I sighed in disgust. "Now, where would I possibly be going?" I slumped over the counter holding my head with my hands. The crack of the screen door made me jump. "Now what?" I closed my eyes and buried my face.

"This is not a time to get sassy, young lady," Mom jested.

I mentally counted to ten.

Warm fingers lifted my chin. I blinked to see John in front of me. His strong hands cradled my face. I closed my eyes as he examined my head.

"That's not so good. You're going to need stitches," he said.

"I'm going to need more than that," I snapped. My belly warmed with the curve of his faint smile. I winced as he touched the skin around the gash.

"Should only be a couple. I'm really sorry." He took a clean towel from my mother and placed it on my forehead. "About lots of things," he whispered. "Maybe we should start over."

John's lingering gaze softened. My eyes glanced over to Chloe who was dragging Voodoo around the kitchen. Her plastic shoes slapped the floor in rhythm with my throbbing head. John left the kitchen. I waited for the slam of the screen door, but it didn't come. I smiled at the sound of the doorbell.

Mom turned from the sink where she had been rinsing out the bloody towel. She shooed me toward the door. "Get up, go answer the door," she ordered.

Chloe climbed up onto the chair next to me. She leaned across the counter on her belly. "Can I just call you Glad? I can't really say that other name you told me. Besides, Glad sounds happier."

"Of course you can, sweetheart," Mom answered her.

"Maggie will be okay. Bad things happen to me all the time," Chloe stated. "My dad says"—she cleared her throat and grunted as she scrunched up her face—"it's all part of life."

I stopped, looked over my left shoulder at my mom and Chloe who seemed so at ease, and wondered if I'd ever feel like that, too.

John stood at the door with his hands in his pockets.

I peered through the screen feeling foolish with the charade. I opened the door. My eyes met his although I could only see him with one eye because my other one was covered with the towel holding my head together.

"Hi there. I'm John McIntyre. I moved in next door and I thought maybe I should come over and apologize for my daughter."

I smiled and took the towel away from my face. "I'm Maggie Abernathy. The woman in the kitchen is my mother, and yes, you probably should apologize for your daughter."

John guided my hand with the towel back to my head. A tingle tickled my spine. "You really are going to have to get stitches. Is your husband home to take you?"

His question hit the nerve. "U-Um," I stammered. "I really don't have a husband. We're divorced." Saying those words felt strange. I pressed the towel to my head.

"Sorry," he mumbled. "I know how that goes. It's just me and Chloe."

"She told me," I said in the midst of feeling lightheaded.

"She tells everyone everything. She has no boundaries, but I guess you already know that," John said, grinning.

"Yeah, I guess I do."

John called to tell Chloe it was time to go home.

"My mom can take me to the emergency room." I turned to prevent another collision as soon as I heard the sound of speeding flip-flopping.

Chloe sprinted past me, Voodoo following behind.

"I don't know if this will help, but I can call ahead and let them know you are coming. It may save you some time." John caught Chloe by her shoulders and twisted her around so she could see me.

Chloe yanked Vooodoo's leash.

"Look Ms. Abernathy in the eye, please," he interjected.

The corner of my lip curled upward. "I prefer, Maggie," I said.

Chloe reeled Voodoo in and clutched him tight. "I'm sorry we bumped heads."

"Me, too," I whispered. I glanced at John who was scrolling through phone numbers on his cell phone. My temple throbbed, making my smile disappear.

Chloe rushed down the porch stairs and vanished around the corner of the house. John paced on the porch as he talked on his phone. I sat on the swing until he was finished.

"They know you're on your way. Hope it helps."

My mom came out with our purses and shut the doors. "Let's go, Mags."

John helped me down the stairs and into Mom's sedan. "I'm really sorry," he said, leaning into the car to buckle my seatbelt.

Chapter 8

I rolled over and squinted at blurry numbers on the alarm clock. Pressing the phone to my ear, I covered my head with the sheet, too tired to move. I grunted as my mom had a conversation with herself. She said she'd be in my kitchen in ten minutes.

"Let yourself in. I'm pretty sure you have a key," I mumbled. Today, I didn't care. I spent most of the night staring at the ceiling with beads of sweat coating my body. This menopause stuff wasn't as great as it sounded. Like clockwork, waking up at least once a night shivering to cold sweat, usually about three-fifteen while the rest of the world slept around me became routine. I'd layer the sheet, the bedspread, and the extra down comforter I kept folded neatly at the end of my bed. Mom disconnected the call and with a heavy breath, I buried the phone under my pillow. Rain plunked against the roof lulling me back to sleep. Twenty minutes later, my phone chimed, again. "What?" I grumbled.

"I'm here, and you have a visitor. A man named Paul Mitchell."

"I know you're here. I can hear you rummaging around down there." I sat up and thought about what day it was.

"It's not like Maggie to oversleep." I heard my mom talking to Paul through the phone. Her voice echoed up the stairs and through the hallway. "This change in her life is wearing her out. You know all us women go through it."

Horrified, I kicked off the covers, slipped into the sundress I'd worn yesterday, hurried to the bathroom, put my hair up in a bun, and scrubbed my face with a cold washcloth careful not to touch the stitches in my left temple. I had exactly no time left to stop her. As I ran through the hall, I stopped in front of the mirror on the wall of the landing then adjusted the straps of my dress to hide any black tattoos.

I trotted down the stairs and hoped that my decision to keep Paul on as my decorator was the right one. I gave a little wave in his direction. "Good morning. Guess, I'm not used to my summer schedule yet."

Mom raised her brow at me. "I'm going to make the coffee and whip up some breakfast." She peered over the top of her glasses. "That is, if you haven't already eaten."

Paul smiled. "We should talk about a few things, get this project going. I got your message about the library. I'll be out of your hair soon so you two ladies can enjoy the morning."

"No. No. Join us. We've got plenty. Just did a major shopping trip yesterday," Mom said.

She stopped in her tracks, turned around and shot me a look through her leopard print cheaters. She had more glasses than Imelda Marcos had shoes. She came back to where I stood at the bottom of the stairs and pushed my hair away from my temple to inspect the damage from yesterday.

"How's that feeling?" she asked.

Paul leaned in. "Ouch." He cringed.

"Really, I am fine. Just a few stitches to hold my head together." Maybe I should have asked them to mend my heart while they were at it.

Mom grinned sheepishly. "She's always brave," she muttered. "I'll get the bacon on."

As Paul and I sat in the great room discussing our plans, my embarrassment subsided. While Paul spoke, my mind wandered to Beckett. The last time we spoke was the day he came to get his books. Shouldn't he be settled by now? I thought he'd call. He said he would. Pretending to be interested, I nodded along with the conversation.

Paul clapped his hands mid-sentence, breaking my trance. "So, I'll get the painter's scheduled and we'll get the ceiling done first."

"Sounds good. A fresh coat will brighten up the oak paneling. Take the window treatments and the oriental out while you're at it. I want something different."

Paul nodded.

"I want an oversized desk, a wooden drafting table for working on my hand-colored photographs, and a place to put my teacup collection."

"Okay then, I'll do some research and get back to you. Would you like to use the oriental in another room?"

I leaned back in my wing-backed chair. "Beckett can have it, if he wants it." I scanned the great room. "Let's ditch these window treatments and repaint in here, too. Something simple. Get rid of the plants, I'm, tired of taking care of them. If Beckett wants them, he can take them. I want a new sofa. Let's move this one into the library."

Paul inspected the rich brown leather he was sitting on. "Yeah. This is a great piece. The silver studs make it." He ran his fingers over the supple hide. "Where'd you get this?"

"Traveling out West. We went to a Dude Ranch when Bradley was fourteen. Beckett thought it would be a great adventure," I chided. "We all ate campfire food for five days and had sore backsides from trotting around on horses. Beckett and Bradley had great horses. Mine was skittish, afraid of rocks, but she was a beautiful Appaloosa. The lodge had a great sofa that we'd hang out on." I gestured to our replica. "And you're sitting on it. Great memories."

"Sounds like a good time," Paul responded as he crossed his legs.

"Yeah, it was. Bradley loved the dirt and the smell of fresh earth. I loved being on a horse under the big blue sky. It really was the best adventure."

My heart warmed, knowing that we had shared that time together. Memories like that overshadowed the petty arguments and quiet evenings Beckett and I had grown accustom to once Bradley went off to college. I worried about Bradley; Beckett worried about finances. I worried making sure the lawn was properly edged; Beckett stressed over his job. I worked harder to get a Master's degree while Beckett took on consulting jobs. Shaking my head, I realized how each nuance had driven the wedge deeper. I got up and strolled over to the heavy oak mantle we spent hours restoring. My eyes caressed the photographs lining the beautiful architectural element. "I have to admit, Beckett looked good on that horse," I muttered.

Mom called from the kitchen, "Hey, you two, you about done? The rain stopped and breakfast is waiting. It's on the patio. And you don't want an old lady to eat alone, do you?"

"You'll have to excuse my mother. You really don't have to stay." I secretly hoped Paul would take the opportunity to leave.

"Actually, it's been a busy morning and I am kind of hungry. Smells great." Paul pushed himself up from the sofa and headed for the kitchen.

I stretched and mumbled to myself, "Sure, just make yourself at home, everybody else does." I followed. The food did smell good. Yesterday, after all of Mom's pestering she provoked me into standing on the scale in the extra bathroom. I figured the doctor's office was light. Guess not. I was down seven pounds. I hadn't been one hundred fourteen pounds since college. The power of stress amazed me.

Mom looked charming as she sat reading the paper. My eyebrows shot up when I saw four place settings. "Um, four plates? Invisible friend?"

She closed the paper and stared at me through narrowed eyes. "Ha, ha. The last time anyone had an invisible friend, it was you. Lily Anderson wouldn't play with you because you snapped her Barbie's head off. You couldn't stand being alone. You said it was the worst week of your life."

"Until now," I joked. Paul pulled out a chair for me. Mom was right. I never liked being alone. Beckett reassured me that I'd find someone when this was all said and done, but I wasn't sure that would ever happen or that I even wanted it to happen. His feeble attempt of making a purse out of a sow's ear only made me think he was full of crap.

"Hey, that whole Barbie incident was an accident." I giggled as Paul arranged his napkin on his lap with exact precision. "Seriously, four plates?" I reiterated.

"Chloe will be here in a minute," Mom said as she put the morning newspaper on the lounge chair behind her.

"What?" I pointed to my head and pushed my hair back showing Paul the stitches. "Oh, I forgot. You already saw them."

Paul wrinkled his nose. "Ouch."

"Can't I catch a break?" I paused, staring into Paul's dark eyes then over to Mom. "Sure, Chloe's father was kind yesterday, but his kid split my head wide open sliding into home plate trying to catch the Triscuit box. Come on. What is she going to do to me today?"

"She's just a little girl. Be nice. You were a little girl once, too," Mom reminded me as she sipped her coffee.

I peeled back the wrapper of my blueberry muffin then broke off a piece of moist cake and plopped it in my mouth. The sugar crystals melted on my tongue sending a jolt of happiness through my bloodstream. Chloe's humming penetrated the dewy air. "Ah, here she comes. Does her dad know she's over here? I am supposed to call, you know."

"Lighten up. He's doing the best he can. Do you know Chloe's mom lives in California? Left her here with her dad. He's a pediatrician, works long hours. And that nanny, I'm not so sure about her, either," Mom rambled.

"Sounds rough," Paul interjected. "Although, this bacon is sinful." He lifted the carafe to warm my mother's coffee.

I sat back, reveling in the fact that Paul felt so comfortable amongst strangers. "Chloe already told me about her Hollywood mom," I said, staring at Mom. Chloe strolled around the corner of the patio dragging Voodoo behind her. "You know, poor Voodoo's face is getting a little worn. Maybe you should carry him," I suggested.

Paul scooted out the chair between my mom and himself.

"He doesn't mind," Chloe said. "He's independent. Dad says, 'It's good to get a few scrapes here and there.'"

Paul nodded in agreement as he helped Chloe get situated. "Your dad sounds like a smart man. I'm Paul. I'm helping Maggie fix her house up."

"Yeah, I know. I seen you before," she replied, carefully reaching for a piece of bacon.

"Saw," I interjected. "I saw," I repeated.

"I thought this was summer vacation," Mom said.

Paul laughed and twisted off the top to his muffin. "Remember that *Seinfeld*?" he asked.

Mom and I laughed.

Chloe snorted. "You people sure are something."

"Hello," a voice called from inside the house.

Chloe shrugged. "It's not J.P. He's at the office."

"Who?" I asked.

"J.P. That's my dad. John Patrick. All his friends call him J.P." She peeled back the paper from her muffin and took a big bite. Crumbs showered down around her.

John didn't strike me as the kind of guy with lots of friends. None of us moved from our respective seats. With Bradley away, Chloe, Paul, and Glad were all accounted for so, I figured things couldn't get weirder. I gulped my juice and peered back at the doors leading to the kitchen just as Beckett poked his head out.

"Looks like a party. Maybe I should come back," he suggested.

"Nonsense," Mom chimed. "There's food in the kitchen. Get yourself a plate."

"Only if it's okay with Maggie," he replied.

His puppy dog expression searched for my approval. "Geez, make me the bad guy, why don't you?" I glanced around the table. All eyes were on me. "Help yourself." I moved the food around on my plate making neat little piles that didn't touch.

The soft breeze blew some of my hair loose from my bun. I twirled the lock of hair and stuck it back in my hair tie. Beckett came out with a heaping plate of fruit and toast. J.P. followed in his footsteps. I eyed Chloe.

"I guess I was wrong. Hi, Dad," she chirped as she gobbled up a strawberry.

Mom and I stared at each other in secret code.

"Sorry to intrude. I thought maybe I'd find her here." John arched an eyebrow in his daughter's direction.

"Not her fault," Mom interrupted. "Not Maggie's either. I invited Chloe to be my guest. Maggie's lived this long, I figured if I could handle her, I could handle Chloe, too."

"Nice one, Mom," I said. "Beckett, this is John, my new neighbor. John this is Beckett." I assessed Beckett's trendy shoes and slacks. *He looks handsome as ever. Damn him. He probably thinks I look like I just rolled out of bed, oh wait, I did.* I wondered if Mom had the gumption to arrange this little gathering. Knowing her, she did.

The men shook hands.

Paul's gaze caught my attention. He slid his chair back and got up. "Hi there, it's nice to meet you in person," Paul said. He shook Beckett's hand. "We've only spoken on the phone," Paul clarified.

That answered many lingering questions. "And John, this is Paul, my decorator, and Paul this is John, my neighbor. Do I have everybody covered?" I asked. Another strand of hair fell into my face. Exasperated, I blew it away. This was just too much work. "If I skipped anyone—"

"You skipped me," Chloe declared. "Beckett, Mr. Maggie, it's nice to meet you." She smiled at her dad. Her front tooth was growing in making her look less like a jack-o'-lantern and more like a troll. "Dad, you didn't ask Maggie how her head was."

John stepped closer to my chair. I could feel his heat as his fingers grazed my skin when he moved strands of hair away from my temple. "No bandage this morning."

I touched the spot carefully as Chloe and I shared a glance, her smile apologetic. "I must have lost it in my sleep. I'm fine." I carefully glanced up in his direction feeling the air change between us.

Beckett leaned in closer. I could feel his breath. He patted my head like a puppy. "What happened?"

Chloe raised her hand. "I happened. We bumped heads. She got stitches, I didn't," she mumbled, trying to hold juice in her mouth and talk at the same time.

Mom slurped her coffee.

I ignored the smirk on her face as I rewound the conversation in my head. Words were pinging from person to person. My eyes went from Beckett to John. A bolt of guilt jarred me for misjudging Beckett and Paul's relationship earlier. I watched the men interact.

"Chloe, you come home after you eat." John's voice was stern. "Nora is cleaning. She's going to take you to the park today."

Chloe frowned. "I'd rather stay here. Glad is way more fun and Maggie will come around."

Waves of heat washed over my body and I rolled my eyes.

"That's not nice," Chloe said. "I'm not allowed to roll my eyes at home or at school."

My mother grinned as she raised her mug to her lips. She slurped her coffee again. I watched her gaze move from Beckett, to Paul, to John, and then to me. The twinkle in her eyes scared me as she scanned the table of misfits. I was getting the feeling that she and Chloe had a lot in common.

Chloe pulled Voodoo up by his string, patted his nubby fur, then moved his head all around her plate. "He likes to eat the crumbs." She grabbed his limp, matted purple paw and made him rub his stomach.

Chapter 9

After breakfast, Beckett followed me into the library.

"You can take the rug. I don't want it. It doesn't go with my teacups." I crossed my arms then glanced at his journal tucked away on the shelf.

"Are you sure?" he questioned. "You picked it out."

"I picked it out for you." I could feel my tongue sharpen and I leaned against the windowsill where my new drafting table would go. The light was perfect for shading in my photographs. "Why didn't you just say something earlier? You could have saved us a lot of time." I wanted to hear the words, not read them.

Beckett rubbed his temples. "I just—"

I waited.

I waited some more.

I slid my back down the wall and sat on the floor, eyeballing him.

He kneeled in front of me. "I just didn't have the courage. I couldn't leave you and Bradley."

Sadness rimmed his eyes. I wouldn't let myself cry in front of him, so I blinked away the wetness. I pushed at his hands when he tried to comfort me. I knew he needed consoling as much as I did, but I couldn't let him touch me. "I'm sorry this happened," I whispered. "Out of all our friends, I thought we were the couple that would last forever."

Beckett stood then left of the room.

I lagged behind him.

He paced back and forth in the great room.

"You can take the plants in here. I don't want them either."

"I thought you liked them," he said.

"I'm tired of taking care of them." I picked at my thumbnail. "I told you that because I knew you liked them. I said lots of things I thought you wanted to hear, needed to hear." My voice trailed off. "I thought it was called compromising."

He came closer. "What?"

The longer I stared at him, the more he felt like a stranger. I didn't know him anymore. I doubted I knew myself. "It's what wives do, right?"

Beckett took a deep breath. He ran his hands through his salt-and-pepper hair. "What?" he asked, raising his voice. "I'm trying to make this as easy as possible and now, you're going to be a bitch." He rubbed his chin and glared at me with a raging stare. "Not once, did I ever say that to you, and do you know why?" He sucked in a pocket of air. "Because you were never one to balk, you were never difficult. What the hell?"

I moved away. Beckett's rare display of anger scared me. His seething tone sent chills up my spine.

"If you weren't happy, you should have said something," he muttered, walking away from me. "I'm not the only one that could have saved us some time."

"I thought I was happy, Beckett. I thought we had everything," I retorted. "You're the one who changed everything. I would have stayed with you forever. Regardless."

Beckett plopped down on the sofa with a thud. "I didn't want to. I had to. The truth was killing me. It was killing you. Didn't you feel it?"

I felt my eyes narrow as I fumed. "No, I didn't." I wanted to hear him say it was his fault again. I wanted to make my burden less cumbersome. We rarely fought when we were married and now there were no consequences for not getting along. I pulled my wedding band from my pocket and put it on the mantle. It was going to take more than a hefty gulp of air to control myself.

"Damn it, Maggie, I couldn't live with myself if I robbed you of the rest of your life."

Beckett got up, came over to me, then put his arm around my shoulder. "I'm sorry, Maggie. I want to make this up to you."

Tears brimmed. "You hired Paul and the lawn service, which I'd like you to cancel. Let's call it even. I'm not sure there is anything else you could possibly do. I think you've done enough."

Beckett lowered his gaze to mask his own tears. He never could hide his sensitivity.

"You can't change who you are. All I ever wanted was you," I whimpered.

"Oh, Maggie." He sighed. "I'll always be here for you."

"I know, but it will never be the same." My throat constricted as my heart withered.

"Bradley's grown. It's time for us to move on. Can't you see it? We'll all be fine."

"Will we?" I snickered, wiping away the stream of tears with the back of my hand. "Just tell me, tell me one thing. Did you ever cheat? What is Paul Mitchell to you?" I wished I could take back the words the minute I said them. I knew Paul and Beckett were only acquaintances.

Beckett fingers slid down my arm, his eyes like tiny slits. "Paul and I met for the first time today. Lois gave me his number and he seemed nice on the phone," he said, catching his breath. "Maggie, I couldn't even admit to myself what was happening. I stayed with you the whole time knowing I'd made a commitment, to you, to Bradley. Never, ever did I cheat," he whispered earnestly.

A spasm bolted through my chest as if I were feeling his pain. I'd caused the hurt in his voice. "Damn it, Beckett."

"What? Would you feel better if I had gone behind your back, made this ugly? I had a family to consider. Believe it or not, I loved you every minute. I still do." His voice trailed off into the electric air between us. "We never fought about this before. Why now?"

"It would make it a whole lot easier to hate you because hating is what happens when couple's split. They don't get along. They fight over things. They make the other person feel tiny. And you have done none of those things," I cried. "You are such a saint."

"Maggie, I could never hurt you that way."

"Damn it, Beckett, will you just stop it?" I shouted. "You're helping with everything. How am I ever going to learn to live alone if you're always taking care of me? Just because you feel bad about leaving me doesn't mean you can smother me with kindness." The words rolled off my tongue with ease. By the look in his eyes, I knew his hurt matched mine. Now, we were even.

"I'd better go. We'll talk later," Beckett said.

I slid the ponytail holder out of my hair then gingerly shook out my tresses trying to ease the tension without making the gash throb. "Maybe that's a good idea." I touched the stitches in my left temple making sure I hadn't opened the wound. The stiff edges of the string poked my fingertips like miniature barbs.

I leaned against the doorjamb. What had I done? My sharp words had wounded Beckett. My heart sank as he loaded his rug into the car and drove away without waving goodbye. He always waved goodbye, tradition. "Damn it." I pulled my hair back, combed it with my fingers, then secured it with my ponytail holder before turning my attention to the soft footsteps approaching.

"You really shouldn't swear, even if you're mad at someone," Chloe said.

I crossed my arms. Her twang of sincerity warmed me. "I know."

"What did he do that was so bad?" Chloe picked up Voodoo. "I still love Voodoo when he does bad things. I know my dad still loves me even when I don't do my chores, trick Nanny Nora, or even break things. Did Beckett break something?"

I sighed. "Yeah, Beckett broke something." My sarcasm tasted sour. I swallowed away the lump in my throat.

"You could glue it or get a repairman."

Chloe handed me Voodoo. He had crumbs in his purple fur and a black smudge around his only eye.

"What happened here?" I asked, pointing to the dark circle.

"He ran into Nanny Nora and got a black eye. Dad wrote him a *scription* for pain."

I smiled. "You mean prescription?" I handed Voodoo back to her.

Chloe scrunched up her nose. "That's what I said, *scription.*" She cuddled Voodoo and kissed his nose then dropped him on the floor. "You really should try not to practice those teacher habits on summer vacation." She put Voodoo's leash around her wrist.

As Chloe stared hard into my face, I knew I had rolled my eyes. "I know, I know. It's a bad habit."

"We all have our vices," Chloe stated with conviction.

I raised my eyebrow in her direction wondering whom she learned that phrase from. I pushed myself away from the doorway. "Let's go see what the others are doing."

Chloe stopped me, her green eyes churning with wisdom. "My dad says you should forgive people."

Her fingers grazed my arms. Her warm touch surprised me, her gentleness alarming. The seven-year-old was right, but I wasn't ready to forgive Beckett, or myself.

"I'm trying to forgive my mom for leaving us. It's really hard," she whispered as she pulled her hand away.

A shadow drifted over Chloe's stare, and my heart wilted. This time I kept my thoughts to myself. *Shit.* This was going to be a love-hate relationship. I followed in her footsteps as she headed for the kitchen. She stopped abruptly, and I bumped into her. Her belch belonged to a drunk, not a young girl.

I cringed, thinking about Bradley, who would have laughed his head off. I patted Chloe's head. Her hair was soft and wispy.

"Excuse me," she chimed. Pride laced her squeaky voice. "Thanks for not telling me to say that. A pat on the head works just fine and it's a lot less nagging."

I nudged her out of my way as we stepped into the kitchen. Mom was standing at the sink washing dishes.

"I have a dishwasher, you know. You don't have to do that," I said, wishing her habits were more similar to mine. My heart skipped a beat when I realized she'd overheard my conversation with Beckett and Chloe.

Mom turned her attention back to scrubbing the bacon pan. "Chloe's right. Forgiveness goes a long way."

I sat on a stool at the counter and folded the napkins trying to make the corners even. I like even. I liked uniform. I liked being married even if I realized we were growing apart, but we really weren't growing apart. Beckett was finding his way and I was in denial.

Chloe pulled out the stool next to mine. I felt pint-sized and young in her company. She patted the top of my head gently like Beckett did at breakfast.

"Just a reminder," she said with her jack-o-lantern smile. "Glad, can we have dessert?"

"Oh, that sounds good. Something chocolate?" I suggested, thinking about the leftover cake in the refrigerator. Chloe's hopeful eyes glistened as she smacked her lips and rubbed her tummy.

Mom turned toward us. "It's too early. Chloe, your dad will have a fit," she said.

Chloe and I frowned at each other.

"I won't tell," she whined. "I promise. I promise, hope to die, stick a needle in my eye." She made the sign of the cross on her chest. "Pinky swear," she blurted out as she made a fist and stuck out her pinky in my direction.

I hooked my pinky finger with hers. Her wet finger made me flinch. "Gross." I sighed and I wiped off my hand on my sundress.

"It's nothing gross."

Mom laughed. "No dessert, you two. Now get out of here so I can finish the dishes."

I raised my eyebrows at Chloe.

Chloe's green eyes held my stare. "We should go. She'll make us do the dishes if we bug her."

After standing up, I scooted my seat underneath the counter. "You're right. Let's get out of here." I wondered where Paul went. Chloe fell from her chair. She rubbed her head then peered up at me with deer in the headlight eyes. I waited for the wailing to begin.

Chloe popped up, shook her body like a rag doll, and smiled. "Don't worry, I'll be fine."

"Good. Now where did Paul go?" I asked.

"He left, darling." Mom carefully washed the delicate juice glasses I inherited from my grandmother.

I was a bad hostess. Mom cooked and cleaned while I skulked around bickering with Beckett. Guilt taunted me like a pesky child pulling at my shirttail. Today, I hurt Beckett, I ignored Paul, and all he was doing was trying to help, but seeing them instantly connect had bothered me. Beckett and I hadn't had that connection in years. Paul secretly understood Beckett. I saw it in his eyes. "I just want to understand," I muttered, deciding what to plant next in the backyard. Jealousy rattled my nerves.

Chapter 10

I beeped myself into the radiation center with my plastic card bearing a barcode especially designated for me. "Too bad this isn't a prepaid Visa," I joked to myself. I had been reduced to a bar code like a can of soup, a candy bar, a box of Cheerios, something to be swiped, and sent down the conveyor belt to the next station.

The vacant office reminded me it was dumb to take the last appointment of the day. Today was my first treatment and I still hadn't shared my diagnosis with anyone.

The impromptu breakfast party, then the confrontation with Beckett had left me spent. This seemed like the easiest of the three scenarios. All I had to do was lay there. The glass window to the receptionist's desk was open, but Debbie wasn't waiting with a smile today. Debbie was blond, caring, perky, and young, all the ingredients for a much-needed cocktail.

I slipped my identification card back into my bag with the baby powder I used twice a day to reduce the redness, the burn, and the irritation from the treatment. Seriously, it was as simplistic as baby powder. It really wasn't, but I was warned not to use lotions because it could cause far worse consequences. The machine would radiate my left breast, leaving me burned and internally scarred over time, but in the long run, probably save my life. I smiled at my own cliché. It felt as if I was robbing Peter to pay Paul. *Let's get this over with,* I told myself.

Promptly after changing into my drab blue hospital gown, I was escorted to the radiation room. The narrow table felt cold and hard. Goosebumps covered my arms. The red stream of bright light on the ceiling caught my attention.

"Here we go, Maggie," Rita said.

Her eyes were kind and offered strength, and I found her smile infectious. "Here we go," I mumbled, careful not to move.

Rita guided my arm into the cradle above my head then exposed my body to the chilly room. She bound my feet with a fat rubber band. I tucked my arm under my side just like we practiced. Being in the exact spot was crucial.

"Today the treatment will be quite short. Over time, the increments of exposure will increase and by next Friday, we will be ready to take the first set of x-rays," Rita instructed. "Bobbi is here to help."

Bobbi leaned over. "You won't be here long," she reassured me.

I carefully moved my eyes from Rita to Bobbi not wanting to contaminate my position. I forced myself to be strong and swallow away the bitter taste at the back of my throat. I smiled, trying to emulate Rita and Bobbi's positive energy.

"You okay?" Rita asked, touching my shoulder.

"Sure," I answered, knowing she saw my angst clearly.

I saw them leave and the thick door shut as I stared at the reflection of the cold room in the plastic ceiling tiles. The shadows and the whirr of the machine were my only companions. Beckoning energy from the heavens, I stared at the decorative ceiling as the red light cut through the silence like a laser beam. Chills crept through my body.

The machine buzzed.

Clicked.

I swallowed, breathing cautiously not to disturb my position.

The machine rotated.

I noted the shadows on the ceiling, remembering the shapes so as to remember them for the future, making them my timetable, knowing when the session would end. Light from the hallway streamed into the dark room as the heavy door opened. I breathed in a sense of relief. Heavenly. Rita and Bobbi rejoined my little party, undid my feet, and set me free.

"Um, we have a silly question," Rita said.

"Go ahead, it can't be weirder than anything else I've heard today." I grabbed Bobbi's arm for support as I sat up and watched Rita shrug away doubt.

"You don't walk with a cane, do you?" she asked, shaking her head. "You know, like a walking cane?"

"No, why?"

She shook her head. "This is so strange. You were the last one to check yourself in and no one else has been here. You sure, you didn't bring a cane today?"

"Nope," I replied, swinging my legs off the table, eager to leave. I stopped when my spine tingled. "Why?"

"You know we check the waiting room regularly. We checked the patient names with the doctors."

"I knew she didn't have a cane," Bobbi interjected.

Rita glanced over to Bobbi then back to me. "Weird," she said.

I shrugged then left to get dressed. I had no clue what their cryptic dialogue meant.

Debbie smiled at me as I walked past her desk on the way out. She held up the cane. "Sure you didn't have a cane?"

I stopped. "Nope."

She put the cane on the counter between us. It rolled to one side. My insides turned over as I touched the name etched into the black paint. *Walter James.*

"No one knows where this came from. We'll have to put it in the lost and found."

That familiar burn seared behind my eyes. I wanted to take the cane, but knew it wasn't mine. I knew I was being watched over.

"You okay?" Debbie asked.

"Walter James was my father's name. He passed four

years ago." I waited for her to tell me I was crazy to make such a phenomenal connection. His spirit brushed against me. I felt him stroke my hair. The wave of emotion pulled me under as I tried to catch my breath.

Debbie touched the cane. "Do you want it? What are the chances?"

I shook my head desperately wanting to take the cane. "I can't take it. What if it belongs to some little old man? That's not right." I took one last look, knowing I may not see my father again for another thirty-five years or so.

"Okay," she chimed. "But what are the chances? Spooky."

I silently said goodbye to the cane.

I'd been wrong about the day's events.

This was the hardest task by far.

The cane haunted my thoughts. *It has to be Dad.* The chills, his name scratched into the black paint metal, the way it'd shown up on the floor at the check-in desk. Finally, someone was watching over me. *Thank you, Dad, I knew I could always count on you. Next time, don't wait so long to show yourself. I promise, I won't be scared.*

A familiar, warm sensation passed over me. I turned the key in the lock of the front door. "If that cane is there on the last day of this treatment, I am going to claim it," I stated as I pushed the door open. "God, I hate it when this front door sticks."

I gasped at the sight of the uninvited visitor. "Jesus," I blurted out.

Mom stared at me with her usual gaze. "So how was it?"

"How was what?" I held up my new books showing her the covers. She didn't need to know it was my reward for surviving the first day of cancer treatment without having a meltdown. "The bookstore was fine. Same old, same old." I set the paperbacks on the table in the foyer.

Mom picked them up. "*The Happiness Project* by Gretchen Rubin. Interesting. I've heard of this before. Maybe it will help."

"I hope." I watched her read the back cover of Lori Nelson Spielman's *The Life List*.

"I'm sure you've got a list, too."

"I do." I said, touching one of the daisies on the purple cover. "And by the way, please feel free to break in whenever you want." I shot her my fierce teacher scowl.

"I have a key," she huffed. "I don't believe that counts as breaking and entering."

"Seriously, you should call first." I marched toward the kitchen smelling heavenly aromas. The sweet seductive smell of dinner washed away any irritation.

"I started the chicken. I figured you could use the support." Her footsteps echoed behind me on the slate floor.

The coolness of the stone soothed my aching feet. "So, I smell. What's on the menu?" There was already a glass of wine poured for me. "Thanks, Mom. This whole thing with Beckett is throwing me for a loop. I can't make heads or tails of it."

Mom sat at the counter and sipped her Merlot. "So this is how we're going to play." She peered over the top of her tortoise shell reading glasses.

Ignoring her, I plucked a strawberry out of the fruit salad. Taking a bite, the red fruit filled my mouth with juicy sweetness I craved. "Play what?" I asked. She was prying. I wondered how much she knew.

Mom's glossy eyes warned me she knew plenty.

I sat back, too stubborn to talk, too stubborn to say I had the 'C' word out loud. The taste of fresh strawberry lingered on my tongue, its potent beauty masking the metallic taste at the back of my throat. I swallowed away the familiar lump then nibbled on another berry, the juice staining my plain nails.

I leaned back against the counter to steady myself, averting her gaze, not wanting to disappoint her. I didn't want her to worry. There was no doubt in my mind that I could fight this battle alone. There was no doubt in my mind that if I kept my breast cancer a secret, even I would believe it was just another bump in the road. Blinders made it easy to dismiss the severity. My breast ached, and I tugged my cardigan closed.

"Marjorie Jean, this is serious. I know."

She was giving me the opportunity to fess up. She was giving me the opportunity to meet my nemesis head on. I watched as she drained her glass of wine. My jaw dropped in awe as she swigged down the red nectar, refilled her glass, and chugged that one, too.

"Wow, that was impressive. I bet you're good at doing shots." I pursed my lips at her sharp gaze. "What? Divorce is hard. How often does your husband take you to dinner, then drop the bomb that he is gay?" I added, reaching for a blueberry.

Mom refilled her glass. Her left pointer finger shot up toward the ceiling. "What!" Her wine almost spilled over the lip of the glass.

I nodded, hoping Beckett's truth would distract her from her original quest to delve into my personal health affairs. I assessed her disposition then peeked curiously into the oven not caring what was on the menu. "Dinner looks great." I gave her a thumbs-up. "It's kind of hot to turn on the oven, though."

Mom gently put her glass on the counter. Her chest rose and fell in time with the deep breaths she was taking to calm her temper. I'd watched it fester as I sipped at my wine. I'd baited Beckett earlier. I silently reprimanded myself for the cruel deed, but yet I tormented my mother with the same insensitive tactics. With a cold heart, I'd stood by and watched her come unglued.

"Listen here, darling daughter, I watched your father negate health issues. I know this must be hard for you, but it's even harder for me to stand back and watch you play the martyr. You don't have to do this alone."

"I—"

"Before you go any further, young lady." She took a sip of her wine. "We will get to Beckett later. It's *you* I am worried about. And if you are making tale about poor Beckett as a distraction, there will be consequences."

I nodded, accepting her challenge. "I—"

"Stop right there." She took another deep swallow of wine.

"Well, if you keep drinking, I just may have a chance to come out unscathed. You won't remember anything if you pass out." Stepping toward her, I picked up the merlot bottle then refilled her glass. "Good stuff."

"What in heaven's name has gotten into you?"

I leaned back against the counter as she caught her breath. She ran her fingers through her hair, took off her glasses, then blinked and rubbed her temples. The vein on the left side of her head protruded. I hadn't seen that expression since I washed dad's car with rocks when I was four.

"Maggie, you can't hide from the fact you have cancer anymore. You need people. You need me. It's one thing to antagonize the handsome doctor next door . . ."

I tuned her out. I hadn't really thought of John as handsome, but he was growing on me. I shook my head, focusing on Mom's lips. They were thin and pursed.

"Your dad kept things to himself and that got him six feet under, God rest his soul." Mom rolled her eyes upward and she mouthed an apology.

The timer on the stove dinged.

I took the chicken out of the oven and turned off the heat.

The ceramic dish clanked on the wooden cutting board, startling us both.

"Oops," I said.

"Not that I could have saved him, but I cannot watch you keep such a giant secret to yourself. Look where that got you when Beckett did that." Her wicked stare unnerved me. "You better not be fibbing about that," she warned.

I opened the French doors to the patio and breathed deeply. The warm summer air filled my lungs. The touch of her hand on my shoulder shattered the barrier between us. "How did you find out?" I asked. The world felt strangely calm.

"I found your doctor's card the other day when I was cleaning up. I know, I shouldn't let myself in, but I can't help it. I want to be here with you. Sometimes the only way I can feel close to your father is by just being with you."

I didn't have the courage to face her. Beckett and I used Bradley as a bandage, too.

"I followed you today when you left."

Swallowing hard, I walked into the early evening air. I kicked off my sandals and sprawled out on my lounge chair. The thick cushion absorbed my weight. I rested my head against the pillow noting the tangerine streaks in the dusky horizon.

"I'm sorry," Mom said.

Her warm hand rested on my shoulder. "What?" I sighed. "You're sorry that I have breast cancer?" Her quick intake of air stopped my words. "Or that you're a snoop." I waited for her chastising tone. When it didn't come, I filled the void the best I knew how. "The grass in the yard is greener than ever. I guess there are some perks to being sick. You get to stay home, hide, and water the lawn a whole heck of a lot."

The sky reddened and I wished upon the whimsical magic of the flickering fireflies to show me the way. I wondered why Mother Nature broke the spark in their tail into short intervals making them blink like they were flying in slow motion. I suspected it was to give humans an opportunity to believe in fairy tales. Lost in the unpredictable flashes of light, tranquility washed over me. The weight in my chest moved across my arms and down my legs, then it left my body. My energy drained, the light dimmed, and the flying creatures before me blinked on and off, in secret code.

When I turned around, Mom was gone.

Chapter 11

The doorbell jarred me from my sleep. I uncovered my head to check the time on the clock. "Shit," I grunted. Ten o'clock. I hadn't slept in that long since I had the flu in March.

"Yeah, yeah," I mumbled, wrapping my cottony pink robe around me. I held the rail as I clonked down the stairs. From my vantage point, I could see through the window to the porch. I didn't recognize the man standing there.

I rubbed my eyes, tucked my uncombed hair behind my ears, then opened the door just enough to speak. "Yes, can I help you?"

"I have a package for Maggie Littleton," he said, fiddling with his clipboard and pen. "You're going to have to sign."

"My name isn't Littleton anymore. It's Abernathy. Does it matter?" I asked.

"No," he replied, shaking his head like Don Knotts.

I opened the door more. He pushed a plain brown box in my direction. "You're not a UPS man." I scanned the front yard. "Who is this from?" I blew a wisp of hair away from my face as he smirked.

"I just deliver them," he stated.

"Yeah, okay, but what delivery agency has customers sign on notebook paper?" I raised an eyebrow. "Give me the box."

"Please sign your full name, Miss."

"This has my mother written all over it." I narrowed my eyes, trying to place the man. His stance was familiar, but I had no clue to his identity. I took the box after scrawling the words *Princess Leia Organa* on his legal pad. "Thank you." I forced a toothy smile and shut the door. I shook the box. Nothing. I shook it harder. Nothing. I carried it into the kitchen and put it on the counter, then poured myself some juice.

There was no breakfast.

There was no unexpected company.

There was no coffee brewing.

There was no anything.

Tired and sluggish, I assessed my package, square, brown, and lightweight. The doctor warned me about fatigue, but I doubted my lack of energy was zapped from radiation. It was still too early in the treatment.

I shuffled back to my bedroom, kicked off my slippers, dropped my robe on the floor next to my bed, and climbed back in. My bed didn't judge. It coddled my weary soul. I pulled the covers over my head and closed my eyes, then uncovered my head just as quickly so I could stare at the ceiling and think about the anonymous package that sparked curiosity. I tried to place the man at the door. His plaid shorts reminded me of camp. My forehead beaded with sweat. I kicked off the duvet willing the air-conditioning to click on then spread my arms across the whole bed. If Beckett were here, he would have gotten a good swift blow. The overhead fan spun, making the rays of light flicker across the ceiling like Morse Code. "These hot flashes suck," I mumbled. "God, I hate that word, *suck*, but they really do."

My hands felt clammy as the dew on my skin spread. In a huff, I scrambled to the shower, dropping my pajamas in my tracks, and quickly turning on the tepid water. I glanced at my thinner-than-usual silhouette in the mirror. If I sucked in my belly, I could see my ribs. If I saw myself on the street and I were a stranger, I'd say, "That girl needs to eat some cake." I faced myself. My eyes focused on my bruised skin, its purple tone reminiscent of ripe eggplant. I carefully touched the healing incision then jerked my hand away afraid to connect with it.

I whisked back the shower curtain and hurried into the refreshing streams of water. I squealed taking in a sharp breath. It was cold. I needed the jolt.

I expected my mother.

I expected a visit from Chloe.

I touched the stitches on the side of my head.

I wanted the water to wash away the year. I worked so damn hard getting my degree, applying for the principal's opening, serving on committees, attending after-hour events to show my dedication, and where did it get me? Nowhere. What did Jenny McBride have, that I didn't? I doubted she even liked kids. I closed my eyes pushing away the disappointment, trying to remember my original desire to guide students into the future with some sort of dignity regardless of their destiny or dreams. I pressed my fingers to my eyelids. How the hell did I become a master teacher to others, but ignore my own wisdom?

Trying to please others and doing good deeds to achieve human worth was tiring. I wanted my footprints to lead others in a positive direction and how would that happened if I continued down the path I had chosen? I gulped for air and water pelted against my teeth. I scrubbed my head vigorously, careful not to touch the stitches, massaging the roots, getting out the particles of disgust, disease, and distain. I screamed into the air, "I want to be whole again."

Cold water washed away the suds, while I clenched my fists. I gave myself three minutes, the time frizz control conditioner needed to do its job, to regain some sort of composure. I turned the water gauge warmer then set the showerhead to pulsate. Jet streams pelted my back, sending messaging blows down my spine.

How was it possible that in one split second my life was turned upside down, broken to bits, and shaken like a cupful of dice? I've seen it before from a distance, and preferred it that way. I counted to sixty, just like the kids do in my classroom when they want to tell me something, but need time to collect themselves. "One, two, three, four, five, six, times ten," I chanted. I grinned at my cleverness. I unclenched my fist, washed out the conditioner, turned off the water, and wondered how I could spend my day being productive.

When I returned to the kitchen, the package hadn't moved. I sipped at the orange juice I'd left on the counter and ran my fingers over the cool brown cardboard pondering the contents, pondering the troll-like deliveryman in plaid.

I rummaged in the drawer for my Pampered Chef scissors, tough enough to do any job, maybe I should have written that on my resume, tough enough for any job. I cut the clear packing tap and opened the box. Inside was a white porcelain teacup. The rim was dotted with pink circles and at every fifth circle there was a pink breast cancer awareness ribbon. A pink piece of tissue paper inside the cup adorned a white ribbon.

The pressure behind my eyes began to build. I blinked away the nagging sensation. I didn't have the energy for a second meltdown. The day was just beginning.

I lifted the gift wrapped in tissue and undid the ribbon. Inside was a necklace. In that instant, I regretted my insensitivity. How did I let myself dismiss my mother's need to reach out? When your child has a disease, you own it, too. It infects everyone no matter how hard you try not to let it.

I fingered the elegant sterling silver charm that dangled from a delicate chain. I was never delicate, just practical, and driven. Bradley and Beckett had been my charms.

The half of heart had jagged edges as if someone snapped it in two. I knew who wore the matching half. I dug through the Styrofoam peanuts to retrieve the card, which confirmed my thought. I read it aloud. "'When you are ready to accept those things that only loved ones can give you, your heart will be whole again. You do not choose life. Life chooses you. Glad.'"

I set the card on the counter then stroked the small trinket wondering how the hell she managed to get the upper hand on all things gone sour. Undoing the clasp, I put the necklace on even though I couldn't bear to wear one more ounce around my neck for it just might make the scales tip with the chip already on my shoulder. I couldn't take another face-plant, but my mother was worth the risk.

With Beckett's rug gone, the wooden floor in the library glistened in the daylight. I imagined the room filled with my things. It was time to call Paul. He needed to get this job done and now. I needed my space, something I never really owned. I poked the numbers on the telephone and waited for him to answer.

"Hi, Paul, it's Maggie. Yup, and first of all, I'd like to apologize for the other day. I didn't mean to leave you hanging. Sorry." I twirled my hair around my finger as I spoke. "Oh, that's great. Really, an estate sale? Can't wait. It sounds perfect. Sure. Tomorrow would be good." My voice trailed off. "Oh, I'm sure it will look great. We have to start somewhere. Even better." I took a deep breath as he stroked my bruised ego from his end of the telephone. "A picture, what a great idea, I'll look for your text. Sure. Bye now. And Paul." I paused. The words got stuck in my throat. "Thank you." I ended the call.

My phone chimed and I eagerly opened the photograph. The desk sat on two black steel pedestals, simple, sleek, perfect. How could he find something so right, even if it wasn't what I had in mind? Underneath he wrote the specs. *63" long, 4 drawers, iron pulls, for the contemporary you.*

"I love it," I whispered into the air.

I took my camera from the shelf and checked the battery. It wasn't my thirty-five millimeter from high school, but close enough. Getting used to it was like going on a first date. This new camera was growing on me, and I wouldn't give it up for anything.

The beach called silently for my company like a long lost friend.

I rummaged through the hallway closet looking for my sea-grass fedora. I did a little jump and knocked it down from the top shelf, then kicked the three scarves that fell with it to the back of the closet. And off I went.

Too anxious to capture the daylight and pressured by the ticking clock not to forget my daily radiation appointment time of three o'clock, I grabbed my keys. I couldn't remember the last time I had gone to the beach. Beckett and I had practically raised Bradley there and somehow its mystique faded away with time. Mom always warned me about the sun's power on a redhead, but I loved the heat that warmed me to the core. Freckles never bothered me as much as they did her. Sunscreen was one of those things I loathed, but couldn't live without. I used to lather Bradley up while remembering not being coated at all as a kid in the midday sun. Mom would sit under a tree with her beach hat and cover-up on, and I'd be in the midst of hot sand and scalding sun. Something about the sun made me feel alive. Even with the doctor's warning, I yearned for that familiar feeling. A few minutes in the sun could only do me good. It was the only thing bigger than me that I didn't feel the need to challenge.

I grabbed my Nikon off the passenger's seat then set out for some great shots. I pictured myself working diligently with paints to hand color these photos at my new desk in my new space with a grin.

Moms and children dotted the shore. Laughter and cries echoed in the sweltering breeze. I pushed my hat down over my brow, made sure my linen tunic covered my chest, then checked the position of the sun. Tiny granules of sand burned the sides of my feet as I trudged to the shore where the water licked the sand. I faced the wind like so many times before. My camera rested against my chest as I removed my sandals.

The cool water rushed over my feet that I had buried in the sand then quickly scurried back to its home. My lips curled as I was reminded of something much bigger. The corner of my mouth touched the clouds when forgotten beach memories brushed up against my mind.

I carefully placed my sandals near the waterline on the shore and waited for the rolling wave to break and froth before me. A helpless hermit crab flailed on its back to recover. I bent down and used my sandal to flip it over. I expected to see a quick getaway, but the creature bathed with the sun on its back, just like I used to. I zoomed in and clicked.

The line of the horizon was still and perfect. The pier of fishermen anchored the floating world. Screeching gulls swooped over their lines threatening thievery. The air tickled my neck like my father's fingers did when I was a child. Chills ran up my spine.

"I do remember, Dad, I do," I muttered, picking up my flip-flops.

I strolled along the beach. A child shouted my name. I peered over the rim of my sunglasses, and smiled. Chloe came bounding toward me. I wrinkled my nose as she splashed along the shore leaving polka dots of lake water on my shirt.

"What are you doing here?" she asked.

Chloe shaded her eyes and gazed up at me through narrow slits.

"Taking some pictures."

"For what?" she asked, picking up a white rock. "Oh, this one's pretty." She bent down and washed it off in the water. "It's pretty windy out here, but I like it. Don't you?"

I soaked in the scenery. "I do." I focused on her stubby nose and quizzical stare as she caressed the wet stone. I clicked my Nikon several times. The sound of the shutter was lost in the rustling breeze around us.

"Take my picture."

"I already did." I snapped another one as Chloe squinted and wrinkled her nose in my direction.

"That's not fair, I wasn't looking." She put her hands on her hips and posed like a top model would. "Let me stand this way." She flipped her hair back. "Tell me to say cheese," she ordered.

"Fine." I rolled my eyes. "Say 'cheese,'" I directed, as I lifted the viewfinder to my eye.

"Cheese," she chimed. "Now take another one, a silly one like my dad does."

"Why not? Get ready," I warned.

Chloe fell onto her back. "No, you get ready. Watch this, a sand angel." She swished her arms and legs.

I snapped three frames as she carved out her mark on the world then I lowered the camera as John approached in my viewfinder.

"Hey, Maggie," John said, squinting into the sun.

Chloe jumped to her feet then rushed into the lake. "Gotta wash this off. Never know what's been crawling around in the sand," she said with a shiver.

"Hi, no office today?" I asked, keeping my eyes on Chloe, who was dunking her head and splashing in the cool lake water.

"Nope, it's a day with Chloe. I figured I'd give Nanny Nora a break. I don't want her to quit."

"Good idea," I said.

Chloe bounded out of the water and stood between us. "Wait, let me do this over here." She jumped to the side and shook like a retriever after an unwanted bath.

I kept an eye on John through my sunglasses as he marveled in his daughter's goofy antics. His scruffy grin tugged at my heart. I wondered what her mother looked like because she sure was the spitting image of him, without the whiskers. I averted his soft stare when he turned back in my direction.

"Let's leave Maggie alone," he said to Chloe.

"See you back at the house she called."

I waved as they left, and the horseshoe tattoo on John's left shoulder caught my attention.

Chloe's words drifted in my direction. "She looks so sad, Dad."

John patted her shoulder.

Chloe glanced up into her dad's face as she kept the pace. "Even when she smiles. I just don't get it," Chloe said.

John took a gander back at me as I studied his profile. I smiled and waved, pretending not to hear their conversation.

Chapter 12

I slid my favorite black T-shirt over my head. Boring, but safe. Checking twice in the mirror, I made sure no one could see the red rectangular patch of skin on my chest that glowed from radiation and not in a good way. I tied my hair back and pinched my cheeks. Paul was on his way over with my desk for the library. I'd spent most of the night printing black-and-white photos thinking about my new workspace with new furniture, without Beckett's imprint. I marveled at the convenience of having a computer and printer capable of producing quality images without going to a darkroom or a convenience store. The photos were sprayed with my "magic mixture in a can," that's what Bradley use to call it, to make my colors stick to the glossy paper.

I trotted downstairs and opened the front door as Paul approached the porch. A truck drove in behind his white Toyota Camry. Excited about the arrival, I opened the creaky screen door. His fitted white button down hugged his lean torso while his black jeans and loafers polished his look.

"Hi," I greeted him.

He ran his fingers through his blond bangs and swept to the side then took off his Ray Bans and hooked them on the front of his shirt. "Hi, it's here. If you don't like it, I have another taker."

"I'm sure it will work fine," I stated, crossing my arms.

"Come take a look before we unload." Paul gestured for me to follow him outside.

Something on the porch swing caught my eye. I stepped closer to see. *Junie B. Jones and the Stupid Smelly Bus*, a chapter book for young readers with a sassy main character. I knew her well. Not only was Junie B. a popular character, but a popular attitude amongst second graders and new neighbors.

"Looks a little young for you," Paul said.

I grinned. "A favorite in my classroom. Kind of reminds me of someone I know. Probably the same someone who left it here." I put the book on the stoop with hopes Chloe would come get it. When Bradley moved out, I didn't miss picking up after him. I glanced over the edge of the porch to flush out young spies.

Paul's long stride was brisk and effortless. I guessed he was a runner. Me, too, but I hadn't been jogging in years. I chose professional growth over personal endeavors such as fitness-probably not the best choice. I grimaced. Beside the truck were two men. I felt my face droop as I shaded my eyes, hoping I was wrong. Beckett's proud grin welcomed me. "Do you like it?" He gestured to the desk.

"I love it, but—" I stopped. "Did you pick it out?" I couldn't take the desk if Beckett orchestrated the deal.

"He's only here to help carry it in the house." Paul reassured me with a grin. "This is Randy," he said, introducing the gentleman in jeans and a Janis Joplin T-shirt. "He's our delivery guy."

Out of the corner of my eye, I saw Paul suck in a breath of air as I focused my attention on my ex-husband. "Can I speak to you for a moment?" I noticed Beckett's eyes dim. I smiled at Paul as Beckett excused himself.

"I'll show Randy where it's going." Paul gestured to Randy to follow him back inside the house.

Beckett stuffed his hands into his pockets. "Maggie—"

"Look, something has to be mine. It can't have any more memories with you attached." His expression pained me. I sighed and lowered my voice. "I know you just want to help, but there has to be a break, a clean break. I have to do something on my own and now you are helping to redecorate? Did we not have this discussion before?" My voice squeaked.

Beckett shifted his weight.

"What?" I grunted.

"I'm just trying to help. I know what you like. I'm good at picking things out. I called to see how it was going and Paul said he was short a guy, and I just wanted you to have what you wanted."

"What I wanted was *not* get divorced, but that didn't happen." I turned away. "One, two, three, four, five, six, times ten." I faced Beckett. The deep creases in his forehead caught my attention, something new. I diverted my gaze knowing I probably gave him the wrinkles.

"What are you doing?" he asked.

"It's not that difficult of a concept," I snapped at Beckett. I rubbed my temples, careful not to touch my healing gash. "When the kids are worked up at school, I tell them to count to sixty before they speak."

"So you get to use higher level math skills since you are older than your students?" The corner of his mouth lifted and a smirk emerged.

"Yes," I hissed, not amused by Beckett's comment. "Look, I know you are finding your way, too, but I need to do this house thing on my own. Please. Did you pick out the desk?" I asked, really wanting to keep the sleek piece of furniture. I crossed my arms then crossed my fingers hoping he would say, no.

"I didn't. Delivering the desk was just an excuse to come over to see you."

I rolled my eyes. "Why? Why is it so damn important for you to find an excuse to hang on by a thread?"

"You just don't get it, do you?"

I leaned on the truck. "I guess not. Why don't you enlighten me, Mr. Professor?"

"His name is Bradley," Beckett said.

I inspected the crack in the sidewalk. Bradley. Beckett was Bradley's father and I couldn't change that. Why did this have to be so difficult? Giving Beckett up was hard enough and now he wants to stay for our son. I felt like a schmuck. I looked up and moved closer to him. "Seeing you"—I sucked in a deep breath—"i-is just too damn hard," I stammered. "Besides, Bradley is in Boston."

He reached out to me. "I'm sorry, Maggie."

Tears blurred my vision. "Me too, Beckett, me, too." I wiped at the corners of my eyes. "You can help them bring in the desk, but then I am on my own." I headed toward the house, up the stairs to the porch, and inside. Clearing my throat, I peered into the naked library where Paul was fingering the books on the shelf. "You three can bring the desk in."

"Are you sure?" Paul asked.

I leaned against the doorjamb brushing away any annoyance with him and his assumption that bringing my ex-husband along to help would be fine. A heads-up would have been appreciated.

"Yes." I searched for the dent in my finger, the one made by the wedding band Beckett gave me years ago, but it had long disappeared.

"I apologize. I thought it would be okay. I should have cleared it with you before I told Beckett it was okay to join us." His words trickled sincerely from his lips.

I lowered my gaze. "It's fine. I guess I need to learn how to react better." The words came out with the rise and fall of my chest. "Apology accepted, and yes, next time if Beckett gets any brilliant ideas, please let me know." A thin smile crossed my lips. "You're just trying to do your job. I know how it feels to be caught in the middle."

Paul rolled up his sleeves. "Oh, yeah?"

"Yeah." I wondered how his forearms had gotten so tan. "I'm an only child. I was in the middle plenty. Let's just get this thing in here. Did you find a drafting table yet?"

"I'm working on it."

"Good, because I have some photos I want to get started on." I rearranged the books on the shelf and wiped the line of dust away with my finger.

"Top priority. Can't wait to see them."

"Really?" I asked, wondering how he would be curious about something I did. "Coloring photos is just a hobby."

"I bet you're good at it." Paul smiled.

Sifting through my cluttered thoughts, I smiled back.

Paul held my stare then opened the front door for me. As I stepped onto the front porch, Beckett and Randy worked to unload my desk from the truck. My gaze drifted back to Paul. I shifted my weight, reminding myself that the trio of men meant well. I realized then that I was on an island all of my own, and I was okay with that.

Chapter 13

Checking the time, I peered over the top of my reading glasses at the mantle clock on the bookshelf holding up Bradley's childhood favorites and Beckett's journal. I continued to color the photograph of Chloe at the beach. I blew away loose strands of hair that hung in my eyes when the doorbell rang again. I stood back to analyze the colors.

"Coming," I yelled as I scurried to the front door. When I peeked through the window, no one was there. I returned to my desk. Just as I chose another colored pencil, the doorbell rang again. The pencil rolled off my desk as I set it down. "Damn it," I whispered, picking it up.

Being on summer vacation allowed for two indulgences; one, freedom of speech; two, free rein to use the bathroom whenever I wished.

I reluctantly went back to the front door. Soft whimpers caught my attention. Slowly I turned the knob, hoping that Chloe wasn't on the other side with some ghastly injury. There, in a crate, sat a wrinkly bulldog with floppy jowls and the hint of an under bite.

I pushed open the screen door trying to locate the culprit. My mother was nowhere in sight. I shuffled to the edge of the porch and kept an eye on the panting dog with the spiked leather collar. "Where did you come from?" I asked, bending down to get a better view of the pup waggling his tongue in my direction. The envelope on top of the cage wasn't sealed.

I read the card out loud. "'I answer to the name Bones. I am about two years old. Thank you for adopting me.'"

Bones cocked his head to the side as his ears perked up while he listened. "Shit," I moaned.

Bones wagged his tail then snorted with excitement.

"What's all the bad language for?" Chloe said from somewhere in front of me.

I jumped. "Geez, you scared me." I looked over the railing and tucked away in the bushes sat my scrappy young neighbor. "Seriously?" Her squinting eyes made me wonder if she was supposed to be wearing glasses.

"Seriously," she said. "I like it down here. It's like a fort."

I watched her flip through the pages of her book. "You can't possibly read that fast," I said.

The dog plopped down then rested its head on its front paws.

"Exactly." I mimicked the dog's exasperated sigh.

"I can if I don't read all the words. Half of them I don't even know," Chloe declared. "It makes me get to the next book quicker."

I went back and peered over the side of the porch at her. Leaning on my elbows, I closed my eyes then lifted my chin to the sun.

"In fact, I don't know most of the words, but I like the pictures. My teacher read my class this book. That Junie B. sure is funny." Chloe shook her head and laughed. "You should read this one."

"I have," I replied. "Junie B. is not a very good houseguest in that episode." Chloe and Junie B. lived on parallel planes.

"Hey." Chloe's pointer finger shot up into the air. "We should have a sleepover, just like Junie B."

"Be careful," I mumbled as she rustled her way out of the bushes. Ogling over the pup in the cage, I had to admit the dog's twitching black nose and brownish-black patch on his right eye were kind of cute.

"Don't worry. I won't let the bushes scratch me."

"It's not you I am worried about. You're pretty tough." I fingered my stitches. They'd be removed in two days.

"Yeah, you're right about that." Chloe hopped up the stairs to the porch one-by-one, teetering as she went.

"I know. You don't want me to crush the plants again."

I put the card down on the swing.

"Wow," Chloe shrieked. "That's a cool dog. Where did you get him?"

I lifted one eyebrow. "You didn't see who delivered this guy, did you?"

Chloe dug in her pocket of her jean jacket. She showed me three one-dollar bills. "Nope."

"Great, an accomplice," I said.

"You are so lucky! I'll take him if you don't want him." She crouched beside the cage. Bones licked her fingers as she tried to pet him through the metal frame.

I briefly considered her gesture. "Seriously, what am I going to do with a dog?"

Chloe unlatched the crate door before I could stop her.

Bones scurried out, jumped on Chloe, and knocked her down. As I bent down to grab him, he plopped down in front of me. His butt went up into the air as his tail wagged to and fro nonchalantly. With one hand on his collar, I spoke gently to him. "Hi, Bones, let's get you back into the crate." After a brief moment of retreat, Bones jumped up and knocked me backward, too.

Chloe got up. "This is fun. You should have gotten a dog a long time ago." She grabbed for Bones' hindquarters, which sent him bolting down the stairs.

"I'll get him," Chloe shouted, skipping in his tracks.

I pushed myself up. "Geez." I rushed inside to the fridge to grab some lunchmeat. I let the screen door slam behind me as I ran back outside. Mom would kill me if something happened to that dog. I imagined the lecture. *You had the poor creature for less than ten minutes and look what happened.* "Yeah, look what happened, Mother, the dog is dead, Bradley is far away, doing God-knows-what, and I've made Beckett gay." I caught myself as I tripped down the stairs and into the yard. I checked the bushes. No dog, no Chloe. They were nowhere in sight, so I headed next door to Chloe's house.

Panic swept over me. "Great, now I'm going to be responsible for losing both of them. Damn that Nanny Nora."

"Excuse me," a rickety female voice said from somewhere behind me.

I spun around, swallowed, and prepared for battle. "What?"

An older woman with bobbed gray hair cleared her throat and stared at me with narrowed blue eyes. "Excuse me," she said even louder. "I am Nanny Nora."

I sized up the haughty woman before me. Chloe was right, Nanny Nora resembled a guinea pig with beady eyes. "What?" I figured if I kept saying "What?" she'd give up. I continued to scan the premises for the escapees.

Nora put her hands on her hips.

Warning myself that this was not going to be good, I stepped closer to her. "Seriously, would it kill you to keep a closer eye on Chloe?" The sound of laughter erupted behind my house. With my back to Nora, I disregarded her presence and entered my yard, then shut the gate behind me. Nora unlatched the gate and appeared thoroughly disgusted. I rushed behind her and shut the gate hoping she would infer my aggravation with the loud slam.

"Excuse me," I said to her, ignoring her steamy glare. My patience faded into the stagnant summer air. Relief washed over me when I saw Chloe lying in my lounge chair stroking Bones' head.

"Excuse me," Nora said, "But who do you think you are?"

I stepped closer to her, accepting the challenge. We stood eye-to-eye. She was on my turf now. "What do you mean '*excuse me*?' You are being paid to watch this little girl. She is over here most of the time. I have never met you.

You have never come over to meet me. I'm not sure you are Nanny Nora. Do you have identification?"

"We'll see what Mr. McIntyre has to say about this." Nora opened the gate and left in a huff.

I shut the gate behind her, waiting for her to return to retrieve Chloe, but she never did. I witnessed Chloe pulling a Cesar Millan by exuding sheer calmness to the escapee.

"How did you get him?" I asked.

She shrugged. "I didn't get him. He got me. I ran back here and he chased me. Pretty smart, huh?"

I plopped down in the chair beside her and patted Bones' thick head. His dark eyes shimmered with innocence. He gobbled up the lunchmeat and licked my hand. My mother had a lot of questions to answer. "Yeah, pretty smart." I leaned back in my chair, closed my eyes, and lifted my chin to the sun. There was something about just feeling the warmth on my face.

"That was pretty good how you handled Nora," Chloe said.

"I'm not so sure I did handle it." Fact was, I was tired of handling things. I was tired of being rational, but I wasn't sure that validated poor behavior. "I'm sure your dad will have something to say about it."

Chloe smiled. "No matter what he says, I'm on your side." She scratched Bones' ears and nuzzled her face against his sagging jowls.

"Thanks, I'll remember that." The sun's warmth calmed me.

"Will you teach me to read better?" Chloe asked under her breath.

I swallowed away the trepidation, choosing not to answer. I was on summer vacation, a time to heal from a year of sickness and letdowns. First, it was losing out on the promotion. Then, Beckett and his grand news followed by the 'C' word. I still couldn't say it, even to myself.

Chloe sighed. "It's okay."

I felt myself relenting. Chloe's eyes held the same carefree, yet sad intensity of the dog on her lap. My mind swirled. My gut twitched as I tried to ignore the moral dilemma.

"You're not gonna swear, are you?" Chloe paused, covering the dog's ears, and squinted with silent warning.

Biting my tongue, I said the naughty words in my head instead. "No," I grunted. "Why does everything have to be so hard?" I kicked off my sandals and put my feet up.

"It doesn't have to be. Look at me. When it hurts, just shake it off. I learned plenty from having a footloose and fancy-free mom."

"How can I turn you down, kid?" My breast throbbed. They told me that was common when scar tissue formed. I rubbed my collarbone then closed my eyes wishing for summer to last for the rest of my life.

"You okay?" Chloe asked.

I stared across the yard, the stillness freezing the world around me like a surreal dream. "Yes," I replied. "Why?" I scolded myself for asking. It's never a good thing to ask "Why?" to a seven-year-old. They have a habit of telling the truth about their observations, which in turn can be brutal. A seven-year-old can make you question your very existence in a split second.

"You really want to ask me that?" Chloe replied with a squeaky voice.

"Sure, what have I got to lose?"

Chloe laughed. "That's more like it. Well—" She paused. "First of all you seem awfully annoyed when I show up." She paused again to wrinkle her nose. "You sure you want my opinion?"

"Here's your chance, kid, let me have it," I replied. "Obviously, my mother thinks I need to learn a lesson or that cute doggy wouldn't be sitting in your lap right now."

"Maybe she just thinks you need a dog," Chloe said with a shrug.

I imagined Chloe smoking a cigarette while drinking beer. "Yup, I've heard that." I wondered if that philosophy applied to neighbors, children, meddling mothers, and ex-husbands.

"Anyway, you seem annoyed with anyone who shows up here. We just come here cause we like you. Is there something terrible about that?"

"Crap," I murmured with a heavy sigh. Chloe wrinkled her nose in disgust then covered Bones' ears. "Did my mother pay you to say that, too?"

Chloe cleared her throat and patted my hand. "Give me a little credit, why don't you. Now what about this reading thing? Can you help me out or not?"

Chapter 14

The porch swing lulled me into a daydream. When John approached, fantasyland quickly came to a halt. "I've been expecting you," I said, not without noticing his brown trousers, white button-down shirt, and Sponge Bob Square Pants necktie. "Nice tie," I joked.

"Nice attitude," he retorted as he loosened the knot at the top of the silk blue tie just above Krabby Patty's head.

"You know Krabby looks like one of those things that dangles at the back of your throat."

"You mean a tonsil?" he asked, his tone ruffled.

"Guess so, but that's what happens when you hang around seven-year-olds most of the time." I pushed the hair away from my face. I liked the way the evening light highlighted the crow's feet at the corners of his weary eyes. "So, I suppose you got an ear full from Nanny Nora."

John cleared his throat and held my gaze. "Got any beer?"

"Must be worse than I thought." As I got up, his eyes brushed against my exposed collarbone. I quickly put the straps of my tank top back in place. A chill ran up my spine. "Follow me." I slipped on my sandals and invited him inside. "Where's Chloe?"

"At a friend's house," John replied.

"That's good, she's making friends." I shrugged as he raised his eyebrow. "Really, that's good. She needs to be hanging out with kids her own age." I rolled my stiff shoulders in small circles, thinking about Chloe's advice. It didn't feel natural. "I need to practice," I coached myself.

"What do you need to practice?" John asked.

I took two Miller Lites out of the fridge and turned in John's direction. The top button on his shirt was undone. His tie was in a wad on the counter, and somewhere between here and the porch he'd rolled up his sleeves. His forearm flexed as he twisted off the top. I pondered his horseshoe tattoo that lingered beneath his shirt. John put his bottle on the counter, took the second bottle from my hand, twisted off the cap, then handed it back to me. He picked up his beer, tilted it in my direction, and said, "Can't drink without a toast."

I tilted my beer bottle in John's direction stumped by his lack of words. Didn't seem to be a problem earlier. "Cheers," I said, clanking my bottle against his.

"Here's to finding a new nanny," he added.

I stopped mid-swig to swallow hard. "Oh crap," I said, rolling my eyes. My gut twisted.

John pulled out a stool and made himself at home. "I have tomorrow covered, but after that, not sure what I'm gonna do."

The pit in my stomach grew as his eyes searched mine for a solution. I took a long draw of ice-cold beer, which soothed my nerves and the brewing hot flash. I put my bottle on the counter and watched John tip it to inspect the contents. "What?" I sheepishly asked.

"This is going well. I figured this would work better than putting you on the spot."

I picked up the Miller Lite and took another long swig. The cold beer was the best thing I'd tasted in a long time. It masked the metallic twang on the back of my tongue. "What?"

John chuckled. "You're something else, Maggie Abernathy." He drained his beer and held up the empty bottle. "May I?"

"Help yourself. I'll have another one, too." I said, before finishing off the first. Not sure of his tactics, I sat patiently as heat crept up my legs into my torso. I patted my cheeks trying to hide the hot flash. I took my second beer from him. "What?"

John chuckled. "It doesn't take a rocket scientist to know that you feel guilty about your behavior today. How's that hot flash working for you? Are you going to be okay?" he asked with a smirk.

I took a long swig, swallowed, and met his gaze. I wiped the sweat from my bottle then rolled it across my forehead.

"I have to be honest here." He paused, drumming his fingertips on the counter. "On one hand, I should tell you to mind your own business. But on the other hand, I've got to give you some credit for having some balls, excuse my French."

I choked on my beer.

"Sorry, it's been a long day." John sighed as he settled into his chair.

I wiped my mouth and rubbed the bridge of my nose.

"Did your beer go up your nose?" he asked.

I nodded, pinching the bridge of my nose harder as my eyes began to water.

"You probably deserved that," he said with a grin.

"Most likely, yes." I lowered my gaze then wiped at the corners of my eyes.

"And besides, it's kind of hard to be mean to a woman dealing with breast cancer." He put his half-empty bottle on the counter.

The hair on my neck prickled. Instantly, my mind sent discontented messages to my mom via osmosis. "I don't know what you're talking about," I said, draining my second beer then pushing the bottle across the counter toward the other empties.

I sat still, waiting for him to break the silence, give up, or change the subject, anything.

John drained his beer, pushed his second empty toward the other three in front of us then went to the refrigerator for two more bottles. He twisted off the tops and slid them in my direction.

"I can play your game, but I'm not sure you want that," he warned.

"I am going to kill my mother." I watched his eyes narrow questioning my statement.

"What does she have to do with it? I think we can safely leave her out of this conversation."

"Seriously?" I asked with raised eyebrows. "Sorry, Mom," I said, realizing he had other resources.

"Can't you just admit it?"

I got out of my chair. "Who do you think you are? You come over here, make me feel guilty for your nanny quitting, and now you are prying into my personal life." I stood my ground as John stepped closer. His fingertips grazed my shoulder as he moved the strap of my shirt to the side and put his pointer finger on my tattoo. "What are you doing?" I thought about slapping his hand away like they do in the movies, but found myself reveling in his electric touch.

"So it's true."

I swallowed away the lump in my throat, the tension in my neck pulled at my shoulder blades. No words came.

John lowered his head.

I begged my eyes not to blur.

"I saw the tattoo. I saw the classic red box peeking out of your shirt when your shoulder straps were off your shoulders outside. Not even your priceless expression can hide this. I noticed it at the beach as you hid beneath your hat and gauzy top, but the breeze blew your collar open and you quickly covered yourself up."

His finger caressed the small black circle. I shut my eyes. His touch was soft, warm, sincere, unexpected. I didn't want to break the connection. I inhaled sharply and met his gaze. "I have cancer. There, I said it."

"Well, that's a good place to start." He kissed my forehead. "Chloe noticed it, too, but in a different way."

"You didn't tell her, did you?"

"Give me some credit, now." He stepped back then sat down on his stool at the counter.

My head tingled. "I think I shouldn't have any more beer," I muttered, staring into the half-empty bottle.

"Yeah, you don't look like a drinker, but with that red hair, I'm guessing the Irish lass in you should belly up and learn how to handle a six-pack."

"Okay," I scoffed with a smirk.

"It would be a start."

I drained my third beer, pushed the empty away, then ran my fingers through my hair, and knotted it on top of my head with the ponytail holder from my wrist. "What a day!" I huffed.

"You're telling me. Chloe's nanny quit, no thanks to you." John sighed.

His pained expression fanned my burning guilt. "Sorry," I mumbled.

"My seven-year-old thinks her mom is coming to visit. Not gonna happen. She says she will, but she never does. And all I've heard about is how your mother bought you a dog, and why can't Chloe have one, too." He unbuttoned the next button on his shirt. "And you want to know what the kicker is?"

I raised an eyebrow at him. "Do I?"

"I came over here with a speech and the intention of putting you in your place, because you, my friend, are just as irritating as Chloe."

"Hey—" My voice cracked. John's pointer finger shot up toward the ceiling, his brow furrowed just like Chloe's had done earlier while having an epiphany in the bushes when I called her out on eavesdropping. Their mannerisms were one in the same. Uncanny.

"No, let me finish before I lose my nerve." He drained his third beer then continued. "And all I can think about is kissing you."

Shocked, I adverted his stare, caught my breath, then glanced back at him. I fought back the urge to lean into his body, to reciprocate his longing because I felt it, too.

I touched his hand, risking that I might find myself in his arms. I closed my eyes as he caressed my fingers. "I—" No more words came.

He pulled away, checked his watch, then brushed his fingertips across my cheeks. "I should go." He collected the empties then put the clanking bottles into the sink.

For the first time since Beckett, I wanted another man. I held his gaze as he approached me without blinking. He swept my hair back from the stitches in my left temple. I closed my eyes thinking about what a mess I was. Cancer. Gash. Divorced. Lost.

"I can remove those stitches when you're ready."

I nodded.

"I really should go." He walked toward the French doors leading to the patio then stopped near Bones who slept like an angel in his crate.

"John—" Frozen, I didn't know what to say. It had been so long. He held my gaze as the rush of heat burned through me, the kind stoked by attraction, not menopause. "I—" I swallowed. I moved toward him.

"I know, Maggie. You're not ready."

He was right, but the yearning to be close to him beckoned. My head and my heart were at odds. He pulled me in. I fit perfectly. For the first time, I knew there would be life after Beckett. The dimple in his left cheek reassured me of that.

"It wouldn't be fair, to either of us," John whispered. "Not right now, anyway."

His musky cologne soothed my nerves while the heat from his body calmed my soul. "I really am sorry about Nanny Nora," I mumbled. Warm lips kissed my forehead sending sparks through my veins, heating my blood.

He strolled into the night, his words trailing behind him. "Just let me know when you are ready. Night, Maggie," he said.

I stepped closer to the door. I was ready, but too chicken to admit it.

Chapter 15

Chloe leaped up the steps, flailing her arms trying to balance. "Maggie, guess what, guess what."

I looked up from my magazine and removed my reading glasses. "What?" I watched her hobble around on sparkly plastic high heels. "Fancy shoes," I said with a smile.

"This is gonna take more practice than I thought," Chloe huffed as she plopped down on her bottom. "Hey, where's Bones?" she asked, unbuckling her silver shoes.

"In the backyard."

"What's he doing back there?" she asked, squinting into the sunlight.

I shrugged. "Hanging out. Exploring his new home, I suppose."

Chloe teetered back and forth. "Man, if I had a new dog, I'd play with him every second. I'd take him for a walk and teach him tricks." She kicked off her high heels.

Guilt sizzled in my gut like the Cherry Pop Rocks exploding in Chloe's mouth as she talked. "Gee, thanks," I muttered as I put the magazine down on the swing next to me.

Chloe got up and came toward me. Her face softened.

"Sorry, Maggie. I didn't mean to make you feel bad."

Her sticky fingers touched mine. She sprinkled a few pieces of candy in the palm of my hand. I popped them into my mouth. The sweetly sour treat crackled on my tongue like firecrackers. I'd forgotten how childhood tasted.

"I just meant that you are so lucky to have a dog. And I want one soooo bad," she whined.

Crap. "It's okay. So, what's all the excitement about?" I asked, licking cherry residue off my hand.

Chloe scratched her head. "Oh, yeah. We just got my mom's call. She hardly ever calls on account she's so busy with her career."

I pushed my foot against the floor after Chloe settled in next to me on the swing. Her father had been so damn handsome last night standing in my kitchen. I touched my forehead where his lips had been. I could still smell his cologne on my sweater as I drew it tight across my chest wishing for John's arms around me.

"You okay?" Chloe said, poking me.

I focused on the freckles dotting the bridge of her nose. "Yeah," I replied softly, although I wasn't sure I was entirely all that okay. "That's good that your mom called. I know how much you miss her." I wondered if she was stunning. After all, she was in Hollywood chasing the dream and Chloe really was the spitting image of John.

"That's not the half of it. She's coming here to see me. I can't wait." Chloe shook the rest of the candy in her mouth.

My heart sank, a little bit for Chloe and a lot for me. I stopped the swing with my foot. "Let's go check on the dog, shall we?" I smiled through clenched teeth.

The swing bobbed as Chloe jumped off, landing with a thud on the wooden floor of the porch.

The last bit of sugar dissolved on my tongue as I pushed myself up from the wooden seat.

"Can I come in with no shoes?" Chloe chortled as she held the door open.

I didn't look back to see if her feet were dripping or caked with dirt. I walked ahead. "Sure," I answered with a smile. "Thanks for asking."

We went to the kitchen and sat at the counter.

Chloe inspected the teacup with the pink ribbons that my mom had sent. I held my breath.

"What's this?" Chloe asked, steadying herself as she climbed into the tall chair. "It's pretty. I like the pink ribbons."

I blew out my angst with a sigh. "Me, too."

Chloe touched the rim gently.

I watched her fingertips caress the edge of the cup with tender loving care. Lost in my own thoughts, I almost didn't hear her words. I tucked my hair behind my ears. This simple gesture made me a better listener. Maybe, that was part of the problem, I just wasn't listening. I wasn't listening to Beckett, Mom, or myself. I pulled out the stool next to hers. My sweater fell from my shoulders, stretched out from years of wear, but I refused to give it up. Beckett and Bradley had given it to me on Mother's Day when Bradley was nine.

Chloe closed her eyes momentarily before taking a gulp of air. Her stormy eyes illuminated wisdom beyond her years. I didn't pull my hand away when she held it.

"I'm sorry," Chloe said.

Pretending she didn't acknowledge my secret, I held her hand. "Sorry for what?"

"Sorry that you have cancer."

My chest rose and fell as I shook my head. "Thanks." I blinked away the wetness. "How did you know?" I whispered.

Chloe leaned in my direction and her hair brushed my shoulder. The tips of her fingers on my collarbone felt like butterfly wings.

"See that dot. I told my dad I thought you had a tumor. You know kids. We notice everything."

"Apparently," I said with a nod.

"So, I said something to my dad because I know he really likes you, even if you don't know it. He's weird that way, always being tough."

"And?" I prompted.

"I told him I saw a dot on your shoulder and on your chest. I begged him to tell me, so don't get mad at him, you know how I can be."

The corner of my mouth lifted. "Yes. I am aware of how persuasive you can be."

"Well, he caved. He swore me to secrecy."

"Well, that didn't happen," I said, not feeling distressed one bit. I caressed Chloe's hand. "Well, now, that wouldn't do any of us any good, would it?" I mumbled, trying to hold back the heave of emotion tickling the back of my throat. I crossed my arms, then put my head down on the cool granite top, staring at the china cup that would remind me of the sickness I hated. "It's okay."

Chloe mimicked my actions by crossing her arms and putting her head down, too. We were two sorry souls just staring at a piece of porcelain painted with some pink ribbons. We sighed in unison.

"Maggie."

"What?"

"Does it hurt?" Chloe asked.

"No. Not anymore," I said.

"Good."

I thought about the cane at the clinic with my father's name on it that I wanted to bring home and would ask for, if it was still there on my last day of radiation. My dad's spirit filled me up. I felt him stroking my hair, whispering silent words of assurance. *You're a tough girl. It's not your time. I'll be with you every step of the way.*

"Maggie," Chloe mumbled.

"Yeah." I moved my head so I could see her better.

"Are you going to die?"

"No," I said without hesitation. The realization that dying could even be a prognosis gave me goose bumps. It took a scrappy seven-year-old to bring the possibility of death to my attention.

"Good," Chloe said. "It just wouldn't be the same without you."

"Thanks," I said, sitting up in my chair.

Chloe wiggled down from her seat. "I think we should get this pity party outside to see Bones."

Chloe stood next to me and her shallow breaths filled the stillness between us. She inspected my bare shoulder then touched the black tattooed dot. "You could turn that into a real tattoo."

"Don't think so, kiddo."

"Why not?" she asked.

"Because—" I stopped myself. *People in my family don't do that sort of thing.* "Getting this one really, really hurt."

"More than those stitches in your head?" Chloe's voice squeaked.

I touched the side of my head carefully. "Yes, way more."

"My dad has a tattoo, you know."

I did know. I pictured him walking on the beach with the horseshoe tattoo on his left shoulder. A tingle ran across my shoulders and down my spine. I slid my stool back, stood up, and stretched. "Now, shall we see about that dog?"

Chloe tugged at my hand. "Please don't tell my dad I told you I know about your cancer. I wasn't supposed tell you I knew."

I pretended to lock my lips.

"Lock it, zip it, throw away the key," she sang.

Chloe's hand slipped out of mine and decided to ditch my sweater. I winced as the door banged against the wall in Chloe's excitement to get outside. With the screeching sounds of a seven-year-old tainting the air, I hurried outside to find Chloe in my lounging chair with Bones who lowered his head as if trying to hide his guilt. My heart sank as I scurried over to my tomato garden. "You are a bad dog, a very, very bad dog," I huffed as I surveyed the damage. I began picking up green tomatoes, ripe tomatoes, big tomatoes, all the ruined tomatoes that littered the ground. I sneered at Bones. "Bad dog, bad, bad, dog," I hissed, glaring at Chloe, who was covering his ears.

"They'll grow back," Chloe shouted in my direction.

"No they won't. He ruined my garden." I held up a red ripe tomato, bigger than one regulation-sized softball. "And he took bites out of most of them," I huffed. "Stupid dog." I shook the ruined tomato in their direction.

Chloe sauntered over. "You still got some green stuff left and maybe some berries."

Bones followed in her footsteps.

I stacked the tomatoes in a neat pile at the edge of the garden, *my* garden, my *ruined* garden.

Chloe crossed her arms over her chest. "I'd say you handled that whole cancer thing a lot better than this."

I narrowed my gaze even more in her direction.

"Just sayin'," she added.

"Crap. Crap. Crap," I muttered.

"Maggie—"

"I don't care. Crap," I huffed as I kneeled next to broken stalks.

Bones hopped in my lap. His tail wagged so hard his hindquarters swayed from side to side. I stared into his dark-brown eyes. He cocked his head briefly before licking my ear. I wiggled as his slobbery tongue lapped at the side of my face.

Chloe snickered. "You are so lucky," she rambled.

"Uh-huh," I grunted, swatting at Bones' rear-end as he trotted away.

"I'll help you clean up. Maybe, that will make it better," Chloe suggested.

"Doubt it." My body drooped. Something welled inside me. The rush of self-pity gnawed in my gut. I pushed back the tears. "Maybe you should head home," I suggested. "Maybe Nora is looking for you."

"Fat chance, sister. She quit, remember?" Chloe snickered.

"Oh yeah, I forgot." I swiped at my eyes trying to conceal my emotions. I jumped when I heard John's booming voice.

"What the heck happened back here?" he asked as he latched the gate behind him. "Chloe?"

"No, Bones," I interrupted, clapping at the dog digging in the flowerbed. I watched as Chloe calmly approached the beast.

She snapped her fingers. "Come on, Bones," she commanded.

Bones focused on her tone. Chloe motioned for him to follow her to the patio. "Stay." She pointed to a spot next to the lounge chair. Bones sat. "Down." She knelt beside him and patted the ground. When he settled, she scratched his head. "Good dog," she praised.

"Impressive," I said. "Obviously, I don't have that talent."

John smiled. "Dog whisperer," he joked. "She wants a dog so bad."

"You can have Bones," I suggested.

"Nope," John said firmly. "Taking care of Chloe is more work than you know."

I challenged his words in my stare.

"On second thought, maybe you do know."

John held out his hand. I grabbed hold as he pulled me up from the littered ground. He squeezed it tight. His green eyes gleamed as they connected with my stare. I glanced toward Chloe then back to John. As much as I wanted to hang on to him, I let go. Nothing good could come from leading him on. It wouldn't be fair to Chloe. I'd seen it all too many times across the conference table on the faces of divorced parents trying out new partners like it was no big deal. "Thanks. Any leads on a nanny?"

"I have a call into an agency. I'll have to warn the next one about you," he jested.

"Ha, ha." Could he have really liked Nora? Doubt it. No one did. "Chloe's better off without Nora." John narrowed his eyes in my direction. "Oh, come on."

He shrugged.

I huffed. "Please." John stuffed his hands into the pockets of his blue jeans that hugged his muscular thighs. I noticed his crisp white T-shirt. "No suit today?"

"Got home early. Had to get the munchkin from her friend's house. No thanks to you."

His words didn't match the glint in his eye. I'd seen that look in Chloe's eyes earlier. Their similar spark for life glowed like mossy embers. Damn, he was handsome. And he wanted to kiss me. "Give it up, doctor," I said. "You couldn't stand Nanny Nora either. I did you a favor."

John stepped closer. The scent of his cologne tickled my nose. I brushed aside the attraction. No one would come out a winner. I glanced over to Chloe, who had Bones rolling over on command.

"Maybe you did, Maggie Abernathy, just maybe you did," John replied.

Chapter 16

Mom didn't pick up so I left her a message on voicemail, again. This was the third time I had called in three days. Maybe she had disowned me as her daughter. Had I really been that rotten? Probably. I hadn't been truly rotten since I was sixteen and snuck out of the house. If I wouldn't have backed into a stupid pole and put a dent in her convertible, she would have never known.

With my back against the refrigerator, I slid down to sit on the floor. I shook away the possibility that I could have offended her that much. She was up to something. My intuition pinched. Bones sat next to me. Between the hot flashes and the humidity, I wanted to be down there rolling around with him on the cool white tile.

I scratched at my armpit. The persistent, nagging itch consumed me. My red skin bothered me constantly. I dragged my purse down from the counter. I bit my lip, trying to ignore the annoying sensation. I dug into the outside pocket for the lotion that Bobbi gave me today after the last session.

I unscrewed the cap. It flipped out of my hand and landed next to Bones. He picked up the tube in his teeth and showed it to me. "Fine. Keep your new toy." I got up and raised my eyebrow in his direction. The sound of plastic echoed behind me as I walked away. His nails clicked against the hard floor. Bones brushed up against my ankle as he trotted alongside me. His pink tongue waggled as he ran ahead, down the hallway, and stopped at the library.

"You're a pill," I said, reaching down to pat his head.

He jumped on me, knocking me backward. My bottom hit the slate floor in the foyer with a thud. Bones grunted at me then licked my nose after sniffing the stitches on my head. The cold stone in the entryway felt more refreshing than the kitchen tile. I cinched up my skirt and pressed my legs against the earthy rock. Bones crawled into my arms. He sniffed my left breast where I had had the lumpectomy. He poked his wet snout under the edge of my T-shirt and his wet tongue licked the red rectangle on my chest. He sniffed at my other breast then licked my collarbone above my glowing skin. I held him close, appreciating his company. "Thanks, friend," I whispered in his ear.

Bones gazed into my eyes.

His tail wagged to and fro with contentment.

"Don't get too excited, friend, I'm still not happy about my garden."

Bones groaned and gave a little *woof.*

"Hey, regardless, you shouldn't have done it."

Bones lowered his head, sniffed the floor, then looked back up. His pitiful wrinkly forehead twitched.

"Nice try."

Bones nudged my shoulder. Then licked my face, again.

"Enough of this gushy stuff, I have work to do."

Bones stood on my left thigh anchoring me to the floor. His piercing bark hurt my ears.

"What?" I moaned. This dog stuff was a lot of work. It was worse than having a baby. "What now? I just fed you."

Bones ran into the kitchen.

I got up and veered into the library. As I walked past the hall tree in the corner, I reached for my ratty sweater. Who was I kidding? It was my security blanket. I touched the frayed cotton on the cardigan's hem. It held momentous memories. Memories I wrapped around me each day like a shroud, trying to keep myself alive. Linus had his blanket.

I had my sweater. Pitiful. I left the sweater on the hook choosing to harbor the memories in my heart, not around my shoulders in an old sweater that weighed me down. Pressure built behind my eyes. How did I get this way? *Control freak.*

With a deep breath, I straightened my shoulders.

I logged on to my computer and played Adele. Her voice pacified me as I contemplated which photo to color next. I stroked each one like a lover. I peeked under the eight-by-ten of my tomato garden photo prior to Bones' invasion. It was side-by-side to another eight-by-ten of a photo I snapped after Chloe and John left that day. Bones sat next to a heaping pile of tomatoes in front of a plot of naked tomato plants. I tugged at the corner of the hidden photo. I hadn't considered myself a stalker, but maybe the police would think otherwise. I pulled at the corner of the black-and-white photo a bit more. John's feet peeked out at me as he walked in the sand. I yanked at it a little bit more. I reasoned with myself. *It's a public beach. I took photos of Chloe. I could explain this if I had to.* I tugged until it was in full view.

Matter of fact, it was the perfect composition. His Hawaiian print board shorts hung from his narrow hips. His muscles were toned, probably from lifting Chloe up all the time, and that horseshoe tattoo begged for my attention. I ran my fingers over it. My eyes lingered like a girl with an obsessive crush. "This is so silly." I ran my fingers through my hair. "You can't even think about that. He's your neighbor. He's Chloe's dad."

Adele's voice chimed in the background. I mouthed the words to her latest tune as I touched the tattoo on his shoulder. "Why are you so damn intriguing?" I carefully put the picture back beneath a photograph of his daughter then picked up the photo of Bones in all his glory next to his pile of fallen tomatoes. I rearranged my paints just as he dropped the leash at my feet. "You're going to have to wait a few minutes."

Bones barked.

"Lie down," I said with conviction.

Bones tested my stare with a playful growl.

"I said in a few minutes."

Bones left the leash on the floor, waddled over to the corner, rearranged his bed, and plopped down with a sigh.

I silenced my phone and got to work. I splashed muted colors onto the photos. The muddy hues reminded me of the twenties. The images seemed to levitate from the paper. Once intently focused, the image of John quit nagging at me, but the photo of him in his swim trunks soon found its way back out from underneath the pile. I moved Bones' photo aside then started carefully painting in John's Hawaiian trunks. The blurry background brought mystery to the composition. He held Chloe's hand as she looked up into his eyes probably asking him why I was so sad. The flush of embarrassment warmed my cheeks. I wiped at my brow thinking that my stitches were due to come out.

I checked my phone. No messages. No missed calls. Nothing. Plain old nothing. Bones gnawed on a grungy piece of rawhide and tilted his head at the sound of my words. "Look who the pitiful one is now."

He snorted then went back to chewing his toy.

I went back to painting the photograph. I wondered why I ever stopped painting photographs in the first place. I knew. With the responsibility of marriage came compromise. Then it dawned on me. I had compromised myself beyond recognition. "Stupid!" I whispered. Bones waddled over and jumped up on me. "I told you in a minute," I said, putting the final touches on Chloe's sun-kissed hair.

Bones retrieved the leash then jumped up on my leg again and dropped it in my lap. I put my paintbrush down on the desk, took off my glasses, and caved to his wishes just as I had done so many times before with Bradley and Beckett. Disgusted with Bones' interruptions, I grunted back at him. "Come on, let's get this over with." I slid my chair back, hooked the leash on the collar, and walked him out the front door.

Bones politely trotted by my side. I thought maybe his intelligence ran deeper than I gave him credit for, after all he did lick my chest in such a caring manner. I once read that dogs can detect cancer. Bones looked up into my eyes as we walked, his short legs scurried to keep up with me, and his tongue waggled. "Yeah, you're probably just making up for the tomato incident. And by the way, I may never get over that."

The shrill sound of a bicycle bell startled me. I glanced back to see Chloe riding on my heels.

"Hey, where you going?" she yelled.

I stepped off the sidewalk onto the grassy patch between the sidewalk and the street trying to escape another injury. Chloe stopped in front of me. Her tires wobbled. Bones didn't seem nearly as frightened as me. "Just walking," I replied, admiring the shiny purple strands of ribbon hanging from the ends of Chloe's handlebars. "I really like your bike."

Chloe pushed the helmet back from her forehead.

"Who is watching you today?" I asked. "Your dad home?" I wanted John to be home. Just seeing him made me feel better.

"No way. He's at work. What did your bike look like when you were seven?"

I smiled. "It was yellow with a white banana seat. I had a white plastic basket on the front that I'd carry my Barbie in."

"Barbie?" Chloe wrinkled her nose. "I hate dolls."

"Shocker," I said.

"You're a funny one, Maggie. I wouldn't picture you as a doll lover."

I shifted my weight telling myself not to go there, but I took the bait. "What would you picture me as?"

Chloe scratched her head. "Not sure. You're kind of hard to figure out sometimes. My dad says you are frustrating.

Not sure why it bothers him, though." She put the kickstand down and got off her bike. "Bones destroy anything today?"

"Nope." Without trying to seem obvious, I wanted Chloe to keep sputtering about her dad. I watched her eyes light up as she lifted her head and shaded her brow to see the tall blonde walking down the street calling her name. "Is that your new nanny?" I asked, hoping like hell it wasn't.

Chloe turned her attention back to Bones. She chuckled then squinted up at me. "No way, that's my mom." Chloe waved her closer. When she got within a few feet, Chloe said, "This is Bones." Her mom scratched his ears and patted his back. "And this is—"

I swallowed hard as Chloe's mom peered over the rim of her Gucci sunglasses.

"This is Maggie. You know, the lady I was telling you about."

I prayed she couldn't read my thoughts through my Ray Ban aviators. I held out my hand. "Nice to meet you," I said politely.

"Oh, don't worry," Chloe's mom said, "they were all good things, I can assure you of that."

My eyes met Chloe's stare. My belly tightened as that familiar wave of heat washed over me.

Chloe reached for the leash. "Let me hold that. You don't look so good." She pried my hand from the leather strap, her little fingers stronger than a death grip. I let go resigning myself to the fact Bones respected her way more than he respected me. I was getting better, but Chloe had a Zen that Bones obeyed.

"I'm fine. Must be the heat." I watched Chloe's mom scrutinize my reaction. "I'll feel better once we start walking."

Chloe straddled her bike. With one hand on the handlebars and one hand hanging on to the leash she rode away.

"Chloe, I'm not sure," I called after her.

Chloe's mom interrupted, "Don't worry, she'll be fine."

I observed the skinny blonde saunter closer as Chloe balanced on her bike with Bones trotting alongside her like they'd been doing this stunt a lifetime. John wouldn't be happy if there was an accident. I didn't want to face him when Chloe was skinned head to toe because Bones made her wipe out. I avoided making eye contact with Chloe's Barbie doll mom.

"I'm Brook," she said.

"Nice to meet you," I said, hoping I sounded sincere.

She lowered her shades, taking a long gander at my face. I felt naked. Summer was my season to go without makeup and glamour. She was everything I wasn't. Her sleek curls hung just below her shoulders. Her perfect eyeliner made her blue eyes pop. It took every ounce of energy not to wither and blow away.

"You look exhausted," she said.

I felt the corner of my mouth twitch as she turned to follow Chloe.

"Thanks," I muttered. *What did I do to you?*

Chloe's mom stopped briefly then glanced back in my direction. "We'll make sure the dog gets home safe and sound. Don't you worry."

I blinked then marveled at what'd just happened as I held the bridge of my nose pushing back the stress. Chloe took the lead on her bike as Bones ran next to her. Brook trailed behind in her cutoff jean shorts as I brought up the rear in my flowing peasant skirt. And then I thought, how ironic, I was the last one in line chasing after something that was mine as it trotted away happily without a care in the world.

Chloe rode past my house yelling over her shoulder, "This will tire him out. We'll be back."

Brook gave a little wave. The sun gleamed off her chiseled cheekbones. Her hair bounced as she trotted to catch up to her daughter. Thwarted, I waved them off before jogging up the stairs to the porch.

"Traitor," I said.

"Well that's a fine hello."

My mother swayed to and fro on the porch swing as she pulled out fuzzy thread from a skein of pink tangled yarn that sat on the cushion next to her. She worked the thick pink strand with one hand and held two wicked-looking knitting needles in the other.

Chapter 17

I nudged my mother's mound of pink yarn closer to her before plopping down on the porch swing. I read the tag. 'Prom dress pink.' Looks like bubble gum." I put the skein in my lap. I pulled at the soft strand of yarn. "I'll get the knot out, you keep knitting," I said to my mother, who had one eye on her knitting and one eye on me.

"Looks like Bones is adjusting well," she said, peering over the edge of her patriotic reading glasses.

"Yeah." I tugged at the yarn. The knot became smaller, tighter, and nettled enough that I felt it fight back. I picked at it like a knotted shoelace. My hands weren't as nimble as they use to be.

"Want me to get it?" Mom asked.

Determined, I grunted, "No." I tugged as I unwound the strand. Just as I thought I had it, the knot became even more unmanageable. "This is annoying."

Mom giggled. "Not everything in life is easy."

I didn't look up. "Duh."

"Don't get sassy, young lady," she whispered.

With a sharp yank, I pulled at the strand of bubble gum, pink yarn as hard as I could. When I looked up, Chloe and her mother were almost back home with my dog. The knot worked its way free, but the one in my stomach didn't. "Sorry," I said, winding the yarn neatly into a ball. "There, that should be easier."

"Perhaps."

My mother stared at me with doubtful eyes.

"What?" I asked.

"Nothing." She sighed.

"Really, you should just say it." I was ready for the tiff.

Brook's long tresses bobbed as she walked. I felt the grimace cross my face. Her appearance seemed flawless. I turned my attention back to my mother.

"Sometimes it's the challenges that bring the best rewards." Mom's fingers worked the yarn like she had been knitting all her life. "That's all I am going to say."

"And?" I prompted.

Mom's chest rose as she inhaled and her eyes darkened, her expression quite familiar. I felt like a child again. Brook was the popular girl like Jenna Morris and I was in tenth grade all over again. I was your average wallflower next to her. I felt the corner of my lip curl and remembered begging my mom for designer jeans, and feathered bangs.

"Just don't go slamming any doors before you know what's really behind them."

"Mom, it's not like life is like *Let's Make a Deal*." I pushed my foot against the floor making the swing sway faster. Chaos erupted in the front yard. Chloe ran in circles and Bones barked. He chased her, his tail wagging wildly. "It's like they're having a conversation." Envy shrouded my very existence.

"Don't you want to know what I'm making?" Mom asked.

"Sure."

One eye on Chloe.

One eye on her model mother.

Chloe had dropped her bike on the sidewalk. Her helmet was in my flowerbed. And her mother was standing like a tall drink of water chirping into her cell phone ignoring her daughter's exuberance. I squinted. I silently assessed her presence. I hated how I felt. Inadequate. Jealous. I judged her for not watching Chloe's every move.

"I'm making hats for the babies at the hospital," Mom said.

My expression softened. I glanced over to my mother. Her smile warmed me. I felt myself relax.

"I chose pink, in honor of you," she said.

My eyes stung.

I scratched at my armpit then picked up one of the finished hats. A lilac purple crocheted flower adorned the downy, soft band. "This one is my favorite. The babies will like these." I paused. "I hate that I have to go through this."

"I know, sweetheart. Being sick is no fun," Mom replied. "You know—" She unwound some more yarn.

"What?"

Mom's forehead scrunched as she worked the knitting needles. She looked the same as she always did. I hoped I had her good genes even if I felt pitiful.

"You're going to be fine. I can feel it. There are some things in life that make you stronger."

I sighed not sure I believed her. "We'll see."

"I know you're tired. And I know it's not fair, but if you own it, you can go on. Life isn't about brewing over spilled milk. It's about moving on when you are dealt a hand of crap. You've raised a darling young man and in my opinion, Beckett didn't deserve you."

"I thought we were talking about cancer."

She batted her eyes over the top of her red, white, and blue glasses at me. "Beckett, cancer, it's all the same shit."

I couldn't help but laugh. "I thought you loved Beckett."

Mom grunted. "Me, too, but when someone breaks my baby's heart, it's hard to see them in the same light. I know things don't always work out, but if he would have been honest from the get go—" She paused as she yanked at the pink ball of yarn and worked her knitting needles.

I shook my head. "I know. I know. Things would have been different." I thought about Bradley. I loved him so much. I closed my eyes thanking God for my precious son. "I wouldn't have Bradley," I said, rearranging the pile of pink hats.

"No, you wouldn't, darling girl, no you wouldn't. And this cancer thing is just another bump in the road. A *sucky* one, but you're doing fine. You need to eat more, but you're doing fine. You're strong, stubborn, like your dad. You'll beat it."

Mom stopped working her needles and patted my knee.

"Hope so." My breath caught in my chest. "I sure hope so." Faces from the cancer center flashed in my mind. My heart cringed for them. I cringed for me knowing human life was tangible. Even with a positive prognosis, there were no guarantees.

"Hang in there, baby girl. Hang in there."

Chloe trotted up the front stairs cradling Voodoo in her arms. Bones waddled behind her. She dropped Voodoo near the swing before going inside to put his leash away.

Bones sat by the front door waiting for her return.

"That dog loves her," I said.

"He sure does." Mom's brow twitched in thought. "Oh, quit feeling like a third wheel. He loves you, too. He's giving her what she needs."

I closed my eyes knowing she was right. "We all need some of that from time to time." Last night, John had wanted to kiss me. Frightened by his invitation, I couldn't go any further. I couldn't allow myself to get close. Hurt is what you get from letting others in. I couldn't do it again. I silently scolded myself for being a chicken. I was never a chicken.

"Chloe needs him, more than you do," Mom said.

I opened my eyes and rubbed my forehead. Mom was making my head hurt. *I* was making my head hurt. My fingers grazed the stitches. They were bumpy and prickly. "Thanks, Mom."

"You're welcome, dear." She took the pile of pink hats for the babies. "I've made twenty-one so far. Not bad for an old lady."

"You're not old. I'm the one that feels ancient."

"This too shall pass," she muttered, as she packed up her knitting things. "I can teach you to knit. We could join a class."

My eye twitched at the thought. "Thanks, I'll think about it."

"Maybe it would be best if you didn't yank my chain. Just be honest. I can see it in your eyes. You have no interest in knitting. First Beckett, damn him, and now you. Just be honest. Do it for yourself."

The hair on my neck stood on end at the tone in her voice. I had no idea how upset Mom really was with Beckett.

"For God's sakes, you only live once," she scolded.

"What's all this mumbo-jumbo about only living once?" Chloe chortled as she let the screen door slam behind her. She took one of the hats from my mom's knitting bag. "This is cute! Someone having a baby?"

The corner of my lip curled. "Nope."

"Then what is all this?" Chloe held the hat so Bones could sniff it. "It's a hat," she whispered in his ear. "Maybe she could knit you a sweater for the winter."

Bones circled around then plopped down at my mom's feet. With a heavy sigh, he rested his head on his two stretched out front paws.

"The hats are for the babies at the hospital," Mom explained.

"Oh," Chloe replied, putting the beanie back in the tote. "Cool. Wish I had someone to make me a hat like this. I don't have any grandmas. They died before I was born."

"I'm sorry," Mom said. "What's your favorite color?"

Chloe's eyes lit up. "Purple."

"One purple hat coming right up," Mom said.

"Will you make Voodoo one, too? So we can match. That would be so cool."

Mom tucked her reading glasses into her tote. She opened her arms. Chloe melted into her embrace just like I did at her age. It had been a long time since my mom held me like that. I longed for her arms to cradle me and now I needed it more than ever. This was turning out to be a banner day. First, I found myself jealous of Chloe's super model mom and now Chloe, herself. I picked Voodoo up from the floor. My fingers stuck to his sticky purple fur. Bones came over, his hot breath warmed my shin. "Yeah, you know, don't you?" I put Voodoo next to my mother.

Bones jumped up on my lap. The porch swing dipped, and my mother yelped in surprise. Bones turned toward her and licked my mom's ear. I swatted his tail when it slapped my cheek. He wobbled and barked before settling down.

I thought I saw pity in his brown eyes.

While they had their moment, my mother's words concerning Beckett lingered in my head. I had no idea she was that irked with him. Although I was relieved to have my mother on my side, a sliver of my conscience was anything but innocent. There was some sense of respite since Beckett moved out months ago. Feeling ashamed, I blinked away the pressure behind my eyes. We weren't meshing anymore and the inadequacy exhausted my efforts. The undertow pulled at the center of my gravity making me inequitable. Finding balance baffled me. It was getting just too difficult to be me, too difficult pretending to be me.

Beaming, Chloe stepped back from my mom. I wished I had my camera to capture the happiness in her green eyes. Brook sauntered up the stairs lagging behind. I forced an inviting grin. How could she live so far away from her baby? What kind of mother does that? There were too many children at school in the same situation. I could never do that to Bradley, but I could divorce his father.

Brook sat on the ledge of the porch. Her sleek legs were unnervingly smooth and tanned. I secretly loathed her.

Chloe began sputtering. "Maggie's mom is going to knit me a hat. It's going to be purple and Voodoo is getting one, too." I inspected Brook's gaze as she smiled at my mother. I didn't like the way her lip curled upward or how easily she made conversation.

"That sounds lovely," Brook said. "Maybe we can sew some sequins on it, too. Make it Hollywood-style."

"Mom says everything is glittery there," Chloe interjected, as she nuzzled up to her mother.

I smiled. I missed loving my mother that way. "Sounds like a fabulous place." I patted my knee to get Bones' attention. "Come on," I whispered. He moved over into my lap, turned in a circle, and sat down. I petted his head. "Good boy," I said in his ear as I bent closer to him. Out of the corner of my eye, my mother grinned. *I'll get there, Momma. I'll get there.* Bones licked my hand, and a sense of release washed over me. At last we'd made a connection and it wasn't at the expense of my garden. "So, Chloe tells us you're a model in Hollywood."

Brook lifted her gaze from her phone. A thin smile crossed her full lips. "Yes, I've done commercials and I model. Maybe you've seen them. I did a campaign for Garnier hair color. The ads ran in *Good Housekeeping, Redbook,* and *Cosmo.*"

Chloe reveled in her mother's presence. Her expression clearly defined. Pride. She loved her mother. Plain, simple, unconditional love, regardless of the circumstances. Chloe's faith ran deep. "Isn't she the most beautiful woman?" She asked, turning to me for validation.

I smiled. "Yes, she is. All mommas are beautiful," I said, patting my mom's hand.

"I bet Bradley thinks you're beautiful." Chloe gave her mom a toothy grin. She leaned in closer to Brook with arms stretched upward. Brook scooped up her daughter with amazing strength. Chloe clung to her mom as she balanced on her mother's hip.

Bradley was six when I'd last hoisted him up. I could barely lift him. He ran into the kitchen seeking out chocolate chip cookies he'd smelled baking. He wanted a better view into the oven, and as I straddled him on my hip, I thought, *I'd better remember this moment. He's so big and I don't think I'll be able to pick him up like this anymore.* Grateful for the intuition, the memory remained preserved in my mind like it had happened yesterday.

"Mom, Maggie has a son. He's old. He's past college," Chloe announced. Her voice softened as her mother rocked her back and forth gently.

Bones' eyes fluttered then closed as his head rested on my lap. His drool seeped through my skirt, but I didn't care.

"Momma says she is staying for a while," Chloe said. "I'm so glad." She wrapped her arms around her mother's neck, squeezing tight.

"That's sounds lovely," I said, truly happy for Chloe. All children need their mothers. Daddies are special, too, but there is something sacred about a child and a mother's bond. I watched Brook's face. Something in her eyes told me she wasn't staying long.

Chloe snuggled her head into the crook of her mother's neck. She was patting Brook's perfect hair. Focused on Brook's dark and ominous expression, I questioned her true intentions when her eyes met mine.

Chapter 18

I answered the door on the third knock. I'd hoped that the person on my porch would go away, but no such luck. Prepared to see Chloe, I opened the door hastily.

"Am I interrupting something?" John asked politely. "I can come back."

"No, I was just reading. I thought you were someone else."

"You thought I was Chloe, didn't you? I can tell by your expression. I'm sorry she's over here all the time," he said, rubbing his chin.

"To be honest, you could have been my mother. She has the same effect on me sometimes."

His green eyes softened and he chuckled.

I relaxed. "It's okay. And yeah, I thought it was your daughter. Chloe can be one tough customer." I opened the door wider. John stood on the other side of the screen door in jeans and a black T-shirt. Transfixed on the way his shirt hugged his chest I forgot my manners. I thought about the horseshoe tattoo on his left shoulder and his crooked smile.

"I just came over to check your stitches." He held up a black leather bag. "They probably can come out."

I pushed open the screen door a crack. "Please, come in."

John reached for the handle and let himself him.

"Sure is beautiful out tonight," he said.

I hadn't noticed it was dark. Stars twinkled overhead while crickets sang night songs. "Yeah, it's beautiful." I stepped back. It had been years since a man had made me come so unglued.

"If we go into the kitchen, I'll take a look. It'll only take a few minutes."

As I gazed into John's rugged face, all I could think about was kissing him. "That's awfully kind of you, but you really don't have to do that." I balked at his proximity then showed him to the kitchen. I sat on the stool at the counter as John prepared to remove the stitches from my left temple. He swept my hair back to inspect the gash. My insides rolled over as his cologne washed over me. I closed my eyes briefly, trying to collect my thoughts, begging myself to not say or do anything stupid.

"Does that hurt?" he asked.

"No, just a little squeamish." I opened my eyes to see a grin cross his lips. I liked the stubble on his face. "Are they coming out or staying in?"

His hand directed my chin so we were eye-to-eye.

I felt my shoulders slump. What was he doing? I knew what he was doing. He knew damn well what he what he was doing.

John opened his leather bag. "I like your Marcus Welby bag," I muttered. When he smirked, my eyes traveled to those sexy creases at the corners of his eyes that told me he must have spent most of his life smiling or joking around. He took out a pair of tweezers and a pair of medical scissors.

"Marcus Welby, huh?"

"Yeah, my dad watched the show all the time."

We were eye-to-eye.

My stomach rolled over again as a wave of heat rushed through my core. Analyzing the origin of my hot flash, I was pretty sure it was physician induced and wished John would hurry up.

"Stop fidgeting and hold still." John said. "Relax. These will be out before you know it."

I rolled my eyes.

"Nice gesture of appreciation. I bet you make a lot of friends this way."

"Hey, I didn't ask you to come over and do this." The intensified heat scorched my veins. I forced myself not to take off my sweater or wipe my forehead.

"What's wrong with you?" John asked.

Embarrassed, I let my shawl drop from my shoulders when he pulled back to inspect me. I lowered my gaze and barely answered him. "I'm just hot." I rolled my eyes again at his grin. Another wave of heat rushed through me as he felt my cheek with the back of his hand.

"You really shouldn't roll your eyes. People will get the wrong impression. Besides, you're too pretty for such antics."

"Chloe already gave me a lecture about this," I said.

John's green eyes twinkled with pride.

He thought I was pretty.

"That's my girl," he whispered, looking down then back to me.

"Oh, crap," I said as the inferno blazed within. I rolled my shoulders trying to loosen the building tension then took a deep breath.

"You don't have to be embarrassed. Hot flashes are normal." His expression reminded me of Dr. Akin. "Now I really am embarrassed." I felt my shoulders tense. How could this guy want to kiss me? How could he think I was beautiful? How did I get to be middle-aged? When did my life veer off course and I missed it? He had a beautiful wife, wait ex-wife, but she was back now. I narrowed my eyes contemplating his motives. *Shit. He probably can read minds.* I forced a smile. In two minutes, I had accomplished everything I had hoped not to. I was a dork.

"Nice smile. I prefer your regular face. You are one big mystery, Maggie Abernathy."

"You know my last name," I said.

"What?" John questioned.

"You know my last name," I said a little louder.

"Of course I do." He paused then took a deep breath. "I also know that you are struggling with life just like the rest of us. I also happen to know that you will survive and your eyes are the color of emeralds. You can still go to your doctor, but I don't think you need to. Do you have any salve to rub on that?"

"Yes," I whispered. Soon the hot flash subsided. I felt a little tug.

"Almost done," John reassured.

I felt another little tug. This time it was my heartstrings.

"Rub some on this scar a couple times a day and you'll be good as new," he instructed like a true physician.

I felt another little tug. John's hand was warm as his finger caressed the tender scar. He turned my face back in his direction. He caressed my cheek, his eyes blazing.

"There. Try and stay away from reckless seven-year-olds," he said, leaning into me.

I closed my eyes as his lips touched mine.

Our tongues lingered and the world stopped when John held me close. Beckett had never kissed like that. I pushed Beckett out of my head and let John's lips linger a bit longer. His firm hands cradled my face. My body went limp, not wanting the moment to end.

He leaned back. "You'll be good as new."

"Thanks," I whispered, swiping at the corners of my eyes.

"Now, now, what's all this?"

Why did he have to be so nice? Why did he have to be so handsome? Why did he have to live next door and have a daughter? Why did his ex-wife have to be here, too?

"I know you're not crying because I kissed you."

I gulped for air hoping to swallow the ball of emotion consuming me. I shook my head. "No," I managed to get out. There was something in his eyes I hadn't seen in anyone's before, most likely because I was too afraid to look. I touched the side of my head where the stitches were. "Thanks. Why are you being so nice to me?"

"Because I like you, Maggie, because I like you. Is that so bad?"

The front door slammed. I jerked my head in the direction of the bang. John went to the front door. When he returned, he was rubbing his head with one hand and holding a purple cat in the other.

He held Voodoo out in my direction. I raised an eyebrow at him. "I know, I know, I felt myself do it. Rome wasn't built in a day," I reiterated, realizing I had rolled my eyes at him.

"Shit." John packed up his doctor bag without haste.

"I'm sorry," I said, but I wasn't sure why. It just seemed like the proper thing to say.

"Why?" John closed his Marcus Welby bag.

I weighed my brewing sarcasm. "I guess my mother had a point when she told me to always lock the door." The disgust on John's face scared me.

"How did we not hear her?" he asked, leaning against the counter.

I had a choice here. I could be honest or just fill the air with empty conversation. I stood up, breathed deeply, and chose to be myself. "I'm going to go out on a limb here." I walked around to the other side of the counter then pulled out a wine glass and poured myself a glass knowing he was would be heading home in a heartbeat and I would be left here thinking about the heat that steeped between us. "She's pretty sneaky." His eyebrow rose toward the ceiling in a split second. "She's seven. She lives for hiding in my bushes. Adventure. She wants to know what's going on." In fact, I did too, but I'd save that thought for another time. I sipped at my wine.

John came closer. He took the glass from my hand and took a long drink.

"Look, you're over here kissing me and Chloe's at home probably crying her eyes out because now she thinks she has to compete with me for your attention or you've just played right into her hand and she's back at your house telling your ex-wife all about what she just saw."

"She knows that I am not getting back with her mother." John drank the rest of the wine then refilled the glass and handed it to me. "And I'm pretty sure I'm not playing into her hand."

This time, I raised my eyebrow. "Really?"

"Damn it, Maggie," John said, "why the hell did Brook have to pick now to do the responsible thing and visit her daughter?"

I sipped at my wine wondering the exact same thing. His deep tone suddenly put us on parallel planes. In that moment, it was as if John and I had known each other for eons. "I don't know. Why does anyone do anything?"

John took another swig of my wine. I watched his Adam's apple twitch as he leaned against the counter rubbing his chin. "I'm sorry, Maggie." He picked Voodoo up from the counter. "I'm sorry," he said as he left in a hurry.

I drained the wineglass. "What the hell?" I refilled the glass again testing my weakling's limit. I didn't jump when the front door banged upon John's exit. I went out to the patio to lie in the chaise. Stars dotted the sky just below the tree line. My tomato garden was naked, my love life in shambles, and my silly self, dodging the unknown, not brave enough to reach out and grab the brass ring. I counted on my fingers the weeks I had left for radiation, three if I wasn't mistaken. I kicked off my sandals, leaned back, and closed my eyes. The blow to my stomach startled me. I sat up. I opened one eye knowing what, more like *who*, I would see. Before I could speak, a wet dog tongue licked my face. I couldn't help but laugh. Bones wiggled his way into my chair as I patted his head then he jumped down, ran into the yard, and picked something up between his teeth.

I squinted, not able to make out what was between his teeth. Trotting back to the chaise, Bones put his front paws up on my chair then dropped a purple book into my lap. I touched the wet cover.

"Shit," I mumbled. "Bad dog, where did you get this?" I wiped off the smudge of dirt. Chloe's name was printed on the cover in fancy silver letters. I waggled my finger at Bones. He whimpered. "Bad dog," I said again, scratching his head, an oxymoron no doubt.

I took a sip of what would be the last glass of wine as my fingers started to tingle. I was feeling all too lightheaded, too quickly. I knew I shouldn't open the book, but nosiness got the best of me. I was surely going to hell.

Chapter 19

Paul Mitchell, interior designer, sat across from me drinking his tall iced Mocha Latte from Starbucks.

"Is that coffee that special?" I asked, pointing to his cup. "Whatever happened to a cup of black coffee in a clunky china cup whether it was winter, spring, summer, or fall? Now they have a flavor for every season and size for every occasion. What's that all about?"

Paul laughed. "You're funny." He reached across the table and patted my hand.

"Thanks. I don't feel funny," I replied. "So are we about done with the library?"

"Yup. I think your rug looks great. You have a great eye."

"Thanks." He kind of looked like Beckett, well-manicured, charming, perfect hair, less gray, maybe a little younger. "Did you order the sofa I picked out for the living room? And the painters are painting tomorrow?"

"Sofa, ordered. Painters will be here tomorrow. It will be done before you know it."

"Good. I hate being out of order." I pushed away the itching sensation from my seared armpit. "I just want it to be done." I wanted more than just this redecorating thing to be done. I wanted the irritation with Beckett to be done. I wanted the infatuation with John to be done. I wanted radiation to be done. I picked up a windmill cookie from the plate and nibbled on the corner.

"What's this?" Paul asked, investigating Chloe's purple diary from the table.

"It's Chloe's. Bones stole it, more like found it in my yard."

"Did you read it?" he asked sheepishly, hooking the latch on the front cover.

"What? Those aren't my teeth marks," I added as Paul rubbed his fingers over the indentations near the latch.

"You did, didn't you? I know that look."

I shoved the rest of my cookie in my mouth, making it impossible for me to answer.

"I'll wait. You enjoy that cookie."

I rolled my eyes. I couldn't help it. I wasn't going to be able to ditch the habit. Besides, it was part of my charm and personality. "Let's just say it was a short read."

Paul waggled his finger at me. "That whole rolling your eye thing. Not very ladylike."

"What are you? My mother?" What was I doing? "You're here to make things look pretty, not criticize."

"Yeah, you're right. Your ex-husband hires me to help you out cause that's normal. Most exes I know have it in for their ex-partner. Let's go check out the living room."

Geez. I picked up another cookie, broke off the corner, and plopped it in my mouth. I scooted my chair back and left the table. Paul seemed awfully comfortable being so personal with me, but I really didn't mind anymore, I was getting used to it. Chloe was doing a fine job breaking me in. I fingered the hem of my shirt. "I like it," I said inspecting the empty room. It felt good to purge old furniture and dusty plants. I'm not sure who thought those were a good idea in the first place.

"What are you mumbling about?" Paul asked.

"Nothing. I might just keep this room empty."

"You're a mystery, Maggie. It will already be pretty empty with only a sofa."

I scowled at him. "Oh come on, there's going to be a rug and I'm keeping my grandmother's antique coffee table. It will get filled over time. Space always does. I just don't want to rush it, this time."

"This time?"

I didn't expect him to understand. In hindsight, I was in love with the idea of marriage, which made Beckett perfect. Of course I loved him, and I couldn't turn back the hands of time, but I rushed it. "Never mind, just sputtering." I allowed him to fill my heart before fulfilling my needs.

"We can get you new plants. I can get you the perfect chair. I found an oversized leather chair and ottoman while surfing the net this morning. Perfect for this room."

I narrowed my gaze. "No, thanks. I think I just want to put my feet up, and get a feel for how things should be before making any more decisions."

"Have it your way, but when you change your mind, give me a call."

"I'm not changing my mind." I looked over to Paul who was standing with his arm propped up on the mantle. I loved the exposed, natural carved wood. "Why do people insist on painting wood?"

"Not sure. Why do people insist on anything?"

"Not sure. Must be something inside that governs our actions. Human beings are strange creatures," I said.

"They're not so strange. They are creatures of habit. People are driven by emotion." Paul ran his hand across the mantle shelf.

"I suppose so, but what makes emotion live, breathe, drive us to rule our actions?"

"Desire."

I sat in the middle of the room with my legs crossed like the children at school when they listen to a story on the carpet. I stared up at the exposed beams imagining myself in a cathedral. The sun flickered in the empty space as it bounced off the trees outside. Paul scuffled across the floor to where I sat. He sat down behind me mirroring my pose with his warm back pressed against mine.

"Maggie, what do you desire?" Paul asked.

"I'm not sure," I answered, not minding that our conversation drifted into the personal lane.

"Everyone wants something. What do you want?" he persisted.

"I used to think I wanted Beckett back. I'm not sure why, but I don't anymore." I picked at my thumb.

"That's probably good," Paul said.

"Definitely good. This is a pretty deep conversation. Am I getting charged extra for this?"

"No. You're easy to talk to," Paul said.

I chuckled, knowing I had been anything but easy lately.

"Beckett's a good man," Paul stated.

"Fine, take his side," I scoffed.

"I'm not taking sides. He talks about you a lot."

My heart hurt, the edges pinched. I stretched my legs out trying to get comfortable with yet another turn in the conversation. I sat silent.

"Maggie, he's really a good guy."

I inhaled deeply, taking in Paul's words. I knew he was right, but part of me still wanted to be mad at Beckett. I touched the scar on the side of my head and cleared my throat. "I know. And I know it wasn't all him. There, I said it. Did my mother tell you to come over and get me to confess?"

"No, I didn't, young lady," my mother's voice boomed. "But it's about time."

I glared at her. "What is it with people around here? You just come in. Is Chloe teaching you how to sneak in without making a sound?"

"Now, now, don't be mad at her. She's just a little girl going through more than you think. We all have our burdens. Don't take yours out on her."

Paul stood up, walked around, and offered me a hand. "She's right, you know. Don't take it out on someone littler than you."

"Fine, gang up on me." Paul and my mom shared a smile.

Paul put his hand on my shoulder. "Painters, tomorrow."

I smiled. "Radiation, tomorrow. Week four. Can't wait for the painters. Can they go to radiation for me and I'll stay here and paint?"

"Nice try," Paul said, squeezing my shoulder.

"I have twenty-five hats made and counting," Mom sang as she strolled toward the library.

"She's making hats for the babies at the hospital. Noble woman, there."

"Noble woman, here," Paul said, giving me a wink.

"Not sure about that, I peeked inside the diary of a seven-year-old."

Paul came closer.

"Like I said before, a very short read."

He smiled. "That's okay. Let me know when you change your mind about more furniture." He meandered toward the front door.

"I told you, I'm not changing my mind. And don't forget your coffee. You left it on the kitchen table." I sat back down in the middle of the empty room to imagine the future. I touched the back of my hand where Paul had touched it earlier. I wasn't accustomed to having others touch me unless they were students in my class. And in that case, seven- and eight-year-olds who gave hugs unconditionally. I thought hard. I remembered a time when Beckett's touch moved me. With a heavy sigh, I realized my time with him seemed like a blur. How could he have kept such a big secret? An unimaginable secret? Beckett was my best friend. My enabler. I sat in the quiet room assessing my part of the relationship. Time had shackled us. We'd spent so much of it appeasing the other, avoiding conflict. I'd spent so much energy trying to accomplish a higher degree, a more prestigious job, that I lost sight of *me*, trying to impress him for the wrong reasons.

I thought about the interview for the position as principal and *bam*, for the first time I didn't fume with disappointment over the whole situation. Jenny McBride could have the position as principal. It didn't matter anymore. I'd finish out my years teaching then retire, to a different life, a less-taxing life. One without phone calls to upset parents, one that didn't require evaluations because I'd judge my own success, one without report cards, and one where I could enjoy Sunday nights and not detest Monday mornings because beginnings were meant to excite us.

"Maggie, you gonna stay in there all day?"

"Maybe," I called to my mother.

I took one last look around. New paint would cover faded walls. A new sofa would be my haven for reading books by firelight, while Bones rested by my side. I put my face into the sun as it streamed through the window then pushed myself to get up and move.

Mom was in the kitchen assessing the contents of my refrigerator. "Glad to see you're eating. I want you healthy. Are you sleeping enough?" She asked, tapping her fingers on the steely door. "When my friend, Jan, went through this, it knocked her off her feet."

"How old was she?"

"About sixty, I guess. Do you want anything at the store?"

"No. Did she live?" I asked.

Mom shut the refrigerator then walked over to where I stood leaning against the doorjamb to the hallway leading to the front foyer.

"I mean, everyone keeps saying, you're going to be fine. How do they know? Truth is, nobody knows."

"Would you rather they say, '*It must suck to be you. What are your chances of surviving?*'"

"Nice." But she was right. "I know it's good to be around positive energy." I wasn't so sure it was good to be around myself. "What's on your agenda today?"

"You," she replied.

"Me?"

"Yeah, you. Thought you could use a day out. We're going to the beach. We're meeting Chloe and Brook there for lunch."

"What?" I didn't want to face Chloe. I didn't want to spend time with Brook. Perfection had its boundaries and that boundary was the edge of John's driveway that touched my front lawn. What could Brook and I possibly have in common?

"It'll be fun. You don't have to be in the sun. I know the rules."

I laughed at her. "What's in it for me? I don't want to go. I really don't want to go," I whined. *Shit. Double Shit. What could she possibly be thinking?* "I think I have plans."

"No you don't. You haven't had plans all summer except to lie around this place and feel sorry for yourself. We'll go to the park. The fresh air will do you good. Then I'll take you to radiation."

"I don't need fresh air. I just need to read my novel in peace and quiet." I held up my new novel by Tracy Chevalier.

Bones barked.

I shushed him.

He barked louder and spun in a circle.

"Shhh."

"That's like telling a crack addict to put the crack down. You're just taunting him. Put the book down. He thinks it's a toy."

I put the book back on the counter.

Bones sat at my feet glaring up at me. He yawned then tugged at the hem of my skirt. "Oh, for crying out loud." I pulled my skirt free. "Bad dog."

"Quit telling him he's a bad dog. He's not a bad dog. You wouldn't tell Bradley or any other child they were bad." Mom stopped talking then whistled and clapped her hands. Bones rushed to her side. Mom got down on all fours to rub his belly when he rolled over.

"I still don't want to go." I crossed my arms. "And you can't make me."

She narrowed her gaze at me.

"What are you, seven?"

"You don't understand."

"Maybe not, but it's already set. Don't be rude. Boy, are you a moody Judy. It just might be fun."

"No," I said.

"Yes," she retorted.

I stood silently, turned on my heels, and walked away. I couldn't possibly face Chloe and Brook. Chloe had seen me kiss her father. Brook was no doubt on the receiving end of that trauma. I went into my library and shut the doors. *Maybe Mom'll leave if I ignore her.* I shook my head at my poor behavior. "I am a bad daughter," I mumbled to myself. I turned on the music and sat at my desk trying to finish painting another photo. The muted colors drew me in. The photo of John and Chloe walking down the beach caught my attention. I didn't need to be the third wheel. John needed to be there for his daughter. I scolded myself for getting in the middle.

"How could you be so dumb?" I chided. Chloe peered through the French doors. She held up her diary. I swallowed hard. I should have returned it as soon as Bones dropped it in my lap. She opened the door. She tugged. The doors always stuck in the summer. They jerked open and she screamed bloody murder.

I jumped out of my seat.

She held her big toe.

There was blood on my floor and on her hands.

Maybe I wouldn't have to go to lunch after all. Maybe she was destined to spend the afternoon with some handsome doctor at the emergency room. Surely, her mother's beauty would get her some extra attention.

"Let me see," I prodded, as she howled louder when I inspected her foot.

Mom came running from the kitchen.

"What did you do to her?" she asked.

"I didn't do anything!" I snapped. "She opened the door and it caught her toe." I stood and rushed to the kitchen to get a towel to catch the blood that was dripping on my slate floor. Thank God, I didn't let Beckett get the white carpet he wanted. The slate foyer was the tradeoff for the tile he'd insisted on in the kitchen.

"Now, now, let me see what this is all about," Mom whispered.

Chloe's face was wet with tears, and her hair stuck to her cheeks that were streaked with dirt.

"Where did you get this dirt on your face?" I asked.

My mom shot me a look.

I reciprocated the gesture. "Where have you been, Chloe?"

My gut wrenched as she held up her journal.

"How did you get my journal?" she asked.

"Bones had it. See the teeth marks?" I replied, pointing to the marred purple cover.

"You read it, I know you did." Chloe's voice quivered.

Mom's eyes silently scorned me.

"I promise I did not look inside," I lied. I hated myself, but I wanted her to believe me and forgive me.

"The tape is broken. The tape wouldn't be broken if you didn't open it," she wailed, picking off tiny bits of transparent sticky residue.

"Now, now," my mother said, rubbing Chloe's back, trying to sooth her. Mom shot me a shamed look.

"Bones had it in his mouth." When he brought it to me last night, I didn't remember seeing the tape. I glanced into Chloe's eyes trying to capture her complete attention, put her in a trance, and make her quit crying. "He slobbered all over it. I cleaned it up."

"I don't believe you," she whimpered.

"Why wouldn't you believe her?" my mom asked, prying Chloe's hand off her foot trying to get a better look at her toe.

Chloe shrugged.

I prayed she'd keep her mouth shut about what she saw last night, but I knew she had no allegiance to me. I was just the kooky neighbor lady that she spied on, took advantage of, and spent much of her time shadowing.

Mom dabbed at Chloe's foot. "This doesn't seem that bad. I think you'll be fine with a few bandages."

Chloe cringed as she examined the gash herself. Her forehead touched my mother's, two manipulators sending messages through osmosis.

I rolled my eyes at the drama.

Both my mom and Chloe responded in unison. "You shouldn't do that."

"I thought my dad talked to you about that bad habit last night," Chloe reiterated.

My palms started to sweat. *Sweet Jesus.* The last thing I needed was an inquisition from my mother. I stared hard at Chloe. The glint in her eyes told me *game on.* I knew the look. I knew the game. I wasn't accustomed to losing.

"Maggie, go get a bandage and a pair of scissors."

"Scissors?" Chloe squealed.

"To cut the bandage so it will stay on your toe," I grunted.

"Oh," she said, sucking in air trying to catch her breath.

Afraid to leave Chloe alone with my mom, I put up my finger in front of her face. "I will be right back. You stay put." I ran to the bathroom, grabbed the whole box of bandages, and a pair of children's scissors with red handles. When I got back, the two were huddled together like Siamese twins. This didn't bode well for me.

"The bleeding stopped," Mom informed me, as if she were a registered nurse.

I set the bandages and the scissors next to her then took the cloth from her hand and wiped the blood from the floor. Bones went running by and slid into the screen door. "What a circus."

Mom took a bandage out of the crumpled box. "These things look older than the hills," she complained.

"I like the ones with Batman on them," Chloe said.

"I'm sure you do, but I don't have Batman bandages."

"Why not?"

"Because I don't have little kids anymore."

"Maybe you should. Maybe it would help."

I narrowed my gaze. I didn't care if my mom witnessed the showdown. Game on.

Mom cut the bandage in half lengthwise and wrapped Chloe's toe. "There, that should work nicely until you get your Batman bandage."

"Thanks, Glad," Chloe said, hanging on to my mother's neck while giving me the evil eye over Mom's shoulder.

"You're welcome," she replied.

"Are we still going to the beach this afternoon?" she asked.

Crap! Nothing good can come from kissing a man, especially when that man lives next door and has a conniving daughter, not to mention an ex-wife staying under the same roof.

"I'm still planning on it, but Maggie doesn't feel up to it." Mom glanced over to me.

Chloe swiped at her muddy cheeks. Dirt, she no doubt picked up hiding in my bushes.

"We can still go," Mom said.

"I don't want to go unless Maggie goes." Chloe pouted. Tears dripped from the inside of her red eyes.

I sighed. *Don't roll your eyes, Maggie. Don't roll your eyes.* I bit my thumbnail, assessing the situation feeling the powers of sisterhood working against me.

"I won't be happy unless Maggie is there, too. Please come with us," Chloe begged.

"I really have other plans," I said. My mom looked puzzled. I was not good at thinking on my feet. Who was I kidding?

"I thought you said you were tired and needed to rest," Mom added.

I rubbed my temple. My head started to pound.

"Please, Maggie, please!" Chloe begged, tugging on my arm. "I won't be happy unless you're there."

A thin smile crossed my mom's lips. She seemed to be enjoying Chloe's charade more than me. "Please," Mom said, getting back up on her feet.

I let out an exasperated breath. "Fine. I'll go. I can rest when I get home." Mom left and I stood toe-to-toe with Chloe. "There wasn't one single word in that diary and you know it."

"You still shouldn't have looked."

Her eyes flickered as I held her stare. I rolled my eyes. "Sorry," I said.

Chloe smiled then limped away, letting the screen door slam behind her.

Chapter 20

I soaked up the glorious Michigan shoreline as boats bobbed in the water that sparkled like a sea of diamonds. Sun flooded out from behind feathery clouds. My friend had painted this majestic scene before and called it, *God.* I loved the composition so much I bought it from him. I'd hang it above the fireplace once the great room was finished. The beach was the place my father would bring me to when I was young. I'd grown up on the rocky shore searching for tiny freshwater shells, fish carcasses, and dreams. Water lapped the land taking me back to a time when he'd held my hand as we walked the beach just like Chloe and John, Dad's strong hand holding mine, letting me know he'd always be there. Because Dad liked to build and do projects around the house, his hands were strong, but so was his mind. There was no deficit of stubbornness or will. His dark hair and eyes burned brightly in my memory, his thick English brow wiser than the night. *I know you're with me.*

I longed for the last day of radiation. That was the day I would allow myself to inquire about the cane at the cancer center. My mother and I watched Chloe splash at the edge of the sandy beach. Her smile stretched from ear-to-ear. Was Mom ever that happy to have a daughter? I was her spitting image.

Dad willed me his mind as my mother gave me her Scottish strawberry-blond hair, green eyes, snarky attitude, and probably an impossible disposition. I slid my sunglasses up on my nose then lifted my face toward the sun filtering through the tree branches overhead. I wanted to be on the beach in my swimsuit, but that wasn't in the cards since my skin was already scorched.

I checked to make sure I was covered.

"You look so far away," Mom said.

"Didn't know you could see me through the Ray Bans."

"See, it's not so bad being here. Chloe's doing her thing and you're doing yours. Wanna tell me what that was back at the house. If I didn't know better, you two need boxing gloves and a sparring ring."

"You know, Dad's been hanging around," I said, changing the subject.

"Yeah, I know." Mom's voice was barely audible. She stared out to the water as she shaded her eyes. "That Brook sure does have long legs. Wow-wee-woo." She fiddled with the knot of hair at the nape of her neck. "Your dad was always a sucker for great legs."

I snickered. "Yeah. I haven't told you, but something happened at the clinic during my first visit." I saw panic as my mother lowered her gaze and the vein pulsated in her right temple.

"Nothing bad, Mom."

"Don't scare me like that. I don't think I could live without you."

Goosebumps covered my arms as a shiver ran down my spine. Sun danced across our picnic blanket as the trees swayed to the summer beat. I smiled, believing it was Dad just stopping by to say *hello* and *I love you*. I knew what my mother meant. "I know. Sorry if I'm a pain in the ass."

"Me, too," she said.

My jaw dropped. "Can I get that in writing?"

"Ha-ha, very funny. And no," she replied. "This is off the record. A child needs to know that parents are human from time-to-time. I've made my fair share of mistakes, but you've always been my baby, my only baby." Her eyes twinkled.

"Thanks, Mom. I know what you mean. Bradley is everything to me, too. I couldn't bear for anything to happen to him." Unexpected emotion came over me, and I had to swallow away the sudden sign of tears. I detested this hormonal rollercoaster. "I love him so much."

"Beckett gave you a gift. Don't be mad at him forever," she advised.

I grimaced. I knew I wouldn't be, but I wasn't ready for my mother to see my soft side yet, another trait I inherited from my dad. Stoic on the outside, soft on the inside, especially when it came to kin. "Did you ever resent my relationship with Dad? He was always so attentive and gave me special treatment when I was a good girl."

Mom smiled. "Marjorie Jean, you're a silly one. Your daddy loved you fiercely. He'd fight tooth and nail for you alive or in the heavens."

"What?" I asked, trying to read her mind.

"I got special treatment, too, when I was *his* good girl," she said, cheeks reddening.

"Stop right there, *Glad*," I commanded, as I covered my ears. "Not something I need to know." I peered down into my T-shirt. The black dot between my breasts bothered me. Scarred for life. So many scars. So many reminders. "So do you want to hear what happened to me or not?"

"Sure. What happened? I'm still upset that you didn't tell me about the cancer when you first found out."

"Whatever. You know now." I unscrewed the cap of my water bottle and chugged the cold drink. "I haven't told anyone. Don't want them to think I am crazy."

"We know you are crazy." Mom chuckled.

"Thanks, Mom. I get it from you," I answered without hesitation. "Seriously. There was a cane."

"A cane?"

I took a deep breath. "I was the last one for radiation that day. After I checked in at the window, they found a walking cane on the floor. And no one claimed it."

"Go on." She waved a hand.

"Mom, it had a name on it. They checked physician rosters and there were no patients with the name. They called the phone number on the masking tape and no one lived at that number by that name" A familiar chill washed over me, a sense of relief in the aftermath. "There was a name scratched in the paint. *Walter James*." I lowered my glasses and stared at my mom. I expected shock. She smiled as she pushed her hair away from her face then fixed her blouse. Her eyes glistened.

"He's a good one to go with you, dear. He was always there, when you needed him most," she stated. "God, I miss him, but I know he's here. He's in the shimmer on the water. He's in the sun warming our faces. He's with you, darling girl. He's with you."

"I know."

The edge of the napkins fluttered as the breeze picked up.

"He knows we know," Mom said, putting another stone on top of the pile so they didn't blow away.

In that moment, the world felt right. Thankful for my family and life, I didn't dislike Beckett. I untwisted my ponytail holder. The wind caught my hair blowing it back away from my face. I checked down my T-shirt once more to see if the black dot between my breasts was still there. It was, but I didn't care. I knew I could handle just about anything that came my way, even if it was Chloe and her *beach-a-licious* mom sauntering toward us. I caught Mom's glance. "What?"

"Be nice," she mumbled.

I grinned. "I am not that horrible. You just said so." I snickered, but the sight of Brook in her black bikini mesmerized me. "Seriously, how did she get that body?" I tried to picture Chloe strutting around like her mom, something I didn't feel comfortable doing. Brook took the ponytail holder from her wrist and tied her hair up onto the top her head in a messy bun. It wasn't fair. She sat at the edge of the blanket in the sun. Her skin glowed with a summer tan or maybe it was a Hollywood spray-on. I checked for streaks and orange creases. I didn't see any. I couldn't imagine John not wanting to be married to such a beauty. I plucked a few green grapes from the bunch in front of me and started popping them in my mouth. They were dry and sour.

"Should have brought wine," I said, reaching for my water bottle. "Thought these were supposed to be sweet and juicy." A raunchy image ran through my mind.

Brook sucked at the end of a strawberry before biting off the tip. The image in my head went from raunchy to pornographic. *Maybe she's practicing to be a porn star. Stop it, Maggie!* I glanced over to my mother, who wasn't paying attention to the big girls at all. Her eyes were glued on Chloe. That was a mother's job, twenty-four-hour surveillance. Brook appeared nonchalant about the whole parenting role, but then again, maybe I was wound a little too tight. I wanted her to seem as if she cared more, for Chloe's sake. Chloe deserved that.

Brook pushed her Gucci glasses up onto her forehead. Rhinestones twinkled in the afternoon light. Even without makeup she was beautiful. *Why are you obsessed?* I knew why. What could John ever see in me if he was with that? Brook was flawless. I was flawed. I adjusted my sunglasses. "These Ray Bans just aren't cutting it anymore," I said, trying to fill the void knowing I wouldn't ever give up the glasses I'd saved my money for.

"I bought mine on Rodeo Drive," Brook said.

Did she spend John's money or her own?

"Honey, do you feel okay?" my mom asked as she touched my hand.

This time, I got the hint. I changed my facial expression. "I'm okay, just a little hot." I chugged the rest of my water, then reached for a fresh bottle in the cooler.

Brook cleared her throat. She leaned back on her elbows with her nose to the sky. My mom glanced from me to her, and my shoulders tensed. I didn't think Brook intuitive enough to figure me out. If she was, she was one cool customer.

"So," she started.

I reached into the bag of Oreos. The crinkling sound of plastic interrupted her thought.

She opened her eyes and stared in my direction. "So, you have a thing for my ex-husband, I hear."

I swallowed hard. *This was precisely why I didn't want to come today*, I wanted to scream at my mother for making me come here. My cheeks burned. What was I supposed to say to that? I ate another Oreo. Who did she think she was?

"Chloe was really upset when she saw you two kissing. You really should be more careful. She's young, you know. She doesn't need this right now. None of us do," Brook said.

I stood up, straightened my skirt, and picked up my bag. "I'll meet you at home, Mom." I tossed her the keys to the Equinox. "You and Chloe will need a ride home. I'll walk. It's up to you whether you want to give Brook a ride or not."

Brook's smirk caught my eye and rattled my instincts. My mom sat speechless. She blinked away the shock as Brook broke the tension long enough to examine her tan lines near the strings on her bikini bottoms.

"Not here, not now. Chloe doesn't need this. Tell her I didn't feel good," I muttered.

Mom put up her hands in exasperation. "What did I miss?"

"Ask Brook. She seems to have the four-one-one." I started to leave, but stopped in my tracks and turned around. "He kissed me. I didn't mean for anything to happen." And then I felt Brook's agenda as her eyes twinkled with mischief. "You're right, Chloe doesn't need this, but she needs a mother who cares."

"Marjorie Jean," my mother huffed.

Creases marked Brook's perfect forehead. I felt a sense of pride. She'd probably have the lines botoxed back in Hollywood, along with her pouty lips.

"Hey," Brook said, standing up.

My mother's face was struck with fear as she continued checking on Chloe to make sure she wasn't paying attention to our catfight.

"Look," I said, "Chloe begged me to come here today. Obviously, it wasn't a good idea. You two finish the picnic although I think my mother would rather crawl under a rock after my little display, but let me tell you something, Brook. I didn't choose to live next door to your ex-husband and your daughter. Chloe sought me out, not the other way around. I'm not sure how you fit into the picture, nor do I really want to know at this point. Your daughter is out there. She won't be little forever. You can chose to chastise me, but I think your time might be better off spent on her." I turned to my mom and took off my sunglasses.

"I'm sorry, Mom. I didn't mean to embarrass you. I hope you and Chloe can somehow finish the day on a positive note." I turned to Brook who looked deflated. "Brook, I hope, you can somehow find it in your heart not to take this out on my mom. She is very sweet. She loves your daughter. And with that, I am going home." I eyed Brook, slid my Ray Bans onto the bridge of my nose, slung my beach bag over my shoulder, then started marched off.

With my head held high, I followed the path out of the park, up the hill, and home. The painters were cleaning up as I strolled up the stairs. The screen door creaked as I opened it.

Beckett was in the living room directing Paul's project. His voice penetrated the empty space as he chatted with them. Of course, he knew just as much about painting as they did. Funny, how he became an expert on most things as the years passed by. Funny, how I never admitted how much it bugged me until now.

"Hi, Beckett," I said, sauntering past him. I dropped my beach bag on the floor. Sweat dripped from my forehead and armpits, my shirt stuck to my back. I trotted upstairs. I yelled back over my shoulder ignoring his presence, "You are going to have to wait."

I began stripping, leaving a trail of garments down the hallway to my bedroom. Locking the door behind me, I went into the bathroom, inspected myself in the mirror, and patted my flushed cheeks. I ran tepid water in the shower then stepped out of my underwear, checking for all the little black tattoos. They were still there. I stuck my tongue out at them, and immersed myself into the cool shower that took my breath away like the birth of my son, the cane at the cancer center, my mother's honesty at the park, Chloe's lack of personal space, the news that I had cancer, and the memory of John's kiss. The scent of Hawaiian soap transported me to a Maui beach under a palm tree, far, far away from the craziness that surrounded me. The trickle running down my back eased the tension.

I let the water run over me until I was cooled down.

My brush caught in my wet hair, but I managed to smooth it out and tie it up on top of my head in a messy bun, like Brook. Mine looked just as good. I wrapped a towel around my torso and went back into my bedroom half expecting Beckett to be knocking at my door. He could be so impatient. I slipped into fresh undergarments and a black sundress that covered me in all the right places. Before heading back downstairs, I slipped on my favorite Havaiana flip-flops. Mom had glasses, I had shoes.

"All done for the day, Maggie," one of the painters said as he walked out the front door with an unlit cigarette dangling from his lips. "We'll be back tomorrow, same time. See ya' then." He nodded.

"See ya," I said as I headed into the living room. Drop cloths speckled with paint protected the floor. A fresh dark khaki hue covered the walls. They'd finish the trim tomorrow. The ceiling beams majestic as ever.

Beckett exuded his usual perfect appearance. "You know what, Beckett?" I saw a flash of panic cross his brow. He hated conflict as much as I did, but then again, I was on a role. What did I have to lose? I felt myself loosen my grip on the reins of my life. "Relax," I continued, "I'm not sure why you're here—"

"Paul said—"

I put up my hand. "Just let me finish. "I'm not sure why you're here, but I don't care anymore."

Beckett stuffed his hands in his pockets and a thin smile crossed his thin lips. "Okay."

"But, why are you here? Or don't I want to know?" Bradley once told me he thought his father was fragile. My heart warmed thinking of my son's observation. Bradley also once said I was tough, braver than anyone he knew. I should have listened to him and believed in myself long ago. Today was honest proof.

"I thought I'd check out the progress. I wanted to apologize for being so pushy." Beckett ran his hand over the mantle. "I just want you to be okay. I'm sorry. And I'll quit pushing."

"Thanks. That's all I want. I need my space."

"Maggie, I know you need space."

I turned toward the front window. The lawn needed to be mowed again. "I feel guilty."

Beckett stood next to me. "Why? You didn't do anything wrong."

I swallowed hard to dislodge the lump in my throat then faced my ex-husband. "Part of me wanted out, too," I said. "I'm sorry." My head drooped. I covered my face with my hands. I couldn't bear to look him in the eyes.

Beckett took my hands down from my face. He held them to his chest. Years ago, my heart would have melted for that kind of attention.

"Maggie, I know."

"Why didn't you say something sooner?"

"I wasn't ready. And I didn't think you were ready either," he said, gripping my hands tighter.

"Oh, Beckett." I freed my hands. "Our foolishness got the best of us."

"Maybe," he murmured. "But we have Bradley and he's pretty terrific."

I wiped away the tears at the corner of my eyes. I couldn't help but smile. "Yes, we do. That, we do." Beckett's eyes flashed with understanding. "By the way, you left a journal behind. It's on the shelf in the library."

"I know. I left it for you. You can read it," he said. "When you're ready."

"That may be a while," I said. "That may be never."

Beckett pulled his car keys from his pocket. "Your choice, Maggie."

"I'd better go check on the beast in the backyard."

"Yeah. He's pretty cool. We played fetch earlier. Good dog. You would never let Bradley get a pet. What gives?"

"His name is Bones. He's a gift from my mother," I stated, as I crossed my arms over my chest.

"Still, he's a great dog. Maybe it's about time you had a canine companion."

"Maybe. I really should go," I said.

"Yeah, me, too," Beckett said as he headed for the door.

Chapter 21

"What did you think was going to happen?" I snarled at my mother. "Did you think we were going to hold hands and sing 'Kumbaya?'" I opened the fridge then grabbed the tomatoes from the counter. "I wouldn't have to buy these," I said, shaking them at my mother, "If it weren't for that dog." Bones barked at me as he danced on his back legs trying to get them from me. "Down." I hissed, opening the crisper drawer, and dropping them in. I huffed then stopped ranting long enough to notice Mom's expression. "Sorry," I said, realizing how awful I was being.

Mom shook her head as she measured out the coffee and dumped it into the filter. Her lips turned down, her eyes sad. I took the scoop from her and put it in the sink. "I'm not handling this all very well. It's not you. It's me. Don't you think I know that?" I muttered. "You were just trying to do the right thing. How would you have known that John kissed me and Chloe saw? And then there's Brook, who no doubt is wondering what the hell is going on." I stopped to breathe. "Everything is such a mess. I can't stand myself."

I let the faucet run, filled my hands with foaming soap that smelled like raspberries, then scrubbed away the day. Steam wafted up over my face. "God, I hate these hot flashes," I crabbed under my breath, pushing the hair back from my face after drying my hands on the kitchen towel. "What?" I shrugged at Mom's silence. "What?"

"You are a mess," she said matter-of-factly.

"Well thank you, thank you very much."

"Seems you know everything. Although I did like the speech you gave Brook at the beach. She *should* pay more attention to her daughter. She shouldn't live so far away, but maybe it's best for their family."

"Maybe."

"You didn't do anything wrong."

"Wait. You're on my side?" I questioned as I stuffed shopping bags under the sink.

"Jesus, Maggie, I'm always on your side."

I stopped and went over to where Mom stood next to the counter. Together, we basked in the aroma while watching the slow drip of coffee plop into the pot. I put my arm around Mom's shoulder before hugging her. "Thanks, Mom."

"No worries," she whispered in my ear. "We're all entitled to lose our minds once in a while."

"You seem shorter," I said, as we held on to each other.

"Gee, thanks," she grunted.

"It's what I am here for." I unglued myself from her side. "But I will have you know I was nice to Beckett today. I think I can bury that hatchet, as Grandma used to say."

"Good girl," she said, touching my cheek. "You are so worried about what other people think. Screw them. Do what's right for you. I'm tired of watching you wallow. It's your time."

"Thanks, Mom."

"That's what mommas are for, but I already think you knew that," she said as she poured herself a cup of coffee. "Now, let's get to the good stuff."

I raised my eyebrow in her direction.

"Tell me what happened with that handsome doctor."

I felt my cheeks glow. "That's embarrassing," I said, feeling heat prickle beneath my skin.

"Maybe, but it has everyone's panties in a wad around here. Must have been something. Now, dish," she commanded, more like a best friend than a mother.

I sat at the counter and fiddled with the grocery bags. "Well, John came over to take the stitches out of my head. And, well, he kissed me and Chloe was lurking in the shadows."

"So, how do feel about that?"

"I felt bad, but we didn't know she was there," I reiterated.

"No, how did you feel about the kiss?" Mom asked, rolling her eyes at me.

"Right there, right there, I get it from you," I jested.

"Seriously, do you like him? It's okay to be attracted to the man. You're a woman. He's a man." She sipped at her coffee. "He's seems like a nice guy."

"He is. I am attracted to him, but it's awfully complicated. He lives next door. He has Chloe and now Brook is here. It's a recipe for disaster."

"Brook won't be here forever. Kiss him again. What do you have to lose? Live on the edge," she said as she caressed her coffee cup with her thumbs.

"I already feel like I am living on the edge." I itched at the red spot under my arm. "I don't have the energy for this."

"Like hell you don't. That's a cop-out. You go to radiation every day. You have people traipsing through your house left and right, and you're dealing with Bones." She leaned down to scratch his head.

"No, thanks to you. If I think about it, you are largely responsible for some of the mayhem around here." I raised an eyebrow in her direction as I scrolled through my missed calls. "Shoot, I missed a call from Bradley," I whimpered.

"Your son is away. You're divorced. That's a done deal. Now you are working on your house. What do you mean you don't have the energy to give the good doctor the time of day?"

"I already did and look where it got me. Besides, I don't think I'm ready," I said, pouring myself a cold glass of lemonade.

"I beg to differ. There's no time like the present. You should have learned that lesson by now, Marjorie Jean."

"Hey, quit middle-naming me, *Glad*."

"Watch it, young lady. I am still your mother."

I got up from my seat and went over to where she leaned against the counter then put my hands on her shoulders. "Thank God." I gave her a peck on the cheek. Her eyes twinkled like fairy dust. I saw my father's memory woven in the golden threads of her irises and I wondered how Mom stayed strong every day without him.

"What do you say we take Bones for a walk," I suggested. "I could use some fresh air before I settle in for the night."

"Let's go," she replied.

Bones barked then pulled his leash down from the chair. We hadn't made it halfway down the driveway when Chloe came bounding across my front lawn. "See you in a bit," I called, giving a little wave.

"Wait." She stumbled on her bad toe. "Yow-za," she yelped. "I forgot about my stupid toe. You really should fix that door."

"You really should be careful." I caught Mom's stink eye. "Fine. I'll be nice," I mumbled in her direction.

"My mom told me you weren't very nice to her at the beach and that's why you left early. Is that true?" Chloe asked.

"Not exactly, but whatever. She's your mom and you have to live with her." I glanced over to Mom who was grinning at me. "I am sorry."

"Oh, okay." Chloe took out a package of Big League Chew bubble gum and stuffed some in her mouth. "Just checking. You know, you could be nicer to her. She doesn't have it so easy. Want some?"

She held the pouch so I could reach in. I pinched a wad of purple strands and stuffed it in my mouth. I cringed at the sweetness.

"Next time you want to kiss my dad, maybe you should do it in private."

My cheeks burned as I crossed my arms and stared at her. She kneeled down to pet Bones who was lying on her feet. "That doesn't seem to bother your big toe."

"What?" she said nonchalantly.

"That hefty dog, with pointy nails standing on your injured toe." I pointed to the bandage. "Nice bandage. I like Curious George. You two have a lot in common."

She squinted up at me. I couldn't tell if she was taking my bait or actually thinking.

"Yup, we do. I'm always into mischief, too." Chloe chuckled. "Well you two better get going before Bones poops out. I'll be waiting for you on the porch swing." She paused to blow a bubble that popped immediately and left purple residue on her lips. "If that's okay."

My mom smiled.

"It's fine," I said. "Only if you go get the Junie B. book you're reading."

Chloe scrunched up her nose at me. "Really?" She hobbled then started to run toward her house. With a short hop at the edge of the driveway, she stopped, and limped the rest of the way home.

"Hey," I called.

Chloe glanced back at me.

"Make sure it's okay with your mom and your dad."

She waved. "See you in a bit. Take good care of my dog," she sang. "I'll be waiting."

"I mean it. Ask your parents. I don't want any trouble."

"Okay," she shouted.

Chloe was lounging on the porch swing when we returned just as she promised. She was singing, "You Can't Always Get What You Want" by The Rolling Stones.

"Classic. She even sounds a little bit like Mick Jagger," I said to my mom.

Chloe held a new Junie B. book. "I got my book. *Junie B. and Her Big Fat Mouth,*" she chimed. "This girl cracks me up. Come here, Bones." She tapped her legs with the palms of her hands. "Come here, boy," she prodded.

Bones trotted right over to her and sat at her feet.

Her crooked smile beamed. "It's a gift."

"I guess so," my mom said.

"Yeah, whatever, why doesn't he do that for me?" I asked as I put his leash over the railing.

"Cause you're too bossy." Chloe put her hands up as if to surrender. "I don't mean to be rude, but if you give him a little slack he'll probably trust you more. We're all part of the pack."

"Thanks, Cesar," I said.

My mother sat on the swing next to Chloe and picked up the book. "You two were made for each other."

"Who?" Chloe's voice cracked as she chomped on her gum. I blew a bubble.

Chloe sized me up and blew an even bigger bubble.

"Show off," I muttered.

She laughed. "Me and Bones? I love him." She patted his head as he licked her hand.

"No, you and Maggie make quite the pair," Mom said.

Chloe and I smiled at each other. More freckles had blossomed on the bridge of her nose. I wished like hell I could be in the sun.

Chloe shook her thumb at my mom. "You're a crack-up. Maggie's way older than me."

"That has nothing to do with it," Mom said.

"Thanks for reminding me," I interjected.

"No worries. It's what I'm here for," Chloe said with a wink.

"You are a pain," I said.

Mom batted her eyes at me to heed warning.

"What? She is." I shrugged.

"And so are you, Marjorie Jean, and so are you," Mom said. "That is exactly what I am talking about."

Chloe gave a deep belly laugh. Her round cheeks jiggled and her eyes narrowed as she chuckled. "I love this lady," she squealed.

I rolled my eyes. "You're weird."

Chloe took a deep breath and settled down. "I know. Can we read now, please?"

I wiggled in-between Chloe and my mom. Bones leaped up on my mom's lap. We were squished together like sardines, but no one seemed to mind. I opened the book to page one and began to read aloud. "Did you finish the last Junie B. book you had?"

"Yes." She shook her finger at Bones.

"What?" I squawked.

"My dad finished it before Bones ate it."

I glared at the culprit.

He tilted his head to the left then started panting.

"You have got to stop that."

"Yeah, he really does. You should see your flowers in the backyard."

"What?" I pointed my finger at Bones, too. He whined then licked my hand. "Bad dog," I grunted.

"Yeah, he can be bad, but we all have our days, right, Glad?" Chloe leaned forward to get a better view my mom. Her elbow dug into my thigh.

"Holy-moly, let's just read," I said.

"Watch your mouth, young lady."

My mom and Chloe both giggled in unison, and Bones sneezed.

Chapter 22

I sat at my new oak drafting table, elbows on top, chin resting on clasped hands scrutinizing my work as the sunlight filtered through the leaded glass windows illuminating my library like a chapel. I chose three of my hand-colored photographs to mat and frame to hang in *my* library. Three is always a good number, one for the Father, one for the Son, and one for the Holy Ghost.

The first photo was of Bones sitting near the destroyed tomato garden looking proud of his efforts. The second photo was a close up of my potted Gerber Daisies that no longer existed, thanks to Bones. The third was a photo of my mother's profile at the beach the day of our eventful picnic. She'd seen more than the water caressing the shore under the bright sunlight. She'd heard more than the spirits in the summer breeze. She was my mother and she was beautiful regardless of the havoc she brought into my life.

The painters banged around in the living room. I couldn't wait for them to be done. I wanted my house back. I wanted peace and quiet.

Beckett's journal sat at the edge of my desk. I moved it yesterday, only brave enough to touch the cover. I couldn't open it. It held secrets, his secrets, secrets he knew he would share with me someday in his own way. I picked up my phone and dialed Bradley's number.

"Hello."

His voice was deeper. He sounded like a man. I had raised a man. "Hi, honey. How are you?"

"Busy," he answered.

"I know. I don't want to keep you. I just wanted to hear your voice. Sorry, I missed your call the other day."

"I know. It's okay. Dad told me he saw you. He said you seemed good. How's the treatment?"

Bradley's voice quivered a tad. For that, I ached. "Okay. I have two more weeks. I'm itchy, but I'm good. Don't worry."

"That's a little hard, Mom. I worry just as much as you do. It's hard keeping up with you and Dad."

I laughed. "You're funny. We'll be fine."

"Yeah, Dad told me you were different with him the other day, too. Way to go."

I smiled and fingered the photo of Bradley on my desk. He was five. It was wintertime. He was wearing the puppy dog hat and matching mittens my mom made for him, his red curls poked out from the edge of his cap. He held a mound of snow trying to lick it. "Some of us are late bloomers. Sorry."

"Sorry for what?"

"Sorry for any hurt. I've made some mistakes."

Bradley chuckled. "We all do. Hey, my company offered me a full time position when I finish this internship. What do you think of that?"

A lump grew in my throat. My baby was a grown-up. He was living in Boston. And I was back home missing him. "That's great. Will you take it?"

"I'd be a fool not to. Six figures. Who would have thought? I love it here."

"I know you do, honey. I'm proud of you."

"I'm proud of you, too," he said softly.

"Why?"

"Because you threw dad a bone. He really needed it. He's not like you. You could survive a nuclear blast if you had to. You're a beast." Apparently Bones and I had something in common.

"Thanks, I think," I said.

"Mom—"

"What?"

"I'd like to think I get that from you."

I inhaled deeply, warding off emotion. "Me, too, darling boy, me too. I love you."

"Love you, too. Can I call you later?"

I nodded, thinking he could see me. I swallowed then rested my forehead in my free hand. "Sure. Talk to you then."

"Sounds good. Bye, Mom."

"Bye, honey." I ended the call and put my phone down. I knew it would be a few days before he got back to me. He was living life, while I was surviving life.

I picked up Beckett's journal and leaned back in my chair. What could possibly be in here that I didn't already know? I opened the book randomly.

Bradley is getting older now. He turned ten today. He's been riding his bike nonstop. Maggie scolded him for leaving skid marks in the driveway, but I think they are cool. Better on the driveway than in his pants.

I laughed and turned the page.

I scratched at the smudge on the corner of the page. Probably blueberry jam. Beckett loved blueberry jam on toast for a midnight snack.

When I see Maggie with our son, my heart goes numb. I want to tell her, but I know it will crush her. I want Bradley to grow up with a mother and a father. They deserve a family. When I think about what my dad did to my family, it still angers me and I can't leave them.

My mind reeled back to a time when Beckett and I lounged by the fireplace during the midnight hour talking about our families. It was something we did once a month. We'd dim the lights, drink wine, and dedicate the time to our families so we could keep them close. I never really knew much about Beckett's father. He didn't come to our wedding. Beckett said it didn't matter, but I think it did. It hurt him.

Beckett's eyes had turned cold when he spoke of his dad leaving when he was twelve and never returning. It wasn't until Beckett started high school that his father contacted him. Beckett said his dad never did tell him why he disappeared like that. *Who does that?*

I thought about Chloe.

I thought about Brook.

I read one more page.

I love her in my own way. I really do. My heart rips open when I think about what I have to tell her. She doesn't deserve this. I should have been braver. I have been such a coward. Forgive me, Maggie.

I shut Beckett's journal. I placed it back on the corner of my desk and patted the supple worn leather cover. Beckett carried a burden I couldn't fathom. How could I have been so insensitive? "I'm sorry, too, Beckett. I should have been there for you."

The corner of Chloe and John's photo peeked out from under my blotter. I didn't keep it with my other photos. I found myself studying it whenever I came into the library. Today was no different. I considered myself a stalker at one point, but then dismissed the claim since I had intentions of giving it to John. "Damn, why does he have to be so attractive?"

"I don't know. Why does he have to be so damn handsome?"

The voice startled me. Brook had her back up against the doorjamb with her arms crossed over her chest. "Did my mother let you in?"

"No."

Her mischievous smile sent chills down my spine. "So, you're accustomed to just letting yourself in?" Her piercing, steely, blue eyes sent a cold message.

"No, the painters let me in. They seem very nice."

Now there's your stalker. She could charm her way into any building with her Daisy Dukes and bare shoulders. "Great." Mother was right. I needed to lock the front door. "So what brings you over? Is Chloe with you?" Bones trotted by. I secretly scorned him for not being a better watchdog then settled back in my chair, and put my hands in my lap.

"No, Chloe's not here."

I waited for Brook to speak. It proved to be a good tactic with upset parents at school and by the expression on her face she didn't seem happy.

"Why did you leave the park so fast? Chloe was upset when she came back and you weren't there. That's not a nice thing to do to a seven-year-old."

"She seems fine now." My hands began to sweat.

"She hides her true feelings well. She was devastated."

"Well, she didn't seem devastated when she was over here reading with me and my mom or when she shared her gum with me or told me she would be waiting on the porch when I got back from walking Bones." I held Brook's stare. She was on *my* turf. "Why are you really here?" My question meant more than she could infer. Brook stepped closer to my desk. I put my elbows back on my desk and rested my head on clasped hands. I watched her as her eyes scanned my photos, John and Chloe's being one of them. Her silence made me grow restless in her presence. "Seriously, why are you here?" I asked again with inflection.

"I don't like that my daughter is hanging out at your house so often. What kind of hold do you have on her?"

"What do you mean? She just shows up. She likes my mom. I think this conversation is about over," I stated calmly.

"She likes you, Maggie. She talks about you all the time. She quotes you all the time. She loves your dog. You let her play here. Are you using her to get at John?"

I felt the hair stand up on the back of my neck. "Excuse me?"

"Oh, come on, Maggie. I've seen your kind before. Single, poor divorced woman, no children around, no man."

I stood up, shoulders squared. "I believe you have overstayed your welcome. I am anything but a poor divorced woman." I stopped, and thought for a moment. Right then and there, I was done playing that card. "I am anything but what you think I am. I don't need to explain myself to you or anyone else. What Chloe and her father choose to do as my neighbors is their business. Last time, I checked"—I took a breath then dug my hands into the pockets of my shorts—"You are a visitor. And as far as your daughter is concerned, I don't believe she has many friends here at her new house. And are you aware that her reading skills are not up to par?"

Brook's eyes narrowed, her brow furrowed, and her cheeks reddened.

"If you and John are together just say so. I'll bow out." *Did I just say that? I didn't even realize I was in.* "So are you sticking around? Are you two a thing again? Because if you are, don't you think you should focus on Chloe, not me?" Wondering how much further to push it, I crossed my arms, mimicking her posture.

Brook huffed, turned on her heels, and left. She sneered at me over her shoulder before exiting the room. "Your mom's right, you should lock your doors."

I followed her out.

One of the painters was on the porch smoking a cigarette. He winked at her as she stormed by. Her flip-flops flapped like her lips. The painter's gaze followed Brook's every move.

Disgusted, I scowled at him.

He lit his smoke then acknowledged my presence. "That didn't sound like it went well."

"Are you the one responsible for letting her in?"

He pointed to his younger counterpart. "Talk to him."

I went back inside. *Jerk!* I hoped I didn't say it aloud. I poked my head into the living room. It appeared to be done as promised. I checked my watch then strolled into the kitchen to pour myself a glass of wine before Chloe came storming in. She'd know how to get in even if the doors were locked.

Bones stared at me.

"Bad painter man, bad, bad younger painter man," I said in the same tone I usually reserved for Bones.

"Maggie," a man's voice called.

I glanced up and the painter man was standing in the doorway to the kitchen. His eyes were round and apologetic, like the bulldog at my feet licking my toes.

"All done. We're all cleaned up. Want to come see?"

I cradled the wineglass in the palm of my hand, the stem between my fingers. "Sure," I said with a smile. Bones followed at my heels. "Come on, boy."

The room was pristine, exactly how I pictured, clean, new khaki paint, and not a lick of furniture. I swung around when I heard the knock on the door.

Paul peered inside. "Anyone in there?"

"Yeah, come on in." I frowned at bad painter man. "Now, he *can* come in," I said, giving Paul a nod.

"Sorry," the younger painter man said, "I thought it would be okay. She said she was your friend."

"Apparently not. Wanna buy a bridge?" I asked, meandering to the center of the great room breathing in the fresh scent of paint.

"Sofa will be here in two days, rug, too," Paul said, from behind me. "You two can go," he said to the painters.

"Thanks." I didn't want them to think I was a total loon. "You did good." I gave them the thumbs-up and a kooky little wave. "Bless you," I mumbled to Bones, after he sneezed. He trotted away, but not without letting Paul scratch his head. When Paul jabbered in baby-talk to Bones, I felt my furrowed brow wrinkle with sarcastic question.

"What?"

"That is so sad, but this room is beautiful. I'd say your work is about done here." I assessed his dejected reaction. "What is it with you guys and your sad puppy-dog faces? Not even Bones looks that pitiful."

"I am going to miss coming over here and seeing you."

"You're sweet," I said for a better lack of words. "You still have to bring the sofa and the rug. I'll see you again."

His eyes lightened. "You're right. And when you change your mind about more furniture. Beckett has my number." Paul stopped himself. "But then again you have my number, too. If you need anything you know where to find me."

I processed his comment. "Beckett will not be calling you again on my behalf. We have come to an agreement. If he does, tell him no." Paul inspected the room further. I set my wineglass on the mantle then buried my hands in my pockets. "This room really is lovely. Can't wait for the rug and the sofa. Will your guys help put my grandmother's table back in here for me?"

"For you, anything."

"Thanks."

"You're welcome." He shoved his hands in his pockets. "When I first met you I wasn't sure what I was getting into."

"Yeah, it's a little crazy around here," I said, reminding myself that I still had flowers to replant in the backyard.

"In a good way. Very entertaining, to say the least."

I snickered. "I bet." I trailed behind Paul as he headed for the front door, thinking how my chaos generated such interest from an outsider.

Paul stepped out onto the porch. "The sofa and rug will be here soon."

The corner of my mouth lifted. "Great." I found myself wanting to be alone as I was consumed with John and the obstacles between us. I wanted to kiss him, get to know him, go out with, explore, but after today that might never happen. I peeked over the side of the porch, half-expecting Chloe to be hiding out in the bushes. She wasn't there, so I went inside, closed the front door, and locked it.

I shuffled through the living room to retrieve my wineglass then meandered to the kitchen to top it off. My book was waiting for me on the lounge chair outside and no doubt Bones was destroying something else in the backyard.

When I opened the French doors to the patio I noticed two small feet sticking out from the Dogwood tree that was more like an overgrown bush. Both of Chloe's big toes now had purple bandages on them. I dismissed the notion to shut the doors, and pretended not to see her. I scratched at the raw skin under my arm, took a quick peek, then put up my feet. My skin was gross. I smeared ointment under my arm, opened my novel, and began to read. From the corner of my eye, I saw Bones scoot under the tree and lay next to her. I heard muffled mumbling, but didn't answer.

"So, you're just going to ignore me, too," Chloe chimed.

I grunted, closed my book, then took a sip of wine and waited for her to crawl out from under the tree. When she didn't budge, I went over to where she was. "Nice bandages. Did something happen to your other big toe?"

"No, I just wanted a matching set."

Innocent bystanders might have thought I was crazy tree lady and wonder how many cats roamed inside my charming stone house as jabbered to bushy branches. "Are you going to come out?" I asked.

"Nope," Chloe replied, popping the 'P' sound.

I heard Bones rustling beneath the greenery. "Why did you think I was going to ignore you?"

"Cause, it just seems like everybody does. My dad works all the time and when my mom finally comes to visit me, she's really not here. She's on her phone or doing something else like shopping."

This was going to be tougher than I thought. I squatted and peered under the tree, thinking, *What the heck?* I lifted the lowest branch and invited myself in. Chloe was stretched out on her back with her hands behind her head. Bones had his head on her stomach. I managed to find a space between the limbs for my head and sat like a pretzel.

"When your sofa gets here, can I come over and test it out?" Chloe asked. "I'm gonna miss that designer guy, he was nice to me."

My eyebrows shot up. Chloe was definitely a stalker. "You were in my house. Listening?"

"Yeah, I came over and let myself in the back."

Apparently, I needed to lock all the doors. "You know you could knock or ring the bell," I suggested.

"I could, but you know me, I forget."

Chloe opened one eye. She pulled one of her hands out from behind her head and started petting Bones.

Chloe sighed. "My mom thought he was cute, but not her type."

"Good to know," I muttered.

"My mom doesn't like you," she stated.

"I know," I said, loosening my hair free from the spindly shoots.

"She's like that you know. She says you push her buttons."

I smirked. It was good to know I wasn't the only one feeling inferior. "I don't mean to." I crossed my fingers behind my back to cover the fib. Not sure it was foolproof, but I thought I should give it a try for old time's sake.

Chloe propped herself up, her eyes filled with doubt. She picked a twig from her messy hair then gave it to Bones who immediately chewed it up. I plucked a leaf from her shoulder. "I'm sorry if I hurt your feelings. Grown-ups can be difficult."

"Don't I know it," Chloe said. "It's not easy having Mom around. She refuses to stay in a hotel. She's always asking my dad for stuff. He says he's *zasperated*."

"You mean exasperated?" I asked.

"Yeah, that's what I said. Geez." Her tone was sprinkled with disgust.

Chloe produced *Junie B. Jones and Her Big Fat Mouth* from her back pocket and handed it to me. "Can we read this?" She wiggled into a pretzel position opposite me. "It's getting to the good part."

Bones got up, spun in a circle, and plopped back down. He laid his head on his paws and sighed. I scratched his ears. "Sure, Chloe, we can read for a bit." I opened to the page with the bookmark. Chloe's eyes studied my face as I read. Then I stopped. "Does someone know that you are over here?"

"Where else would I be?" she chirped.

"Where's your mom?" I asked.

"Out buying stuff. Dad's home."

I found my place on the page and kept reading.

Chapter 23

The sun nudged the horizon. My eyes strained to see the words as I continued reading to Chloe. I swatted at a mosquito on my neck. "I think we'd better give this up for tonight." I crawled out from under the Dogwood. "Are you coming?"

"I don't want to," Chloe sniffled.

"Oh good grief, you'll be one giant mosquito bite if you stay under there. Bones needs his dinner," I said, poking my head back under the tree. "So do I."

"Can I feed him?" she asked.

"Sure, but the only way to feed him is to come out of there. Let's go," I ordered. "Come on, Bones. Dinner." He jumped up and scooted out across Chloe's feet. I waited for her to crawl out then offered her a hand up.

"Wait," she gasped. "Voodoo's still under there. I have to get him."

Before she could crawl back under the tree, Bones ran under the branches to retrieve the dusty purple cat.

Chloe smiled. "Bones likes me. And Voodoo, too." She brushed off her jeans. Bones dropped the raggedy stuffed animal at her feet and bolted for the kitchen doors. "Look, Voodoo has a broken toe. Just like me." Chloe pointed to the purple bandage on the cat's foot.

"You don't have a broken toe," I reminded her.

"Well, it sure feels like it. Stupid door," she groaned.

"Yeah, stupid door." I put my hand on her back and guided her toward the house. "Go in. The scoop is in the bucket with Bones' food. I'll be there in a minute." I watched her trot in the house after Bones before going next door.

Surprised that no one had investigated her disappearance, I figured I'd better let John know where his daughter was. With one hand on the gate Chloe hollered my name.

"Can I eat with you, too? Voodoo doesn't want to go home yet," she called.

"Stay there. I'll go check with your dad." Brook had warned me off, but I felt sorry for Chloe. She was caught. I opened the gate then slammed it behind me. Percolating rumbles from a motorcycle came from John's garage. I wondered if he had a guest. Weary of running into Brook, I cautiously approached the garage. John was sitting on a Harley Davidson revving the engine. I waved to get his attention, but he was too engrossed with the bike. I waited for the rumbling to subside then I yelled his name.

He nodded to me. His eyes were dark and clouded with angst.

My stomach twisted. "Sorry to bother you, but Chloe is over at my house. She is feeding Bones and wants to know if she can stay for dinner." I stepped closer to John. "She says Voodoo doesn't want to come home."

John tightened his grip on the sleek handlebars giving the engine one last rev.

I jumped at the unexpected roar then waited for an answer. His organized garage was impeccable. All the tools hung over the workbench, the wrenches placed by size. Two bikes were parked against the wall, Chloe's bike with the banana seat, and a man's black mountain bike. Fishing rods hung from the rafters. I shivered at the thought of the dangling hooks. With all of Chloe's mishaps, I thought John would know better. I inhaled a deep breath of air as my eyes returned to his solemn face. "I can tell her to come home."

He swung his leg over the seat of his Harley "You sure are a lot of trouble," he started.

I raised my eyebrow at his remark. "Not sure what you mean." I crossed my arms.

John's temple twitched. "First, you get the nanny to quit. Then, Chloe gets attached to you."

"Wait, that was not my doing. She comes over on her own." I stopped talking as he put up his finger in my direction. Both my eyebrows went up as I was silenced.

"She loves your mother. Now Chloe's mom is here and you've managed to get under her skin, which by the way is costing me more money with each passing second. Lord knows what store she's buying out now."

I put up my pointer finger in his direction just as he had done to me moments earlier. "Not sure what you mean, but that has nothing to do with me and I'm pretty sure you know that." My head pounded. John's jaw line unexpectedly soften, laugh lines emerged around his luring eyes. He was clean-shaven today, and damn attractive. "I'm sorry if I've caused you trouble." My heart ached for him. "Like I said, I'll send Chloe home."

John grabbed my forearm as I turned to leave. He spun me back around. "We haven't had this much upheaval since Brook and I split three years ago."

His Adam's apple wobbled when he swallowed. His eyes stared through me. The heat from his body penetrated my skin like tiny waves of lust burrowing into my pores, making my insides crumble. I tried to yank my arm free.

"And yet—" He took a deep breath. "You are still so damn beautiful."

"Please, please stop saying that to me," I said. "This is a mess. I don't think I have the energy to do this with you."

He leaned into me, our noses almost touching. He squeezed my arm. "Well, you better find the energy because I'm not backing down."

"What about Brook? She's here. And Chloe. I can't do this to Chloe. I see it all the time at school with parents and it just doesn't work."

"Stop with the excuses, Maggie. I'm not one of your parents from school."

"Yeah, but you're my neighbor, Chloe's dad. And Brook warned me to stay away." His eyes turned dark like the rush of a sudden downpour. "I shouldn't have said that." I shook my head. "That's between me and her."

"She's not even part of the equation. She's not here for Chloe. She's here for money. This is how she rolls. She'll be gone soon. Chloe looks up to you and she loves your mom. Please don't turn her away because of her unreasonable mother."

I thought about Brook accusing me of using Chloe to get to John. I wondered what his motive was. Dads seek out moms for their children, too. My mind froze. "I'm not going to befriend your daughter just because you keep coming on to me." At the flash of hurt in John's eyes, I immediately regretted my words. He lured me closer. Our bodies touched, waves of electricity igniting between us. The night sky darkened intensifying our united emotion. "Please, nothing good can come from this."

"Are you sure about that, Maggie?"

Suddenly, John's arms were around me. His lips pressed against mine. They were warm and soft unlike the tone in his voice. I closed my eyes, cautioning myself, but couldn't stay strong. I caved to his sexy self. He leaned me back after the kiss, his hands held my arms. As I gulped for air, his fingers release me.

"You tell me there is nothing there and I will leave you alone," he said.

Speechless, confused, and alarmingly attracted to him, I forced myself to say nothing.

Brook parked her rented BMW at the end of the driveway.

"I have to go. I can't go another round with your ex-wife. She'll always be here. That's too much." My words were heavy. I didn't want it to be true. "Mommas don't leave their babies. I know. I have one," I said matter-of-factly. I couldn't read his expression. "Should I send Chloe home?"

"No. She can have dinner at your house. I have some things to settle with Brook."

I crossed my arms and hung on to myself, somebody had to. Nobody was going to take care of me, except me. My shoulders tightened as disappointment crowded out the exhilaration I felt from John's touch.

John sighed. "Damn it, Maggie. I never thought I'd find a woman like you. Matter of fact, I was content being by myself." He paused and touched my cheek.

His hands smelled like motor oil and testosterone. The urge to lead him on taunted me. "Call me when it's safe for Chloe to come home. I have no plans. Bones could use the company while I work."

"Work on what?" he asked.

"Just a project." A project that involved him and his daughter. Chloe, the girl with no boundaries, high-top tennis shoes, purple bandages on her big toes; the girl with limited reading skills, a crazy mother, and a mangy, stuffed purple cat named Voodoo. The girl that was changing my world.

John wiped his hands on the bandana from his back pocket. "Chloe really loves Bones, doesn't she?"

I nodded. "Yes, she does. If you want him, he's all yours. That offer still stands."

John shook his head. "No way, I've seen what he's done to your yard."

"What if I trained him?"

"No," John said, snapping down the studded leather strap of his saddlebag.

"John—"

"Yes," he said quietly.

"I can't. Good luck with Brook."

Chapter 24

I closed the French doors from the patio to the kitchen. Chloe sat next to Bones on the floor next to his dish. He was munching and crunching while Chloe painfully tried to sound out words in her Junie B. book. "Your dad says you can stay for dinner. He'll call when he wants you home." Her frustrated expression drifted up toward me as I headed for the refrigerator.

"These words are hard. Most of the kids could read these books in my class last year."

"You're going into third grade, right?"

"Yup. I stink at reading."

She cringed, admitting her problem. "Bradley had a hard time learning how to read," I said. "He used to come home from school with his head hanging low. He thought he was stupid."

"I know the feeling, especially when your—"

I pulled my head out of the refrigerator. She stopped, put the book down, then gathered the crumbs of food that Bones had dropped in front of his bowl, and let him lick them off the palm of her hand. "What were you going to say?"

"Never mind."

"If you've got something to say, just say it. I won't get mad." I put my head back in the refrigerator. Nothing looked good. "Want to order pizza?"

There was no answer.

I shut the refrigerator to see if Chloe was still there. She had her head buried in the crook of her arm at the kitchen table. Muffled sobs and hiccups escaped as she cried. I approached quietly then sat across from her and played with the breast cancer teacup my mother had sent me.

Bones stopped eating and plopped down in front of his bowl. He was in love with her. I could see it in his dark sad eyes as his brow furrowed with concern.

"I have an idea." I'd heard what John said, but I couldn't help myself. "If you go to puppy school with me, we can work on your reading even more."

Chloe's shoulders stopped shaking and the sniffles slowed.

I handed her a tissue from my pocket. "Here, wipe your nose." She took the tissue and inspected it with a grimace. "It hasn't been used," I said.

Chloe dabbed her damp cheeks. She swiped at her eyes with the back of her hands. "Thanks. What did you say?"

"Bradley's a really good reader now. He's got a job and everything. In fact, he's got a great job and lives on his own." I was happy for him, but living without him proved more difficult than I imagined.

"You must miss him," she whimpered. "Did you teach him to read?"

"Yup," I answered. "We had to work really hard." I bit my lip remembering how painful it was for him. "Mostly he needed confidence. He needed to know he could do it. He also needed to understand that not everything comes easy."

Chloe swiped at her nose with the tissue as I spoke. Her hair was matted down. She was a hot mess, but then again, who was I to judge?

She stuffed the tissue in her pocket. "Dad is always saying something about everyone has their brothers, mothers, *doe-thers*. Oh, I don't know," she huffed.

I grinned at the old-fashioned lingo, thinking not many people speak to their children like that anymore. It had shamefully gone by the wayside. "Everyone has their druthers," I said as she scratched her head. "He's right, you know." I wondered what else he was right about.

"Will you really teach me to read instead of just reading to me?"

All year I'd longed for a break from teaching and suddenly I found myself right back in the swing of it. "When do you turn eight?"

"August seventeenth," she answered.

"August is the best month for a birthday. Bradley's birthday is August twenty-second."

"My mom's pretty mad at you. I'm not sure she'll let me go to dog school with you and Bones. And my dad said, no dogs."

"Yeah, got that." I sat back in my chair and crossed my legs. "Do you want pizza, or not?" I picked up my phone and started dialing the neighborhood pizza joint as Chloe nodded yes. "I'd like to order a ham and mushroom pizza." Chloe wrinkled her nose as I spoke. I leaned over to her. "What do you want?"

"Ham and pineapple," she said. "Please?"

"Make that ham and pineapple. Thin crust."

Chloe rubbed her stomach and gave a little smile.

"Thanks. Yes, please deliver it." I listened to the teenager with the raspy voice on the other end of the phone. "Yes, that's my address," I answered before hanging up. "Have any ideas?" I asked Chloe.

"About what?" she replied.

I rolled my eyes at her lack of focus. "How to get permission for dog school in trade for learning to read."

"Yeah, don't ask my mom!" Chloe snorted. She put her hands on the table in front of her, one on top of the other. "You got a better shot at asking my dad."

I wasn't sure about that. "We'll work on it." I didn't know why it was important for a trade. I could have just told her I would help her with reading without dog school, but then again I knew why, she had a way with Bones that I didn't understand. We could learn something from each other.

Chloe told Bones to eat the rest of his dinner. Bones pushed himself up with his front legs and did as he was told.

"I just don't get how you do that. I tell him to do something and it's a crapshoot."

Chloe smoothed her hair back from her face. She had her daddy's green eyes and his laugh lines. "It's all in the delivery."

We both laughed.

"Let's go watch television until the pizza gets here," I suggested.

Chloe slid her book across the table. "Will you finish the chapter first? I'm at the good part," she said with a wink.

"You said that last time," I reminded her.

"They're all the good parts. I love that girl." Chloe jerked at the purple string on her lap. Voodoo came flying off the floor and landed with a plop on the table knocking over the saltshaker. "Woe there, kitty cat," she said as she quickly put the salt shaker upright, but not without leaving a mound of white crystals. "I'll get that later."

I got up. "I'll get it now."

"You always have to do stuff now," Chloe said. "Why? It's not like it won't be there later." She squinted and stuck her finger in the salt.

"Don't know. I just want it done now."

"You're impatient. That's what my dad calls me."

I went to the sink and moistened the sponge under the faucet. Chloe was right. There were lots of things I wanted right away, hence marrying Beckett way back when.

"My dad says sometimes things take time. That I just need to slow down." Chloe patted Voodoo's head and stood up. "You gonna clean this up?"

I returned to the table, wiped up the salt, then tossed the sponge toward the sink. It landed on the counter by the toaster. "Better luck next time." I took Chloe's book and we meandered into the family room.

Chloe plopped down next to me on the sofa, her leg touching mine. She snuggled in with her head on my shoulder.

I quickly inspected her for anything creepy that she may have picked up outside, then I checked my clothes, arms, and legs to see if I hosted any unwanted crawling creatures, too.

I opened the book. There were a few crumbs stuck to the page. As I looked closer, I realized it was dog food. Listening to Chloe read to Bones had been painstaking. The words had scraped my ears like nails on a chalkboard. I thought about John and Brook who seemed like two educated individuals. I hoped this was just a hiccup for Chloe. Reading was so important. Liking it was half the battle.

"Can Bones sit with us?" she asked.

"Sure," I replied.

"Come on, Bones," Chloe chimed as she patted the cushion. "Cesar says dogs shouldn't be on the furniture unless they are invited."

"Kind of like people."

"Huh?"

"You know. You shouldn't go into other people's houses without being invited."

Chloe leaned back, pulled her legs up, and crossed them. Bones lay on his back with all four paws in the air. Chloe rubbed his bare belly and Bones snored.

"You are really good at that," I said, finding my place in the book.

"I love animals. I used to have fish, but they died. They're not very good pets. You can't walk them or pet them."

"Yeah, you're right about that, now let's see what happens here."

I read while Chloe peered into the book as I tracked the words.

The phone rang at nine o'clock. I was in the library touching up John and Chloe's photograph. Chloe had curled up with Bones on the sofa after pizza and zonked out. "Hello. Yes. Actually, I have to wake her up. I'll go get her." I smiled to myself.

"I'll come over. She's exhausted," John said.

"Sure thing. See you in a few minutes." I put the phone down and waited in the foyer for John. When he came to the door, I pictured him riding his orange Harley through the streets of Grosse Pointe. *Rebel*, I thought, liking the image. The creaky screen door pierced the summer air. John grinned and came inside. The dim light in the entryway glowed in the stillness. "Hi," I said. "How did things go with Brook?"

"She's impossible, but you don't want to hear about that."

"I suppose you're right. About earlier—"

"Yeah, I'm sorry."

I wasn't sorry, but I didn't have the gumption to admit it. "No worries." Butterflies tickled my stomach when John stepped nearer. I wanted to know about Brook, wanted to know what happened when I left, and when she'd be going back to California. John's emerald eyes spurred my curiosity. He held my stare. The scent of Old Spice drifted by, and longing clawed at my willpower. I swallowed, hoping to disguise my wavering senses. It wasn't right, but, damn, it was tempting. The hair on my forearms prickled when John touched my hand.

"Really, I am sorry about earlier. I have a lot to work out," he said. "But I hope—" He paused to move closer.

With one more step, he'd be on top of me. I couldn't take my eyes off him.

"Thanks for entertaining the munchkin," John said.

"Any time," I replied.

"That's progress." His words were faint.

"It really was no trouble. No one even got hurt this time around." John snickered. "Phew."

His breath brushed up against me like a lover. I grinned. "She's in by the television." I pointed toward the kitchen. "Back there and to the left. I'll show you." I led the way.

"We read part of her Junie B. book." John tripped on the back of my foot when I stopped abruptly. We were nose-to-nose as he caught me. "Oops." My nervous laugh caught in the air between us. "I have an idea."

"What?" John said. "I'm almost afraid to ask."

"It's not that bad. Really, it's not." I took a deep breath. "I was thinking that I wanted to take Bones to dog school, but then I thought it would be good if there was another person. Chloe spends a lot of time with Bones, and well"—I hesitated, not quite sure how to spit out the exchange—"I'd like Chloe to come to dog obedience school with me."

I saw a flash of hesitance in John's eyes. "Wait, before you say no, I'll work with Chloe on her reading if she goes with me. She is really good with Bones. I feel like a dog owner flunky, not that I wanted to be a dog owner in the first place, and as you know, I've tried to get rid of him several times, but my stubborn neighbor just won't comply." I did my best to look pitiful without killing the effect.

"Brook is not going to like this."

"Brook does not live with you and Chloe."

John lowered his voice. "Brook is Chloe's mother and while she's here, she can make life a living hell. Did we not discuss this earlier?"

"When's she leaving?" I couldn't believe I asked.

"Not sure. Depends on how fast she feels like she's gotten what she wants."

"Why does she stay with you?" I blurted out. "It's weird."

John's thin smile grew. "I didn't think you cared."

"I don't." I refrained from rolling my eyes.

"Where else is she going to stay? We try to be civil for Chloe. She doesn't have family around here and we have way too many bedrooms. And if you have forgotten, I'm out a nanny."

"It's still weird," I mumbled. "Can Chloe go to dog school with Bones or not? I'm admitting I need help."

"I know. And I am enjoying every minute of it. Let me see what I can do. It would be good for her. She doesn't have many friends."

"When school begins, she'll make more friends," I reassured him.

"She's still really mad at me for moving. She needs to learn to read better and we never seem to find the time to practice."

I raised my eyebrow at him. "Oh come on, you're a doctor. What doctor doesn't have the time for that?" I prodded. He averted my gaze. He hemmed and hawed.

"She throws a fit when I try to help her."

"Ah-ha. The truth comes out. You need me," I said, searching his eyes. I wanted *him* to need me, too.

"I just don't have the energy to fight with her when I get home. As you know, the last nanny wasn't any help and now she's gone, no thanks to you."

"Yeah, we've already established that some time ago. I said I was sorry." I inched closer. "Here's my chance to make it up to you. I can take Chloe off your hands for a bit and she can work on her reading." *God, what am I getting myself into?* Brook would put the kibosh on this whole idea, for sure.

"I'd better get my daughter."

John's words grazed my ears as he reached for Chloe who slept like an angel. A chill ran down my spine. There was something about the way he moved. His jeans hugged his hips. I needed to keep my distance, although I wasn't showing great restraint. When John scooped up his daughter, a murmur escaped her lips, and I smiled.

"Dad," she mumbled.

"I'm here to take you home," he whispered in her ear, giving her a peck on the cheek. "You've had a busy day, princess."

Funny, I never thought of Chloe as a princess.

John trudged back to the front door carrying a human rag doll. I did my best not to check him out from behind, but it was impossible. What was I supposed to focus on?

"Let me get the door," I whispered as I scooted past him in the foyer. He stopped directly in front of me, grinning at Chloe who had her eyes shut, and was practically snoring.

"I am serious about dog school," I said.

"I know, princess," he said with a sly smile. "Goodnight." His lips touched my cheek.

Chloe hadn't been the only one kissed by a prince.

Chapter 25

Two days passed. I hadn't seen Chloe. I hadn't seen John, and I hadn't seen my mother. Besides going to radiation, I spent my time cleaning out closets and coloring photographs. Like a seventeen-year-old trying to decide on what dress to wear to the prom, I even made a list of pros and cons of getting involved with John. Were we already involved? I didn't think a couple of kisses quantified anything. I threw the list away as soon as I finished it. It was silly to think we could mesh. It was foolish to test the waters. I needed to live by myself.

Beckett had left behind little things here and there. I believed he had purposely done it to keep one foot in the door. I mustered up the courage to read Beckett's journal in between cleaning frenzies. After radiation, I collapsed on the sofa with Bones. In fact, I read it to Bones, even if his eyes eventually closed, while he rested his head on my lap. I didn't finish it, though. I read the passage dating back to the last anniversary we spent together. Beckett must have spent hours logging his thoughts, orchestrating the synopsis, hoping that I would understand when the time came.

I should have felt like a fool, but I didn't.

I carried the last of three boxes into the garage. Beckett said he'd be over to get them by seven. I opened the box labeled *knickknacks* and put his journal on top of his college pennants, little league trophies, and Scout paraphernalia. I kept the plastic container of tennis balls for Bones. Maybe he'd like them instead of my flowers.

I tossed the canister on the workbench, touched the cover of Beckett's journal, and closed the top. With a heavy sigh, I commended myself on my own progress. It was time to let go and Beckett was letting me.

The garage was the place where Bradley painted his derby cars, the place where he hit the workbench with my car the day he got his driver's permit, the place where Beckett taught him to tie fishing knots, and how to build a birdhouse. Distant memories conjured up long-lost spirits. They swirled around me like an invisible cyclone, reminding me that *we* had purpose.

I envied couples that stayed together, like my parents, especially in today's world, but for some maybe it's not meant to be. I supposed not all stories had a happy ending. Mom said I wasn't a failure, and I thought maybe she was right because I believed in love and loyalty. A twinge of longing nipped at my heart. *Hope.*

I wondered if being divorced had become commonplace due to means. I shook my head. My armpit burned, reminding me that I had other pressing issues to deal with. Divorced or not, I wanted to keep on living. Dr. Masterson, my radiation oncologist, reassured me that my treatment was going well. I trusted her judgment. I should have known her when I accepted Beckett's marriage proposal.

Beckett scuffled up the driveway slowly. He was dressed in khaki shorts and a navy polo. "No class today?"

"No class. It's good to have a break. I really should think about not teaching in the summer. That would be a treat. You would know."

I narrowed my eyes at him. We'd had this disagreement before. I viewed summer vacation as a blessing, a time to rejuvenate, and take care of Bradley. Sometimes Beckett thought I should be slaving away at some summertime gig for a few extra bucks that would eventually be spent on childcare.

"Your boxes are over there," I said, pointing to the workbench. I hoped he wouldn't open them, knowing the journal would spark discussion, and I didn't want to rehash the past.

"It's quiet around here today," he said.

"Yeah." Trails of dust gleamed in the cascading light flooding the garage. "It's nice."

"Paul said he delivered the sofa yesterday. Is everything done?"

"Yup. It's done." I hoped Beckett didn't want to come in. The awkward air between us unnerved me. There was nothing left to say.

"Good."

Beckett went to his stack of boxes and opened the top box. I winced as he took out the journal.

"Did you read this?" he asked.

"Yes," I answered. Then I hoped there wouldn't be a quiz.

"You don't want to keep it?"

I shook my head. "No." I paused, waiting for that familiar pang of loss that Beckett had left me with, but it didn't come. "I really don't." I watched his face. His brown eyes were solemn, his temples grayer. "Are you mad?" I asked.

Beckett put the journal back in the box and closed the lid. "No, Maggie, I'm not mad."

A wave of relief lightened the heaviness I felt in my chest. "Just thought you might want it back. It's pretty personal." And it wasn't mine to keep. Keeping the relic would be an unyielding weight on my conscience each and every time I saw it on the shelf.

My treasures needed to fill the space and no one else's. There was a long life ahead of me. What was in the past was going to stay in the past. Bradley reminded me of the important things, things that mattered, and times that'd shaped us into family. "You need it more than I do," I said.

Beckett's eyes glistened, and I knew I had made the right decision to give it back.

"Thanks, Maggie," Beckett said, lifting the top two boxes. "I'm going to take these to the car then I'll come back and get the last box."

His tall, lanky body seemed trim as ever as he walked down the driveway. I moved the third box from the corner then decided I'd carry it to the car for him. I handed the ragged box to Beckett when he finished rearranging the back seat.

"You didn't have to do that, Maggie. I said I was coming back."

I didn't appreciate his tone. My mouth curled downward. "I know. I was just trying to help," I said quickly.

"I was coming back to get it."

"What's the big deal?" I asked.

"That's just like you. You're always a step ahead. Sometimes you should just let people do what they're going to do. I told you I was going to get the box."

The jab deflated me. I wasn't going to apologize. Why should I? "I was just trying to help," I repeated, unsure what he wanted from me. "Surely, you understand the concept."

Beckett sighed. "Never mind." He took his keys out of his pocket. "Paul said he thinks you have a thing for your neighbor."

I glared at Beckett. "How is that any of your business?"

"It's not, but you should consider the ramifications."

"Are you serious?" I quipped. "Would you like me to give you dating advice?" Obviously, he'd forgotten the scene at the restaurant when he told me I'd find someone as I sobbed out of control in public.

Beckett narrowed his eyes and glared at me. "You're hilarious."

"Just sayin'."

"Not sure you know much more than I do," Beckett shot back. He got into his little eco-friendly hybrid, started the engine, and rolled down the window.

"I think we should both keep our personal lives to ourselves," I scolded, leering into his car.

Beckett smiled. "You're probably right. I just know being alone isn't your thing."

I rolled my eyes. I didn't need anyone. "Right now, I just need myself. Thank you very much. I'll figure it out." I took a breath. "I'm gonna take one day at a time, my way," I lectured.

"Point taken. You can stop now. And so will I." Beckett put the car into gear. It drifted in reverse toward the street. He leaned his head out the window making sure the coast was clear then glanced my way one last time.

I waved goodbye, not sure of when I'd see him again.

That was like Beckett, he had to have the last word. I closed the garage door then strolled toward the house. There was a world of quiet waiting for me just inside the creaky screen door that had been the threshold of many nuances. I peered over to John and Chloe's house. All was quiet there, too.

Chapter 26

My left temple throbbed, as if Chloe had knocked me in the head all over again. I put the phone down and started to paint an orange moon in my photograph. I'd taken the photo on a field trip last fall, a congregation of black-and-white heifers adjacent the perfect barn, more interesting than the pumpkin patch where my class trudged along paths harvesting perfect pumpkins to carve jack-o-lanterns. I colored in the spots on the cows with a rainbow of colors. One cow graced pink spots, another lime green, another turquoise, and another lavender. I would tribute the color scheme to Easter eggs. Each brush stroke calmed my nerves as I processed the cancer lab's words. I didn't want another week of radiation. I thought we were on the straight and narrow. She said it was precaution. I thought it was overkill. But then again, what did I know? I put my paintbrush down, scrutinizing my color palate. The cows captured my attention sparking an idea to make multiple black-and-white copies for further artistic endeavors. I envisioned a Christmas tribute with green-and-red cows, a Fourth of July tribute, a Valentine's Day tribute with pink-and-red cows, a Saint Patrick's Day tribute; my mind wouldn't stop. It was a children's book in the making. I never thought about writing a children's book, until now. I made a note to make reprints. I wouldn't know if I didn't try.

The phone rang and John's number flashed on the screen. "Hello," I said.

"This is Chloe. My dad's on his way over. Be prepared," she said in a hurry.

The abrupt disconnection pierced my ear. "What was that all about?" I said to myself. The doorbell rang as soon as I put the phone down on my desk. Bones skidded to the front door, barked twice, then sat down and snapped at a fly that buzzed by his nose. "Get it, Bones," I said.

He barked again in my direction and snorted as I yanked on the heavy oak door. John had his hands buried in his pockets.

"That's some face," I said, opening the screen door to join him on the porch. "With all the rain, the lawn needs to be mowed," I noted. "The bushes need to be trimmed, too." I peeked over the railing for tiny feet or prying eyes in the hedge. "What's going on?" I asked, watching John rub his temples. I knew the feeling. My breast ached today. Must have been the weather.

"So, Chloe is all jazzed up for dog school," he began to say.

"Great. Bones needs some manners. And I need some help." I knew I could brave the experience alone, but didn't want to. Chloe already had a better rapport with Bones and besides if I thought about it, there wasn't anyone else who'd want to go with me. Maybe Mom, but then I wasn't so sure I would want to go.

"Don't get too excited yet. There are some conditions," John said.

I backed onto the porch swing and gave it a nudge to get a slow sway going. "Must be Brook. Why does she hate me?"

John grunted. "She doesn't hate you."

I rolled my eyes. "So you've said. And yes, she does," I declared.

John sat on the porch half-wall. "She wants to go with you two, to dog school." He lowered his voice. "I think she's jealous. In some weird way she doesn't want to lose her daughter to you."

"What?" The squeal in my tone surprised me. "You can't be serious."

"I am. And Chloe is all torqued up about going. Brook said yes, then she said no. Then she said yes, as long as she could go, too."

"Great." I forced a smile. I thought about Chloe and then pondered her manipulative mother. This was a bad idea. "What's wrong with her?"

A shadow drifted over John's steely gaze.

"Sorry, don't answer that. Now, what am I supposed to do?" The sway of the swing slowed.

"It's up to you," John said. "I'll understand. Chloe is a different story, but she'll bounce back if you don't want to go. Disappointment is a big part of life."

"Don't I know it," I stated.

John's lips curled upward with the hint of a mischievous smile as he moved to the other end of the swing. It swayed like a lazy summer breeze. The quiet between us seemed like a long-lost friend.

"Your skin looks really irritated," John whispered. "Does it hurt?"

I touched the red, flaking area beneath my arm. I'd forgotten I was wearing a little tank. The fresh air felt refreshing against my raw skin. "Not really. It's itchy. And ugly."

"I'm sorry, Maggie."

I wasn't sure what he was apologizing for. At this point it could be anything. I wished I had chosen a different shirt or had something covering my peeling skin.

"I'm sorry you're sick. It's not fair," he added. "You don't deserve this. Nobody does."

"You're right about that. Cancer sucks the big one," I replied, making eye contact. "I love summer. I shouldn't have to spend it going to treatment everyday wondering what the outcome will be. And now, I have five extra sessions." I held up five fingers. "The doctor called today." John's caring eyes warmed my heart. Raw, bruised, hurt, I swiped at the corner of my eye. His tenderness surfaced at the least expected moments.

He scooted closer to me.

After a hard swallow, I allowed myself to face him. "It's okay. It's what I have to do."

"You're a strong woman, Maggie. I haven't met many people like you."

"Some days, I'm not sure I'll make it," I said softly.

"You will," John said, playing with the strand of hair that had fallen across my cheek. "You will." He chuckled, putting his hand on my shoulder with a tender squeeze. "If you can do this, and survive your crazy neighbors and their antics, you can do anything."

The warm weight of John's hand grounded me. It felt good to have someone besides my mother care. I needed her because my world was small and her antiquated presence was essential, but I longed for someone else, something else. I was becoming fonder of her quirky habits as we began growing older together. Funny, how time and a little serious illness can change a person's perspective. Now, I had the attention of someone else, a man, reaching out to me. John challenged me, made my nerves bristle, but he was kind, compassionate. Something about him beckoned me to explore the possibility that he just might be *somebody*, even if he had a seven-year-old child, and an ex-wife. Were the planets going to align bringing peace and harmony or was I in the path of destruction and heartbreak? Only time would tell.

"So, you have a motorcycle. How come I've never seen you ride it?" I asked, changing the subject to something that didn't involve feelings. I hoped John wasn't the kind of guy who was going to call his chopper by a woman's name or suggest it was an extension of his manhood. That would be a deal-breaker.

"Well—" John made a clicking noise with his tongue against the roof of his mouth. "I don't actually know how to ride that well."

I laughed. "Then why do you have a Harley? That's a serious bike."

"I'm really not a motorcycle guy," he said.

"Yet." I shifted my weight and put my arm on the back of the swing. My skirt fluttered as we moved back and forth.

"Not sure, I ever will be. Truth is, I bought it thinking I could just ride, get away, tune out the world on bad days, and feel the wind in—" He touched his head, letting out a guttural chuckle.

I laughed then touched his head without thinking. His extra-short haircut on the side of his head was stubbly. "You kind of look like a biker, not a pediatrician." I thought about his left shoulder. "I saw the tattoo at the beach. What's that all about?"

"Reminds me of growing up on the ranch. My dad collected horseshoes. You should see them sometime. He has hundreds, tacked up inside the stable, in the house, even has some in his truck. He's the one who urged me to be something other than a Montana rancher. Now, I'm here." His voice trailed off.

"You don't want to be here?"

He shook his head. "Not sure. I thought it was the right thing to do for Chloe. She needs neighbors and a school."

Bones nudged the screen door open with his nose and joined us on the swing. His weight jerked us closer together and he nuzzled in-between us.

"Here's the beast that stole my little girl's heart," John said, scratching the dog's head.

"Better a dog than a boy," I interjected.

John made a face. "I guess so. What's your story, Maggie?"

I cringed. "Well, you know I'm divorced. I have a son named Bradley. He's twenty-two and lives in Boston."

"Yeah, I get that, but why are you here?"

"I grew up here. My job. I only have a few more years until I retire."

"You look too young to retire," John scoffed.

I snickered. "Nice try, doctor, or is it cowboy now that I know you're really from Montana?" I ran my fingers through my hair then continued. "I bought years through the school district I work in. That purchase, one of the good decisions I made, will help me get out early. And I am looking forward to it."

"What about your mother?"

I smirked. "She's funny. She's got so many things going on, so many friends, sometimes I rarely see her. She's the opposite of me. I like my solitude."

"Maybe you would like my dad's ranch." John rubbed his chin. "What do you do in your spare time, the time when Chloe's not bugging you?"

I fingered the wood of the swing. "I love to read and I just started hand coloring photographs. I really enjoy my camera and this summer I've had time to work with it. Would you like to see what I'm working on?"

John stopped the swing, and Bones' creased forehead showed his loathing reply to our decision to go inside.

I stood up, my legs a little shaky.

John held the door for me.

"You coming, Bones?" I asked.

He put his head back down between his paws and shut his eyes. Soft whimpers escaped his jowls before I even stepped inside the house.

"This is a big house for one person," John commented. "Love the new living room. Gonna get more furniture?"

"Nope. I'll fill it up as I go. Starting over, I want new memories," I said. "This is my workplace." John's eyes scanned the wood paneling in the library.

"My dad would love this room. It reminds me of his ranch." He went over to the window and rested his hand on the ledge. "Even the light in here feels like God's country."

I smiled. "There is something about this house that is like a sanctuary." I showed John my photographs of Bones in the ruined garden, a photograph of Chloe, and the cows.

"You did the photographs on the wall?"

"Yes, I just finished them the other day and put them in frames. I love that photo of my mom," I said.

"It's great. And Bones, he's something else, isn't he?"

"Yeah, hence the need for obedience school."

"You're just an old softy. You think you're all big and bad, but you're really a marshmallow on the inside," John said.

I sighed. "Like my dad," I said, touching the photo of my mom. Dad was there, too. I wanted him to be alive. I wanted him to know me. I knew he did, but on a different plane. "I miss him. He passed away a while ago."

"Sorry, my mom is gone, too. I know how that feels. It's like a kick in the gut you never recover from. You have to force yourself to breathe," John said softly.

"Yeah." The sting of loss lingered as I blinked away sorrow. I hadn't cried this much since Beckett and I separated. Even the words *breast cancer* hadn't caused a meltdown. That was a kick in the gut, too, but I was able to recover. "Were you close to your mom?"

John faced me. His eyes gleamed in the deluge of afternoon light. "Yeah. I guess you could say I was somewhat of a momma's boy. I think my dad thought I should have been tougher."

"Maybe learning how to ride that Harley would change that." I shifted my attention from the photographs back to John as he leaned over my desk. I liked how he chuckled. Wicked mystery waggled at the corners of his eyes, and I wondered what he wasn't sharing.

"Maybe." He hooked his thumbs in the pockets of his jeans. "So let me see what this is all about."

He picked up the picture of Chloe and ran his finger over her face. "I hope you don't mind. I couldn't pass up the moment. You can have it, if you want," I offered.

"She takes after me, poor kid."

"Yes, she does, but I'm not so sure that's a problem."

"So you're admitting I'm handsome?" John came around to my side of the desk.

"Maybe. You'll just have to wait and see," I whispered, meeting his warm green eyes.

He rested his arms on my shoulders. "You sure are one hard woman to read, Maggie Abernathy. First, you're all surly like a tomcat on the prowl, then you're all sweet like warm molasses on a summer day."

"You should let that cowboy in you out more often." My voice trailed off just like my mind. Who was this guy? I shut my eyes trying to collect my thoughts and resist his proximity. God, he smelled good.

"Maybe I will, only if you're good."

His soft lips kissed my forehead. Trickling heat warmed my blood from the top of my head to soles of my feet. The pain in my breast, gone, the irritation from Beckett, gone. My heart danced and the world seemed a little bit better. Actually, a whole hell of a lot better.

Chapter 27

Bones and I strolled along the pathway near the lake. I peeked over my left shoulder at the thundering footsteps behind me. Chloe was running at full speed. She yelled my name into the wind as our eyes met. I stopped. Bones danced on his hind legs then rolled onto his back as soon as she was upon us. Chloe panted and flipped the hair away from her face to see. Her injured toes seemed to no longer be a problem. Her neon-pink toenail polish gleamed even on a cloudy day.

"Hi, stranger," I said.

With a heavy sigh Chloe kneeled down to rub Bones' belly. She gulped for air then started to speak. "My dad says I can't go to dog school."

She delivered the disappointment through sad eyes, followed by a sigh. For a moment, I thought maybe Bones had been teaching her some of his tricks. Bones' hind leg twitched as Chloe scratched his neck, his dog tags jingled beneath his wrinkly chin.

"You like that, old boy, don't you?" Chloe said, bending closer to his face. She giggled when he slurped her nose.

This wasn't fair. I thought I could escape this conversation, but I was wrong. "Sorry, Chloe, I think I should do this on my own. I have to learn how to handle Bones by myself."

She squinted into the sun and batted her eyes at me. "My dad says stuff like that. I think you two are in cahoots, as Glad calls it. Cahoots," she repeated. "Cahoots. That's a funny word. Sounds like something Junie B. Jones would say."

"Sure does. And no, we're not." My brain twitched then

I let it go. "I am just trying to respect your mother." Then I prayed for zero questions.

Chloe got up and Bones followed her lead. Granules of sand pelted my legs like tiny pebbles when he shook back and forth, as if someone had given him a bath.

I brushed off my shins then handed Chloe the leash. "Where's your mom today?" I held her worried stare.

Chloe pointed. "She's over there by that big orange umbrella. She's catching her rays. That means getting a tan in Hollywood language."

I nodded. "Oh." I didn't look. Didn't need to be reminded of how I didn't look in a bikini, never did, or ever will. Bones knocked Chloe backward on her behind then crawled on top of her, licking her ear. I couldn't help but grin as I watched the scene unfold. She laughed and rolled around trying to hug him. It was more than puppy love.

Chloe squealed, "Sand in the mouth. Sand in the mouth."

Bones wagged his tail harder and continued the licking fest as Chloe wiped at her tongue. Finally, they both stopped thrashing, put their noses to the sun that broke through the hazy clouds, and stretched out on their backs.

The breeze brought Brook's voice closer, and Chloe sat up. "Here comes my mom," she said with raised eyebrows.

"Don't worry. I'll behave," I reassured her.

"You're funny, Maggie," Chloe said, hopping to her feet.

"Chloe, Chloe, are you okay?" Brook hollered.

I slid my sunglasses from my head into place. Chloe's quizzical expression amused me. Then I glanced at Brook then back to Chloe. "What?" I asked.

"Chloe," Brook barked. "Are you okay? Did that dog hurt you when he jumped on you?"

I marveled at the act as Brook tucked Chloe's hair behind her ears, inspecting her from head to toe. "I think she's fine," I said.

"Oh, Maggie, it's you," Brook said with distain. "I didn't recognize you with the hat."

I smiled. "Yeah, it's me. Hi, Brook," I said, forcing myself to give a little wave.

"You should really rethink taking that dog to obedience school. He's going to hurt someone someday," Brook continued.

"Yeah, okay, maybe if he licks someone to death and I don't think that's really possible." I caught Chloe's smirk out of the corner of my eye. "Chloe, are you okay?" I said, mimicking her mother, leaving out the pawing dramatics.

Chloe smiled. "Yup. I'm great," she chirped.

Brook frowned. I wanted to ask her if her lawyer would be contacting me, but knew better not to. I'm sure John would hear about this. Bones rolled over and got up on all fours. He licked his chops then started to pant. His dark eyes surveyed Brook. He meandered over to her as we spoke. I kept one eye on him and one eye on Brook as she continued her rant.

"Maggie, I don't know who you think you are, but I just want my baby to be all right. You don't have to be so sarcastic."

Before I could tug on Bones' leash, his leg was up. Brook's stature must have resembled that of a tree or a fire hydrant. Brook seethed as she ran into the lake to wash off the dog pee that dripped down her shin.

"I'm so sorry. I'm so, so, sorry," I stammered, trying to stifle the laughter.

Chloe's mouth hung open and her eyes bugged out of her head.

"Ohmigod, I am so sorry." I glared at Bones. "Bad dog."

He wagged his tail, validating my secret thoughts. Humor washed over his dark eyes, pride filled his stance. Maybe he was my kind of dog after all. Maybe this was his way of making up for the ruined tomatoes and uprooted flowers in my garden. I knelt and tugged at his collar. I waggled my finger at his nose, chastising his behavior.

Chloe ran after her mom. "Just rinse it off, Mom. I got bird poop in my hair once. This is way better," she announced as her feet splashed through the water trailing after Brook.

I pretended not to watch her display and kept my attention on Bones. "You are not helping the cause," I scolded.

Bones grunted and gave a little *woof.*

Brook sauntered out of the lake. The ends of her hair were straggly and damp. She didn't appear to be much like a super model now. Chloe tried to hold her hand, but Brook shook her off. Chloe wrinkled her nose and stared up at her mom who was rambling, "I don't know who you think you are, Maggie, but this is not the end of this. I will be sending you a bill."

The words spewed out and over my lips before I could stop myself. "For what? New skin." I don't know what came over me. I covered my mouth with my hand. Chloe stood like a statue on the verge of crumbling. "I'm sorry, honey, I shouldn't have said that, and Bones is a very bad dog, right now."

Chloe meandered my way. She reached out her hand and I took it. She wasn't trying to console her mother. She wanted to be consoled. Poor baby, I thought, and I wasn't helping. I squeezed her hand trying to soothe her rattled nerves. "I'm sorry," I said, crouching in front of her. Bones came and sat beside me. Chloe's furrowed brow stoked instant remorse within me.

"That's just like you," Brook said. "You're nice to her, but horrid to me."

"Chloe, why don't you take Bones down to that drinking fountain and get him some water. I'll be there in a second. If it's okay with your mom." I paused and peered over the rim of my sunglasses at Brook. "And, if it's okay with your mom"—I put my finger up to stop Brook from talking as she puffed out her chest like a peacock—"we'll get you a frozen cherry Icy."

Chloe squeezed my hand then took the leash off my wrist.

"It's okay. I promise we won't fight anymore," I added softly.

Brook gave her a little wave and a reassuring nod. Chloe and Bones trotted off. I waited until Chloe was out of earshot. I put my finger up again toward Brook, cautioning her. "Look, I'm not sure what I've done to piss you off, but this needs to stop." Brook huffed and crossed her arms like a hormonal teenage girl. "I am sorry. Bones just went"—I restrained myself from smiling—"went on your leg, but that is precisely the reason I wanted to take him to obedience school. Obviously, he needs to work on his manners. Chloe is better with him than I am."

"That's obvious," Brook said.

I ignored her. "I thought I could learn something from your daughter. They're like two peas in a pod." I focused my attention on Chloe who had her hands cupped and was scooping water from the fountain for Bones. I could hear her sharp voice telling him to sit and stay, and he did.

"You're a piece of work," Brook whispered under her breath.

"I am going to pretend I didn't hear that. I am going to go over there"—I pointed to Chloe who was splashing in the beach shower—"and get my dog. I will apologize to her for the scene." I took two dollars out of my pocket and handed it to Brook. "Why don't you get Chloe a cherry Icy and we will go our separate ways?"

Brook smirked and pushed her Ray Bans, like mine, up on top of her head. I wondered where her Gucci sunglasses went. Her bloodshot eyes appeared tired. I wondered if she was going to cry or if she was some kind of special vampire that could stand the sun. I thought I saw fangs when she opened her mouth.

"You are really something," Brook said.

I held her stare.

I have been head-to-head with the best of them.

I didn't budge.

I waited for the silent mercy.

Brook blew out a pillow of air then marched ahead of me kicking up sand as she sauntered toward her daughter. I let her take the lead. I didn't say I would walk with her, I only promised not to fight.

Why didn't Brook just hold Chloe's hand? I asked myself. *That's all Chloe wanted, and needed.*

Chapter 28

John's motorcycle rumbled as I put the last dish away. The deep grumbling thrusts jostled my concentration. Each rev of the engine sounded furious. I'd like to blame it all on Brook, but I knew I was just as much to blame. My chest fluttered at the thought of confrontation with John. I could handle Brook. With her I had nothing to lose.

The rumbling stopped.

My doorbell rang.

It was Chloe. Her red cheeks and blood-shot eyes grabbed my attention. "Chloe, what's wrong?"

"I want to go to dog school with you," she wailed.

I ushered her inside, contemplating Brook's appearance. I was harboring a fugitive and there would be hell to pay if caught so I shut the screen door then the front door, and locked it behind me. "I'm sorry, Chloe, but there's not room for three people at dog obedience class," I lied. That would cost me. I silently begged the heavens for forgiveness. Surely, He would understand sparing a child's feelings.

"I want to go. My mom is being so difficult," she sobbed. "I hate it. She always makes trouble when she comes around." Chloe gulped for air. "I spend all my time waiting for her and it's always a disaster."

Chloe wiped her nose on the sleeve of her sweatshirt. "Come get a tissue." She scooted into the kitchen in front of me. "Where is your mom? Does she know you're here? Does your dad know you're here?" How could he know, he was in his garage revving up a machine he doesn't know how to ride.

"Boy, you have a lot of questions. Mom's out shopping, again. Dad is in the garage playing with his motorcycle. I just left."

I shot John a text hoping he would see it. If the engine were to stop, I'd venture over. Intuition told me to stay home in a locked house and take my chances. "Chloe, you can't just leave when things don't go your way. Moms and dads need to work things out." I offered her a stool at the counter, patted the granite top inviting her to sit, and put the tissue box in front of her. "Want something to drink?" I asked, getting a glass from the cupboard.

"Whiskey," she said, slapping the counter.

"What?" I asked, not believing my ears.

"Didn't you hear me? Whiskey," she repeated.

I went to the refrigerator and got lemonade. "Kids don't drink whiskey. I don't drink whiskey," I explained.

"That's what daddy wanted. Figured it would be good for me, too."

"Oh boy." I paused, listening to the waning motorcycle engine. I figured my doorbell would be ringing when the Harley's purr totally subsided. "Chloe, whiskey is liquor."

"You mean *elllllcohall*?" she asked with big eyes.

"Yes, Chloe. It's for grown-ups, not kids."

"I had a boy in my class once that said he used to go to the bar with his mom and she would leave him in the car."

I let out a hefty sigh. "Oh boy, that's not good, but I knew a boy like that, too. Only, it was a girl. How about some lemonade?"

Chloe shoulders slumped forward. I knew the feeling. "Okay. Can I have it on the rocks?" She asked, leaning over the counter. "That's ice," she told me, "but you probably already knew that."

"Yup." I went back to the fridge with her glass, filled it with ice, and showed her the glass. "Good?"

"Sure." She blew her nose again and set the tissue on the counter.

I found the disinfectant wipes under the sink and handed them to her after popping the lid open. "You want some pretzels?"

"Sure." Chloe wiped the counter off. "Where's Bones?"

"He's in the backyard," I slowed my speech, rethinking the last time I saw him. "Why?" I asked, not sure that I wanted to hear the answer.

"Just wondering," she answered, hopping off her stool and heading for the French doors to the patio. She swung them open, checking her feet. "Don't want to lose another toe."

"You never lost a toe," I reminded her.

"Close enough. Bones. Bones," she called.

Chloe gazed at me strangely. Worry creased her forehead. Her eyes were glossy with hidden agenda.

Oh no, here we go, I told myself. Something wasn't right. I felt the twist in my gut.

"Bones!" she yelled at the top of her lungs.

I went to the door.

I clapped my hands for him as I searched the yard. I peeked under the Dogwood. "This is almost as bad as the time I lost Bradley at Sears," I muttered, feeling the exasperation build. I know, I tried to pawn Bones off on John, but I would never wish *the beast* any harm. Maybe, I shouldn't refer to him as *the beast.* I stopped searching long enough to notice Chloe's lack of concern. "Where is Bones?"

Chloe seemed like she was going to explode. Her flushed cheeks turned even redder, if that were possible, and her eyes glossy with tears.

I knelt before her. "Chloe, where is the dog? I just want to make sure he's not lost or hurt." The open gate caught my attention. I ran out calling for Bones.

John came running out of his garage.

"Bones!" I called with my hands cupped around my mouth. I ran back to Chloe who was still in my yard. Her feet stuck out from under the Dogwood tree. I crouched down trying to dial down the hysterics, but I wanted my dog back. "Chloe, do you know where Bones is?"

"No," she said.

John stuck his head under the Dogwood tree, too, and wiggled her toes. "Open your eyes, Chloe. We need your help. Maggie needs our help. You don't want Bones to be lost, do you?"

Chloe opened her eyes and sat up. "I don't know what happened to him. Mom said she was going to fix the problem."

I fell back on my heels in disbelief.

John questioned Chloe sternly. "What do you mean, she's going to *fix the problem*?"

"She couldn't possibly do something horrible. Could she?" I asked, horrified that Brook would hurt Bones.

John sighed. "She was pretty mad when she came home. Doesn't sound like you helped the situation any," he added sharply.

"Hey," I barked. "It takes two."

John eyed Chloe. "Sometimes three." He dragged Chloe out by her feet. "Where's the pooch, kiddo?" Chloe wiped her eyes. "Does Mom really have him?" John sighed when Chloe pretended to button her lip. "Maggie is really scared, honey. Remember that time you got lost at the County Fair?"

Chloe nodded.

John's left temple twitched intermittently with his jaw.

"That's how Maggie feels. She doesn't want Bones to be lost or worse, hurt," he said calmly. "I will be a lot less mad at you if you tell the truth. If you don't tell the truth, you will be in big trouble, little lady."

Sighing, Chloe left the yard. We followed her to John's house, where she produced a happy dog on a leash about five minutes later.

"Sweet Jesus." I studied John's scowl then focused on Chloe as she sat on her front stoop with my dog. "Well played. How did you know?" I asked John.

"Brook's nuts, but she loves animals. She wouldn't harm a flea," he said. "Sorry, I'll deal with Chloe."

We marched up to the stoop when Chloe refused to make eye contact.

"What's the deal, Chloe?" John demanded politely.

She wouldn't budge.

"Give it up, Chloe. We can stand here as long as you like," he said, with crossed arms and a look that only a father could produce.

There was silence.

About two minutes later, which seemed like an eternity, she huffed and handed her dad Bones' leash then patted his head. "Sorry, old boy," she apologized, sounding like Peppermint Pattie.

My patience ran thin, but I stood doing my best not to intervene.

"Fine," Chloe huffed. "He was in my room. I thought if I blamed it on Mom, you'd be less mad at Maggie."

Surprised at her response, I had to hand it to her. I scowled, keeping in tune with John's frown.

"That wasn't very nice," he scolded, holding her chin in the palm of his hand.

"You promised if I told the truth, you'd go easy on me," Chloe reminded him, as she searched his face for forgiveness. "I don't want you to be mad at Maggie. Mom's gonna leave and Maggie's not going anywhere," she yelled. "I just wanted to go to dog school with Bones and Maggie," she declared, before stomping back inside the house and letting the door slam behind her.

John handed me the leash.

"Thanks," I said.

He put his hand on my forearm. "I heard about the beach."

"I figured you would," I said.

"She's not going to be here forever, you know."

"I know." I took a deep breath. "But you can't expect me not to be me. It happened. I didn't tell Bones to lift his leg on her. She said she was sending me a bill."

John shifted his weight. "It wouldn't have been for new skin," he said, taking a deep breath. "She was worried about her spray tan streaking."

I couldn't help but grin knowing I was right about Brook's fake bronze skin. "Sorry, it just came out. Look, I don't want to be someone else's mother. I've already raised my son. And I have to say, he was a piece of cake compared to Chloe."

"I bet," John said, kicking at the grass. "I don't believe I asked you to raise my daughter." His eyebrow arched.

I clambered for words. "I'm not going to ignore her. It wouldn't be right. And it wouldn't be right to let Brook talk down to me, especially in front of your daughter. Chloe's right, you know, her mother's going to leave, you said it yourself, and you're going to be stuck living next to me, the sarcastic, mixed-up, crazy neighbor." I searched his eyes for a glint of understanding. When I didn't see it, I headed home. "Come on, Bones," I said sternly, and he followed.

Mom was standing on the porch absorbing the scene.

"Oh, geez," I said. "Nothing good can come from this."

Mom flung her tote over her shoulder. "What was that all about?" she inquired, following me inside.

I bent down and let Bone's off his leash. "This dog has caused quite a ruckus around here. And it hasn't stopped."

"You've had quite the summer so far," Mom said.

I gave her the evil eye over my shoulder as we went into the living room. I plopped down on my new sofa. Bones started to jump up then I gave him the evil eye, too. He trotted away. I propped my feet up on my grandmother's table, crossed my ankles, leaned back, crossed my arms, and sulked. I glanced over at my mom who was sitting at the other end of the sofa leering at me. "What?"

"This is more action than you've had in a long while. It's kind of exciting, don't you think?"

"What?" I said, feeling more annoyed than when I was outside bantering with John. Then she grinned. "I've seen that twinkle in your eye before." My speech was slow and deep.

"This is getting good. You don't even realize what you're doing." Mom threw her head back with a giggle.

I stared into the fireplace. "You're making fun of me."

"Hardly, darling. You're scrappy. I love it. It's about time you stood up for yourself. Jesus, all those years with Beckett, everything seemed so even keel. Life is not about being on an even keel. Sometimes the boat tips over and you surface for air. Sometimes you think the boat is going to tip over and that's when the wind hits the sails and you have the ride of a lifetime. Sometimes it's about going against the grain, knowing in your gut it's the right thing to do. It's about taking chances."

I internalized her speech and sighed.

"Oh, for Pete's sake, Marjorie Jean, let it go. Brook is being a pain in the you-know-what and you are calling her out on her bad behavior."

Mom had her feet up on the table next to mine.

"I like what you've done with the place," she said, nodding. "A little sparse, though."

"I want to fill it up as I go."

"What?" she asked.

"I don't want to buy a bunch of stuff just to have it. I want to make new memories. I want this place to be mine," I explained, waiting for more criticism, sounding like a bossy thirteen-year-old, tired of sharing a bedroom with a little sister.

"It's about time. I knew you'd bloom in your own time. It was always so easy for you to go along with Beckett." Mom removed her knitting needles and yarn from her tote bag. "Sometimes things don't work out for a reason, you know. You might not see it at the time."

"You think I'm a pushover," I said.

Mom unwound the purple yarn, put her yellower-than-the-sun reading glasses on, and started to knit. The blue metal needles clanked together as she began humming a random tune. She stopped, turned in my direction, and said, "Not anymore." Singing to the rhythm of her knitting needles, Mom worked the yarn through her fingers like a pro.

"Is that for Chloe?" I asked.

"Yup," she said, glancing over.

"She'll like it."

Mom nodded in agreement. "She's got a lot on her plate right now.

"Don't we all," I mumbled.

Chapter 29

I put the leash on Bones and explained to him that we'd leave the house quietly like fugitives on the run. He tilted his head as if to question the lecture. The treats were in the car along with the dog obedience registration form. Guilt riddled my nerves as I scanned the yard for a seven-year-old girl dragging a purple cat around by a string. I rear door to my Equinox and ushered Bones in quickly. He jumped immediately into the front seat and eyed me like, *What's the hurry, lady?*

I backed out slowly, more cautiously than usual, ready to evade Chloe. I lied to her about canceling the registration. I learned from crime shows, everyone eventually gets caught, some nearly get away with it then bam, one little slip-up happens or some long-lost bystander produces a shred of evidence. I'd have to face the consequences when the time came.

Luck was on my side. There wasn't a soul in sight as I backed into the street. No one stirred at Chloe's house. I pictured Brook lying at the beach in her black triangle bikini while Chloe ran wild with other abandon beach urchins.

The drive through town was quiet, but then again it was that time of the season when the neighbors evacuated for their summer homes in Harbor Springs or Traverse City. It sounded like too much work to me. One home suited me fine. Bones hung his head out the window sniffing the air. His back twitched every so often.

Petco seemed vacant. Relief came over me. I was nervous about taking Bones in a busy parking lot. I was more nervous about not being able to control my dog in class. I didn't want to face an instructor who would tell me I was an unfit pet owner.

I was afraid Chloe would be waiting for me with crossed arms and a death stare, while Brook pinched her nose shut in a room that smelled like liver treats and hot breath.

I managed to get Bones into the store. His fast pace tugged at me as he walked ahead. The automatic doors startled him as they jerked open. His nose twitched and he pulled me inside toward the birdcages. The clerk smiled, and I pretended I was in charge, praying to the dog obedience Gods.

Bones traipsed over to the aisle lined with dog beds. I'd get Bones one for the library and put the old bed on the patio. He sniffed a fluffy rectangular one that was lined with fabric resembling lamb's wool. Bones stepped on it, whirled in a circle, and plopped down. I knelt beside him. "Apparently, we can agree on something. We'll get it on the way out," I said, patting his head. "And some treats and an antler bone. I hear you dogs like that sort of thing."

I hadn't told Bradley that Nana gave me a dog. He always wanted one, but with Beckett and me working full time, I didn't think it would be fair to have a pet. When school started up again in the fall, leaving Bones would be hard, but I'd have Mom to check on him or find a dog camp. Leaving him alone all day would eat at my conscience. Bones stretched, kissed my nose, and trotted toward the dog's schoolroom at the back of the store.

We were the first ones there. I sat in a metal folding chair. Bones bit at the leash. I told him to sit. He didn't. He rolled on his back and panted, ready to entertain anyone willing to watch. I tugged at the leash. When that didn't work, I produced a dog treat. Bones sniffed it wildly then gulped it down. He drooled for more then coughed up the morsel I had just given him. "Chewing would be a good idea," I said as I continued prodding him to sit and relax, unsuccessfully.

A Golden Retriever trotted in. With its head held high and perfect posture, it walked right past Bones without giving him a second look. The dog's owner smiled. I secretly accused them of cheating. You weren't supposed to come to obedience school with more manners than you were expected to leave with. With my eyes glued to the perfect canine, I didn't see the instructor come in. Bones did. He greeted her with two paws on her left thigh and a sloppy hello. My arm jerked as he jumped up on her.

"Get down," I commanded.

Bones ignored me.

"Hi there, pup. You must be Bones." The instructor produced a treat from a small pouch on her belt then fed it to the Golden Retriever sitting nicely beside us. She glanced at me with a roster in her hand. "Got the list of names and breeds right here. This is going to be a small class. We're waiting for one more dog, a hound named Cleopatra."

"Hi, I'm Maggie. And Bones has already introduced himself. Sorry about that," I said, trying to coax him down on all fours.

"Down, Bones," the instructor said in a stern voice, smiling with a gleam in her eye.

Bones put all four paws down on the floor.

She bent at the waist. "Sit," she said in a sweet voice.

Bones sat.

She gave Bones the treat.

Figures, I said to myself. I needed Chloe. She'd know what to do. She wouldn't be afraid to own the room. What was my problem? I could stand in front of twenty-seven kids daily and tell them what to do, and how to do it. How could this be any different? Bones was just one relatively stumpy dog with an under bite.

"What's your dog's name?" I asked the woman with the Golden Retriever.

She smiled. "His name is Wagner."

"He's pretty," I replied. He was a little too pretty by my standards and a little stuck-up. I watched as Bones followed the instructor around, with her pouch of treats.

"Cleopatra should be her any moment. My name is Tracy. I'll be your instructor."

Wagner's owner smiled. "I'm Heather."

Heather had feathery, blond Farrah Fawcett hair. I read the obedience flyer. *Six sessions of this might kill me.* Bones wagged his tail as the third student entered the room yanking at her owner's leash.

"I'm Tanner and this is Cleopatra."

Tanner was tanner than George Hamilton and a little too good-looking. I wondered if his parents were mannequins.

Heather sat a bit taller thrusting her boobs out as she said, "I'm Heather." She reached out and shook Tanner's hand. Bones sauntered toward them investigating the exchange.

This was going to be interesting. Bones snorted. I wondered how he'd feel about dropping out. Six sessions was going to be one long haul. Bones finally settled at my feet, and waited. "Good boy," I said, patting his thick head.

"Now if you say that with a perky voice and put some zest into it, your dog will respond better," Tracy instructed.

She came over, patted Bones on the head, produced a treat from her pouch, then told him to sit, which he was already doing, then began speaking to him in a high-pitched gooey twang. That wasn't part of my repertoire. Straight-forward was my game, either you did it or didn't do it. It all seemed black-and-white to me. I knew Bones preferred Chloe's voice to my cynical tone. Maybe if I had Farrah Fawcett hair men would ogle over me at dog school and the trainer would forgive my weaknesses as a pack leader. Maybe, I didn't want men to ogle over me at all, I knew I didn't need Tracy's approval cause I'd figure it out like I always did. Chloe could run this class without a doubt. This was going to be an excruciating six sessions.

Silent sarcasm kept the session lively.

I patted Bones on the head and wondered if he could read

my thoughts. He wagged his tail, which I took as a signal for *Yes, I can read your thoughts.*

I did my best to be an active listener. I participated to best of my ability, but by the end of class Tanner and Heather had given each other their telephone numbers, scheduled doggie play dates, and traded flirty glances. I was on my own island and it was deserted. I longed for Chloe. I'd spent most the hour thinking about her and how she would interact with Bones appropriately and please Tracy at the same time.

I picked up the phone and couldn't believe what I was about to do, but I had to finish obedience school. Members of the Abernathy family did not quit. "Hi, it's Maggie. Can you meet me in five minutes? Yeah, just ring the bell." I nodded and disconnected the call questioning my motives all over again.

I rambled to myself quietly as I paced in the living room. There was plenty of room with only a sofa and my grandmother's table. I didn't miss the dusty plants or Beckett's furniture.

I inhaled deeply before answering the door.

Brook was on the porch in her cutoff jeans and baby blue tank top. A herd of fairies cautioned me, but in true fashion I ignored their warnings and everyone knows that when fairies speak, you listen. Evidently, I was possessed. "Hi there, come on in."

Brook took off her Ray Bans and hung them on the front of her tank top, which made her even more disgustingly attractive. Her hair was perfectly wavy. She reminded me of a younger Daryl Hannah, but it was hard to read her icy, blue eyes.

"So, what's this all about?" she asked.

Courage percolated in the pit of my belly and I let it fill me up. "I would like to apologize for my behavior." I breathed deeply. "I am sorry." Brook inspected my house.

She didn't seem to have any interest in what I was saying. *Shit. This was a mistake.* She sauntered past me and into my library. What was she doing? I stepped in front of her. I leaned on the edge of my desk trying to hide my photographs.

"John showed me the photo you snapped of Chloe." She ran her fingers through her hair and tilted her head as if she were posing.

"Oh?"

"So why am I here?" She asked, fiddling with her sunglasses.

I held her stare. "I want Chloe to go to dog obedience school with Bones. I think it's unfair that you won't let her go unless you go, too," I said, lowering my voice. Maybe if I supplied a treat and spoke to Brook like a baby, she'd respond. Bones did. So did Tanner.

Nothing.

I stood quietly, waiting. I felt groomed for another round in the game.

"I guess you would feel that way, but how do you expect me to react? She's my daughter, not yours," Brook said.

There it was, my foot in the door. "You're right, she's *your* daughter. I should have been more sensitive to your feelings." Brook's posture softened. "What can I do to change your mind?" A flash in Brook's eyes let me know I was on the right track. *Make it about her,* I told myself. God, how I hoped she didn't have some unreasonable request.

"You really snapped all these photos?"

I nodded. "Yeah." She picked up the Christmas Cows I had colored earlier that day. I liked the red-and-green spots on their backs. With a black drawing pen I'd inked in a wreath around one of the cow's heads. I colored the sky a faded midnight blue and added gold stars. I painted a Charlie Brown Christmas tree next to the barn then inked in a string of white lights.

"Can I get a copy of the picture of Chloe you gave John?" she asked.

"Yes," I said. "What size?"

"An eight-by-ten. I don't have very many pictures of her. An updated photo on my mantle back home in Hollywood would do me good," Brook explained.

"Black-and-white?" I asked.

"Sure. I like black-and-white."

Brook wasn't making me work too hard for her acceptance. Distant distraction crept across her face.

"There's more," she said, examining the bookshelves. "Is this your boy?"

"Yes, his name is Bradley," I answered. That was all I gave her. He was mine.

"I'm not wealthy by any means and I could use some new headshots of myself," Brook said, staring me in the eye. The angle of her cheekbones in the midday sun was defined, rigid, toned. "What are you asking me?" She was going to have to say what she wanted, spell it out or no deal.

Her eyes clouded over like murky puddles as she spoke. "I'll let you take Chloe to dog obedience school in exchange for headshots. Chloe doesn't know it, but I am going back in a week. She's going to have a hard time with this, but I can't stay, I have work." Brook flipped her hair back.

I doubted she had work. Who doesn't stay for a child? Her agenda was something I couldn't grasp, nor wanted to. What was she missing in her life that she had to go to Hollywood to pursue a career when she had a beautiful daughter here? How could she leave John? He was beautiful, too. I sat down at my desk and let her list her demands.

"I want some indoor shots and some outdoor shots." Her eyes lit up. "We could go to the beach. I could rock out my bikini. I've been working out."

I smiled as if I approved of her self-indulgence and asked myself if I could handle it. I also reminded myself that Brook wouldn't be here forever.

Chapter 30

With my back against the wall, I tapped my toe. I checked my watch as if I had a pressing engagement. I did. Her name was Claire Cook and I needed to read her new release. Beads of sweat dotted my forehead. I craved my bathing suit, but that would have to wait until next year. I was covered appropriately and ready for Brook's shoot as if I could do her justice. Yesterday, we shot indoors.

Chloe had helped bring over her mom's outfits. I pictured a casual, free-spirit sort of look with faded denim, a white T-shirt, an oversized rancher's belt, and some boots. I guess I had cowboy on the brain after hearing John tell me about his dad's ranch in Montana. Brook had a different agenda. First, she wore a slinky top and skinny denim. Next, she had a black low-cut sheer shirt, paired with leather pants, and stilettos. Then, she had a large cable-knit sweater that hung off one shoulder with leggings and thigh-high riding boots. I was coordinating a fashion show as well as taking photographs. Later I'd have to sit with her, discuss the photos, and get them printed for her. Five days and ticking, then she was leaving. My thoughts were of Chloe, and I wondered if she knew about her mom's plans.

I watched people come and go from the bathhouse. No Brook. Really, how long could it take to put on some triangles? I got tired of waiting and wandered away. My phone buzzed with a text. *How's it going? John*

I stepped into the shade of the frozen Icy stand. "I'll have a frozen cherry and cola mix, please," I said to the clerk, digging two dollars out of my pocket.

"Small, medium, or large?" she asked, adjusting her headband back into place.

"Medium, please." I hammered out a reply to John while I waited for my treat. *Haven't even started yet. Waiting for model to primp. Who does this, anyway?*

A new text buzzed in. *You asked for it. I have said this before, you're one hard lady to read. How's Chloe?*

I took the frozen drink from the clerk and handed her my money. "Thank you," I said with a smile then sat on the vacant park bench sending out another reply. *As usual, I have nobody else to blame but myself. Hey! I thought you were still mad at me for the other day.*

I waited for John's next response, but when it didn't come I thought maybe I shouldn't have reminded him he was upset with me. I liked it better when he wasn't. I slurped my drink and was glad cola was on the bottom. It was my favorite, the sweet dark taste reminded me of Saturday nights at the pizza house with my girlfriends and football games. I kept one eye on the bathhouse door and one eye on Chloe who was building a sand castle with two boys with curly black hair in navy blue Speedos. I nicknamed them the Mark Spitz boys wondering if they were here on vacation from Europe.

I gulped down a mouthful of frozen drink then winced at the instant headache from the sugary cold. I pressed my eyes shut and rubbed my forehead, begging for relief. A shiver of childhood ran down my spine.

"Maggie, are you okay?"

I opened one eye. "God, that hurts," I said, clenching my teeth. My eyes blurred from the pain, but I did my best to focus on Brook. A soft gentleness lingered in her eyes like warm blue seas I hadn't noticed before.

"What's the matter?" she asked.

I pointed to the frozen drink on the bench. "Too much cold." I massaged my forehead with hopes of rubbing the pain away. "You ready to go?" I asked. Brook had on a different suit today. It was a nude-colored crocheted bikini. The design filtered through her opaque flowing cover-up. Did she ever not look fabulous? Did John still think she looked fabulous? I glanced over at Chloe who was standing on top of a mound of sand, probably someone else's sand castle no doubt. "She seems like she was having fun."

Brook peered over the top of her sunglasses. "Yeah, I sure will miss her. It's rough being so far away."

I picked up my Icy, then my camera bag, and scouted for the perfect place to shoot Brook's photo. "Then why do you live so far away?" I asked, remembering Mom saying that curiosity killed the cat, but I threw it out there, risking backlash.

Brook stepped into the sunshine then put her hand on her forehead to shade her eyes. "I like that spot over there." She pointed to a big rock with tall wild grass in the background.

I waited for her answer. It was less rude than some of the other things I had said to her since her arrival. I padded toward the rock, digging my toes into the sand, and repositioning the strap of my bag as it pulled my top from my shoulder. I prodded a bit more. "Hollywood is far away."

"Not that it's any of your business, but since you won't let it go, that's where the jobs are. If I want to model and act, I have to be in Hollywood. Chloe understands, if that's what you're worried about." Brook kicked up sand as she walked along side me.

I wasn't so sure I believed her. She didn't seem too attached to her daughter. "Does she ever come and visit you?"

Brook shrugged off my question at first. Then she stopped. With the sun behind her head, glowing like a halo, I couldn't see her eyes behind her shades. I don't think I would have wanted to either. By the creases in her forehead, I considered I had crossed the line.

Water lapped the shore keeping a steady rhythm. A white foamy layer bubbled on the sand as the water returned home to the lake. Brook pushed her Ray Bans up on top of her head. The breeze swept loose locks of blond hair across her sharp cheekbones. I marveled at her reaction. A heavy warm feeling held my feet planted in the sand as I watched Chloe out of the corner of my eye.

"It's not that easy," Brook said. "I never wanted a baby."

Chloe's laughter drifted through the air. Gravity tugged at the corners of my mouth with sadness. How was that possible? Beckett and I had such great problems getting pregnant and all I ever wanted was a child. No words came. The quiet rift stabilized.

"There, I said it. Are you happy?" Brook snapped quietly.

I chose my words carefully as I tilted my head into the sun for warmth and strength. "I'm not trying to get under your skin. I'm trying to understand." I peered toward the rock then pointed. "Let's head over there, the sun is in the perfect place."

Brook gathered her lose hair and twisted it into a spindle to one side of her head and let it fall over her collarbone.

"Snapping an impeccable photograph would make me happy."

Brook sighed. "How do you do it?"

I put my face to the breeze, watching the horizon thinking it was my responsibility to define life, not let missed opportunities seed regret. Brook strolled, dangling her sandals from her fingertips. I kicked off my flip-flops, bent down, picked them up, and caught her staring at me. Her serious gaze solely focused on me, and I asked, "Do what?"

"Keep on going. There aren't many people like you," she said. "You poke, you jab, but you always come back for more regardless."

"I guess I don't see things the same way you do." The rush of cool lake water washed over my feet.

"I never meant to get pregnant. John seemed excited, and I pretended." She paused. "I bet you think I am a terrible mother."

"What would make you think that?" I responded, trying to hide judging thoughts as I put my head down, and continued to put one foot in front of the other.

"You stayed married until your boy left," Brook said.

He wasn't just *a boy*. "His name is Bradley."

"You wanted him, right?" she asked.

"With all my heart and more," I answered. A thick warm chill filled me. My heart swelled, prompting me take a breath. "I love him so much. Sometimes, he's all that keeps me going."

"It's not that I don't love Chloe. I do, but there's this invisible yearning to go do all these other things. All I ever wanted was to be a model. I can't do that here," Brook explained.

The rock grew bigger as we neared it, and the scent of wild grass tickled my nose. I glanced back over my shoulder. Chloe skipped behind us, kicking water, her arms swinging like she didn't have a care in the world. And there we were, Brook and myself, leading the way. "I'd like to believe that all mommas love their babies. It would just be too sad if they didn't. And if they don't, I hope they get love from someone else. Mommas come in all shapes, sizes, and ages. Sometimes you don't even have to search for them, they're just there," I said, thinking about my students, kids, Chloe, and Bradley. "Everybody chooses their own path whether you are seven or seventy," I continued. Chloe's singing grew louder. "Do you come to see Chloe because you ache to see her or do you just come when your schedule allows?"

Brook stopped.

I stopped. A strange calmness floated between us. I waited for Brook's fiery words. Shame clouded her blue eyes. She chose her path. I chose mine. And Chloe danced behind in our footsteps.

"The ache hurts. I know it well," I said, trying to console her.

Brook swiped at the corners of her eyes. "I just want to know she is okay from time to time," Brook whispered, glancing back over her shoulder at Chloe, who was chasing the boys.

Chloe waved and skipped toward us.

I nodded. She did love Chloe, but in her own way.

"You are so irritating," Brook mumbled. "I really don't like you," she said, sliding her sunglasses back to the bridge of her nose. "Sometimes—"

"I know." I moved over, allowing Chloe room to scoot in-between us. The aroma of hot dogs and Hawaiian Tropic drifted through the air.

Chloe grabbed her mom's hand. "Where you guys going?"

I pointed to the big rock at the end of the beach. "Up there to take some pictures."

"Cool, can I come, too?" she asked, seeking her mom's approval.

Brook pushed Chloe's damp hair away from her face. "Sure," she said, putting her sunglasses on top of her head so she could see her daughter's glow. Brook smile softened her chiseled features.

"I'll stay down here and shoot up, then work my way up to where you are." Brook climbed up the rock and Chloe shimmied behind. Chloe's hips mirrored Brook's. I set my camera and waited for Brook to get ready. She ran her fingers through her hair. Her glamour faded and I smiled to myself. "Chloe," I yelled. "Wait over there." I motioned to a grassy spot behind Brook.

Brook wrapped her fingers around Chloe's hand. "No, I think the pictures would be much better with her in them."

Chloe's smile grew. She hugged her momma from behind.

I snapped the first photo.

Chapter 31

Mom came into the library with a tall glass of lemonade. "You've been in here for hours."

"Yup," I said, distraction not an option.

"I took Bones for a walk," she said, making herself comfortable on the worn sofa from out West. She put her feet up on the ottoman and sipped at her drink.

"Thanks. Was he good?" I asked.

"Depends on your definition of good. He's back in one piece."

I peered up from the photograph I was painting. Her arched eyebrow cautioned me. *Don't ask, don't ask, don't ask,* I told myself. Mom dug her knitting out of her tote next to the chair. "How many hats do you have now?" I asked.

She shrugged. "I stopped counting."

"I should be done here in a minute. Do you want me to cook you dinner?"

"That would be nice. I invited the neighbors over."

"What?" I rolled my eyes. "Is that why you cleaned out the refrigerator and brought a cake?" Mom's eyebrow twitched as she focused on her knit one, pearl two even more intensely. "You always have an ulterior motive." Mom's familiar smirk appeared in the seam of her aging lips. I always thought of her and saw her as middle-aged. Sometime when I wasn't looking, I took her middle-aged place, which made me ache knowing she was growing older.

"Must be where you get it from."

Her knitting needles clicked.

"*Touché*," I answered, not making eye contact. "What are

we having? What time are they coming?" I asked dabbing at the puddle of paint. "Exactly who is *they*?" I asked, stroking the midnight-blue paint across the sky of my photo.

"I don't know what we're having. That's up to you. They'll be here at seven, and they would be Chloe, John, and Brook. Chloe is bringing a friend. I believe her name is Bella."

I thought I'd heard Chloe mention Bella before. "Great." I had two hours. "That's one way to get me out of the library. You're interrupting my creative swerve."

"Sometimes interruptions add brilliancy to the madness," Mom said.

"So you say," I mumbled.

"It's a matter of fact. I'm sure your dinner will be lovely, now quit fretting," she ordered. "I finished Chloe's hat. I'll give it to her tonight." She held it up.

I peered over and squinted. Adorable. "When did you get so fashion savvy?"

"Brook helped me."

I sighed. "Of course she did. I like the sequins on the band and the pearls in the center of the flower. Chloe will love it."

"Hope so, what are you giving her?"

I stopped painting. "What do you mean, what am I giving her?"

"Didn't she tell you?" Mom asked.

"Didn't she tell me what? I don't think it's her birthday," I said, washing out my brush and putting my paints away.

Concern washed over Mom's expression, and my chest tightened.

"She's going to Hollywood with her mother."

My heart skipped a beat in the sting of disbelief. "For a visit?"

Mom was quiet. The corner of her mouth sagged.

I slid my chair back, glancing over the photos of Chloe and her mother that were sprayed across the floor next to my bookshelf. "I don't believe it." I grabbed my keys, my purse, and a gulp of fresh air as I left the house.

The screen door slammed behind me and I drove away with tears in my eyes.

Mom was gone when I got back from the store. I found the quiet house a bit unsettling. I dug out the biggest sauté pan from the cupboard and arranged my ingredients on the counter. I'd splurged and bought jumbo shrimp. I reached back in the cupboard to get a large pot for orzo then filled it with steaming water and put it over a high flame. I drizzled in some olive oil and salt. The fresh spinach was hearty and beautiful against the store-bought cherry tomatoes that I had to buy, no thanks to Bones. I squeezed the lemons and waited for the water to boil.

I set the table in the dining room, but then changed my mind. I needed to be outside without a ceiling, confining walls, a place with plenty of air. The doorbell rang as I carried the stack of plates to the patio. "Come in," I yelled.

Determined to be ready before the guests arrived, I continued straightening up my house. I couldn't lie to myself. It was not going to be easy to sit across from Chloe thinking she was going away with her mother.

"Let me help you with that," John said.

He took the heavy stack of plates from me. "Is it seven, yet?"

"No, I figured this wasn't your doing and thought you might need a hand. You have to be exhausted."

A knot filled my throat, and my heart. John understood. For the first time in a long time, I didn't mask the truth. "I am." I opened the French doors for John, and the rush of warm, summer air washed over me. I arranged the placemats on the table outside as John arranged the place settings.

"Thanks for having us over," he said.

"No problem. You really should thank my mother," I said over my shoulder as I went back inside.

"I will."

John followed me. He put his hand on mine as I reached for the tray that held the silverware and napkins. A rush of heat ran through me. It wasn't a hot flash. His emerald-green eyes held my attention. "What?"

"I came over early because I wanted to tell you something."

I wanted off the hormonal rollercoaster holding me hostage. I held on to myself as sadness dimmed his beautiful eyes. I couldn't take much more. "What is it?" I murmured. "Are you leaving, too? Are you going to Hollywood with Brook? And Chloe?" I couldn't see him leaving his daughter.

He snickered. "No, I am not going anywhere. I told you before, I'm not with Brook. I could never survive out there. I'm having a hard enough time here in the Midwest. So you know Chloe's leaving?"

"Mom kind of let the cat out of the bag. Why? What gives?" I asked, narrowing my eyes.

"Ever since you took her to the beach to do that shoot, Brook's been different. She thinks Chloe should try it out there with her."

I grimaced.

"I know what you're thinking. I don't want her to go, but if I don't let her go, Chloe may never forgive me. Some things she's going to have to learn on her own."

"Who? Chloe or Brook?"

The corner of his lip curled toward the ceiling. "Both, I suppose." John's mountain twang rolled off his tongue as he rubbed his chin.

His stare brightened.

"What?" I said in my usual way.

"So," he said with a snicker, "you really do care."

I rolled my eyes and looked away.

"Admit it, you are attached to Chloe," he said, touching my chin and redirecting my attention.

"I just don't want to see her get hurt," I said, my words teetered on the verge of tears. The rumble of the boiling water reminded me I had forgotten about the heat. I dumped the box of orzo into the pot. It bubbled and rolled.

John leaned against the counter.

"That's all," I said.

"That's all, my foot," he said.

"What if she decides she wants to stay with Brook?"

"You are full of questions," he said, putting his hands on my hips.

"Sorry, this isn't any of my business," I whispered, staring into his soulful eyes. We were nose-to-nose. A hint of concern crossed his stare.

"We'll cross that bridge if and when we get to it, and that's a big *if*, Maggie."

John slid his hands around my waist and clasped them behind my lower back. "You sure do have a way with people," he said. "I'm not sure what you said to her, but you got her thinking, that's more than I could ever do."

"I'm sorry?" I said, not sure where we were going with the conversation.

"I'll let you know later if an apology is in order," John said with a twinkle of hope flashing in his eyes.

I smiled. "I sure as hell hope I don't owe you one."

John laughed. "Do I scare you that much?"

His breath synced with mine. "Sometimes you do scare the hell out of me." I closed my eyes and let him kiss me until the hiss of water kissing the burner tore me away. John took the potholders from me and slid the pot off the heat. "I'll finish in here if you could finish the table," I suggested.

He pulled me close again and held me, his words in my ear. "You can't always control what happens around you, but you sure can pray like hell that it all turns out for the best."

I wrapped my arms around his neck then leaned back to get one last look before mayhem arrived for dinner. "Thank you."

"You're welcome," he replied.

"Kiss me again, before they get here."

"So, you do like that, huh?" John joked and pulled away. "I think you just may have to wait for the next one."

"So you're admitting there's going to be a next one?" My body quaked with uncertainty. I had never really played this game before. I stirred the pasta with anticipation.

John came from behind and drew me close. His lips brushed against my ear. He took the spoon out of my hand, moved me away from the stove, and up against the wall. My stomach rolled over with excitement as he lifted my chin.

"It's sooner than you think," he said in a deep seductive drawl.

I closed my eyes, and his lips brushed mine, teasing, taunting. I wrapped my arms around his waist and held him close. When he finished kissing me, he smoothed the hair back from my face. His fingers caressed my hot cheeks. His smile ignited my desire for more.

"If your cooking is as good as your kissing, well—" He paused then stepped back giving me a sexy smirk.

"Well, what?" I said.

"Let your imagination run wild, Maggie, just let it run wild," he said, picking up the tray of silverware and napkins.

I strained the pasta then melted some butter in my sauté pan before adding garlic then the shrimp.

The front door slammed shut then Chloe and her friend skipped into the kitchen.

"Wow, wee, wow, that stove must be hot. You're cheeks are flaming," Chloe said, yanking on Voodoo's string. "Where's Bones? Bella wants to meet him." She knocked herself on her head. "Where are my manners? Maggie, this is my best friend in the whole wide world, Bella. Bella, this is my bestest neighbor, Maggie."

I smiled. "Nice to meet you."

"Bella's my best friend from my old house." She beamed.

Bella smiled and came over to the stove. "Nice to meet you, too. Is that cake for dessert?" She grinned and pointed to the chocolate monstrosity my mother had displayed on the cake stand.

"Yup," I answered. "We should just skip dinner and have cake. What do you think?"

"Really?" Chloe giggled.

Bella tilted her head in Chloe's direction. "She's just yanking your chain."

Chloe hopped up on the stool to see what I was doing. "That smells good. My dad doesn't cook like that."

Bella wiggled her way up on the stool next to Chloe's. "Neither does mine. Neither does my mom."

Chloe yanked on Voodoo's string.

I guarded my food from the purple straggly cat that could end up anywhere, at any time. "Can I set a place for Voodoo and Bones? Voodoo wants to eat with him tonight. Just like me and Bella."

I stirred the shrimp one last time before setting aside. "Sure, if you can find him. "We're eating on the patio. How about you take Bones' dish out and put it next to the table." I reached into the cupboard for a bowl. "Here's a bowl for Voodoo."

"Thanks," Chloe said. "Come on, let's find that dog."

Mom came in with Brook. She had a purple party bag decorated with sparkling purple ribbon. Brook was wearing a plain cotton sundress and flip-flops. Her hair flowed over her shoulders like curly ribbons, her makeup flawless. I touched my hair remembering I hadn't seen myself in a mirror all day. So focused on dinner and the fact I was going to have to say goodbye to Chloe, I forgot about taking time out for me and the five minutes at radiation did not count. They were used to seeing me in my not-so-fancy, faded checked blue hospital gown, and yoga pants.

I sautéed the spinach then mixed in the orzo, shrimp tomatoes, and lemon juice. "Mom, would you mind taking this off the heat and putting it into this dish."

"Sure, honey, everything okay?" she asked.

"Yeah, just need a minute to clean up." I'd need more

than a minute and a team of professionals to look like Brook. I scurried away from the kitchen.

Hustling up the stairs to my bedroom, I didn't have time for a revelation about my wardrobe choices. My favorite khaki shorts and white T-shirt would do. I washed my face then rubbed in some tinted moisturizer, brushed on some mascara, swiped my cheeks with blush, and raked my hairbrush through my messy tresses before pulling them back in a messy bun at the nape of my neck.

My sandals banged against the wall when I kicked them off. I slipped my feet into beaded flip-flops then put on the necklace Mom had sent me. The half-a-heart hung around my neck on a silver chain. By the time I returned to the party, I hadn't skipped a beat. John, Brook, and my mom were on the patio sipping drinks. The girls had Bones on his leash teaching him to heel, and the table was set beautifully.

I poured myself a glass of wine, swirled it around as I leaned against the stone pillar at the corner of the patio. I studied the interaction as the adults mingled. Mom was her usual self, socially beautiful knowing exactly what questions to ask, knowing when to listen, and when to speak. John attended to my mother as if they were old friends. Mom could make anyone into an old friend in no time at all. I sipped my wine, letting it sit in my mouth, allowing myself to savor each swallow. Brook stood to the side watching the girls with her arms crossed. She shifted her weight from side-to-side as if she were nervous.

Chloe told Bones to sit. He did. She unsnapped the leash from his collar. She told him to lie down. He did. I loathed the commitment to next week's dog class. With Chloe off to Hollywood in a few days, I would definitely be going solo. Chloe touched Bones' nose with her pointer finger then scratched behind his ear. He rolled in the grass and Bella clapped.

"We'd better eat before it gets cold," I announced, gesturing to the table.

John pulled out a chair for my mother then pulled out a chair for me. The girls sat beside each next to Mom.

Brook's eyes flashed with caution as John helped her with a chair. "I got it, but thank you," she said.

The brush off sent a thread of relief down my spine as I'd spent so much time trying to decipher their feelings for each other. I did a better job at second-guessing the facts than anyone I knew. John backed away without hesitation. He sat down and put his napkin in his lap. Mom offered to dish the girls up. Chloe rubbed her belly as she sniffed the food.

"What's Voodoo having for dinner?" I asked, inspecting the dinner bowls set for the animals.

"Tuna and cheese," Chloe answered.

I smiled. "Yum. And when will Bones get to eat?" I pointed to the yard. He was still lying where Chloe told him to stay.

Bella craned her neck to see.

Chloe giggled. "I almost forgot. Bones, come," she called, hitting the side of her leg.

He popped up and trotted to the patio then went straight to his dish, stuck his wrinkly nose in, and gulped his food.

"Good boy," Chloe praised him. "I'm really sorry I can't go to dog class with you." She looked to her mom who was sitting quietly with a gleam in her eyes. "Did they tell you?" Chloe asked, taking a bite of pasta and shrimp. A few grains of orzo dropped from her lip, bounced off her chin, and went onto the ground. She began talking with a mouthful. "Bones will get that, don't worry."

"I'm not worried," I said, "and yes, they told me. California is a long way away. I bet you're excited," I added with a smile.

"I sure will miss you, Chloe," Bella said, buttering her bread. "Can I come see you there, too?" She took a bite, chewed, swallowed then continued talking. "You sure do move a lot."

Chloe shrugged.

Mom asked her questions about packing. I tuned her out and thought about Chloe. Did she mean what she said about her mother earlier? She said she knew her mom was not reliable. She cried about moving and leaving Bella behind. She seemed happy now with her mother's invitation. I raised my glass. "A toast. Here's to new adventures," I said as everyone raised their glasses to mine. Chloe and Bella couldn't reach so John leaned in their direction to make sure to clink glasses with them. Bones gave a little *woof*, snatched up the spilled orzo, and waited patiently for more.

Brook remained quiet.

A disconnect flickered in her eyes when I leaned in her direction to clink my glass. What was she possibly thinking? I ignored it and held my plate out for my mother to fill.

She smiled. "I knew you'd find something to whip up. You always do," she said with a wink.

Brook nibbled at her dinner. Her appetite made mine look ferocious. Although mine had gotten better, thanks to Mom's intervention, I couldn't help but sense Brook's uneasiness. So, I did what Mom did. I smiled, chatted with the girls, and thought about the hot kiss in the kitchen.

Chloe spotted the purple present bag. "Hey, who is that for?" she asked, nibbling at the end of a shrimp she was holding with her fingers.

Mom put her fork down. "It's for you, a going-away present. I think you already know what it is."

Chloe shoved the rest of the shrimp into her mouth and wiped her hands on her napkin. "Can I open it now?"

"I guess so. If it's okay with your mom and your dad."

I was sitting between a man and his ex-wife whose child spent most her time hanging with me or spying on me. This weird scenario nagged at me, but the kiss in the kitchen didn't seem weird at all. It was anything but weird. I let go of my own uneasiness when John winked at me. "I say, open it now." I handed the bag to John, who handed it to Chloe.

Brook forced a smile. It wasn't a smile I'd seen when snapping her portrait.

"It's just what I wanted." Chloe wiggled off her chair and hopped over to kiss my mom.

Bella smiled. "Now, that's a hat with pizzazz. I wish I had one just like it." She wiped her hands on her napkin then touched the beaded flower. "It's so pretty."

The willingness to make Bella's wish come true sparkled in Mom's eyes. She couldn't hold it in. "I can make you one, too. It may not be exactly the same, but then you will each have one, like sisters."

Chloe and Bella laughed. "I gotta go look in the mirror," Chloe chimed. "Come on, Bell."

Bella wiggled out of her chair and the two girls disappeared into the house.

"I bet we won't see them until dessert," I said.

Brook rearranged her food on her plate while the three of us finished our dinner.

Chapter 32

I'll be over in a few, John's text read.

I checked myself out in the foyer mirror then went into my library. I sequenced the cow photographs. Today, the Fourth of July Cows and the Christmas Cows were my favorite. When the doorbell rang, I hollered, "Come in." I glanced over the top of my glasses, then back down again, reveling in the color. Part of me felt silly for what I was about to request.

John peeked around the corner. "Sundays are good. No work. Not on call."

"I agree. No radiation." I smiled, liking the way my project was coming along.

"What's this all about?" John asked.

I took off my glasses and leaned back in my chair. "I feel silly. I know Chloe is about to leave with Brook. And I was wondering—" I paused. "I was wondering if she and I could have a sleepover before she left," I said, fidgeting with my hands.

John smiled a sheepish grin. "She eventually wears you down and you have no choice, do you?"

"Pretty much. I don't have a going-away present for her and I thought it might be fun. Do you think Brook will let us? I wanted to run it by you first." His expression soured as I said Brook's name. "What?" I tucked my hands under my thighs to keep myself from playing with them.

"It might be better coming from you, but I think it's a great idea. They leave in three days."

"How about tomorrow night? That will give her time to spend with you before she goes." Like a kid, I crossed my fingers.

"She and Brook are out right now getting a few things. Why don't you give her a call in an hour or so," he said, taking a breath. "You really don't have to do this," he added, leaning against the desk and crossing his arms. His biceps flexed, filling his sleeves.

"I want to. It's going to be strange not having her around," I said, fidgeting with the brushes on my desk. "Bones will miss her."

"I will miss her. As much as a handful she is, this is going to be hard," John said, straight-faced, his temple twitching.

"Not to go all *Maggie* on you, but do you think Brook will actually keep her out there full time?" I asked.

His eyes grew serious as he contemplated the consequences.

"I hope not, but I don't know," John said, shifting his weight. "Chloe needs to find out on her own what it would be like and Brook badgered me into trying this."

"I'm sorry."

"You should be." He pointed his finger straight at me. "She wouldn't have ever done this if it weren't for you."

"What did I do?" I asked cautiously.

"She told me about your conversation at the beach, about how mommas love their children and what her motives were for the visit." John paused. "It doesn't help that Chloe likes you, really likes you."

I tried to hold back the smile. "She likes me?"

John came around the back of the desk. He took my hand and pulled me up. I kept my eyes focused on his emerald-green beauties. "Just about as much as I do. She adores you, even if you are difficult, but then again, so is she."

With his hands wrapped around my waist, he tilted his head, and put his lips on my neck. Heat waves ravished my body. I closed my eyes and let him nibble. A soft moan escaped my lips.

Breathy words tickled my neck.

"There's more where that came from," John whispered.

"I bet there is," I said, rubbing his forearms.

"Maybe we can have our own sleepover," he suggested, running his fingers across my collarbone.

"We'll see," I answered, picturing him naked. I still didn't think it was a good idea.

"You pick the day and the time," he said, "and I'll be there."

"I don't know if I can do that to Chloe. What if it doesn't work out?" I pictured tears, revenge, or a missing dog. What was I doing, egging him on like this? Suddenly aware that hearts could be broken, most importantly, mine, I stopped. The thought of living next door to a jilted lover left a foul taste in my mouth. "I couldn't stand it if our relationship turned ugly."

Uneasiness shrouded John's determined eyes.

"I'm sorry," I said.

"Would you quit being sorry? Maybe you should decide what you want. Maybe you're still not ready."

"I'm not ready? What does that mean?" I asked, pulling back. I didn't consider myself, *not ready.* "I just want to be sure."

John rubbed his chin and shot me a look. "I don't think that's possible. How can you ever be sure?" he asked, lowering his gaze and the tone of his voice.

"Maybe you're right. Maybe I'm not ready." How would I ever be sure?

"When you figure it out, let me know." John exited the room then turned just outside the library door, and walked back to where I stood.

I crossed my arms, bracing myself.

He put his hands on my shoulders. "I know what I want."

He held me close and kissed me softly, letting his lips linger, even after the kiss was over. My hands found his waist. My heart took a nosedive as he left the room. I picked up my phone to text Brook. *Can you please call me when you get home? Maggie.*

I went back to my photos. They'd morphed into quite a summer project. Actually, the summer itself had turned into quite a project, leaving little time for wallowing in self-pity, until right now. I'd never expected to fall for the guy-next-door, let alone the guy-next-door with a seven-year-old daughter, and an ex-wife. I wondered if Beckett's partner would ever look at me with judging eyes. Who was I to make such criticisms? Rash scenarios flashed through my brain like a crazed teenager. Maybe John was right, maybe I wasn't ready, but damn, he was making it impossible not to think about him.

I heard the rumblings of his Harley Davidson. I cringed to think that I caused this episode of engine revving. "Really? If you're gonna have that thing, learn to ride."

The doorbell rang.

I left my desk to see who was there. Brook waited for me on the porch twirling her sunglasses in expected supermodel mode.

"Hi there, come on in," I said.

"Are my photos ready?" she asked with a glint of intrigue behind her crystal-blue eyes.

"Kind of. I wanted to talk to you about something else," I said. My clammy palms started to sweat so I jammed my hands in my short pockets and admired her freshly painted gray metallic toenails. "I like your toes." *You geek,* I said to myself.

"Thanks, Chloe and I just got back from getting pedicures," she replied.

I braced myself then said, "I was wondering if you would let Chloe have a sleepover, here with me before she leaves. I didn't get her a going away present and I thought it might be, fun."

"Aren't you a little too old for that sort of thing?"

Ouch. "I don't think you're ever too old for a sleepover," I said, trying to read her thoughts. "I was thinking tomorrow night so she'd have time with John before you flew out." I hoped she'd go along with my plan. "I'm really gonna miss her," I said, my voice barely audible. Brook pressed her lips together and stared at me. That little voice inside my head prepared me for rejection. How could she be so cold? It was for Chloe.

Who was I kidding? It was for me, well, for both of us.

Bradley hadn't had a sleepover since he was twelve. It seemed so long ago when I'd pray that he and his friends would just go to sleep, I'd be the one all out of whack the next day, and crabby. I didn't know if I had it in me. Was this one of those things that just sounded like a good idea?

"I'll think about it," Brook said.

"Fair enough," I said.

"Can I see the photos?"

I thought that was a bold request after making me wait. But, really, what was the harm? She would have many nights with Chloe, maybe I should have suggested she go out and celebrate at the bar, cause you can't do that with a seven-year-old in tow. "I have them on my desk." I showed her inside my workroom.

"I remember," she said quietly.

Was it me? Tension seemed to plague our every conversation. I treaded lightly. I didn't want to anger the beast. I studied her expression as she picked up the photographs one-by-one inspecting the images. Fierce lines defined her profile. A prickly heat came over me, and beads of dew formed on the nape of my neck. This was crazy. She was just a woman, the most unpredictable kind, the kind of woman with apprehensive motives. I wasn't sure if Brook wanted her daughter to herself or worse, her husband. John reassured me that wasn't the case, but Brook's moods swung to and fro like a pendulum on steroids.

"You did a fabulous job," she said quietly.

I detected shame. "You didn't think I could take the photos?"

"No, it seems you do everything well."

Goose bumps covered my arms. Thank you," I said, not so sure that was a compliment. Brook didn't say anything else. She fixed her attention on the photographs. I stood back, letting the air settle between us.

"I feel like I should pay you something," she said.

"No, I told you I'd do it for free."

I didn't want anything from Brook except a little time with her daughter to say goodbye. I thought back to Chloe swinging on the porch singing "You Can't Always Get What You Want" by The Rolling Stones.

John revved the Harley engine louder.

"What did you do to him?" Brook asked.

"What do you mean?"

"I saw him come home and now he's in that garage making a bunch of noise. I'm not sure why he has a motorcycle, if he's not going to ride it. Stupid, if you ask me."

"Don't know. I asked him about the sleepover and he thought I should ask you." I kept my eyes on her, searching for clues. Something behind Brook's eyes worked like my mother's fingers when she was knitting.

"You sure there wasn't something else?" she asked.

"Not that I can think of," I said.

Brook walked out of the library. "If you change your mind about being paid, let me know. I'll get back to you about the sleepover."

Her slim hips swayed as she sauntered out the front door, her blond waves bouncing in time with her stride. This was going to be impossible.

Chapter 33

Shivers crept through me like cracking ice as I waited in the quiet radiation room. Bobbi made sure I was in position. She called out the coordinates to the new girl.

"Your skin looks pretty raw," she said.

"Not too bad," I replied, resisting the urge to look.

She moved me around to make sure I was centered on the table. Wouldn't want to accidentally radiate my heart.

"Grab some more lotion before you leave. Remember, you meet with the doctor today," she reminded me.

"Got it," I said.

"Be right back, lay still."

Music played overhead. I watched the heavy, lead door slowly close in the reflection on the ceiling just like all the other days, and I'd kept my eyes glued to that spot to see it open back up again. The rubber band around my feet dug into my skin, but I wouldn't complain if it meant beating cancer. With my arm over my head in the brace, the other arm tucked under my side and my feet bound, there wasn't much to do but lay still and stare at the ceiling. The squeal of the machine rang out, the machine shifted position with a *click, click, click*, and I waited for the last radiating zap. The line of infra-red light on the ceiling twitched. I counted the days in my head. I would be done in one week, which equaled five sessions, but then I remembered the extra week. *Damn*, ten sessions. That sounded shorter than two weeks, but I'd still have most of August to rest.

Chloe would be gone in three days.

The door opened, and I removed my arm from the brace.

"Your arm getting sore from holding it over your head?" Bobbi asked.

I wiggled back into my robe while she took the thick band off my feet. "No, not really."

"Here," she said, holding out her arm to help me off the skinny hard table, "let me help you up."

I ran my fingers through my hair then twisted it, making a loose bun at the nape of my neck.

"You know, you don't have to take your hair down every time," Bobbi said, handing me a sample-sized bottle of lotion as I fixed my gown.

"I know." I didn't want to admit that I wanted my head flat against the table every time just to make sure I was in the right position, because I wasn't coming back, and I didn't want to be responsible for radiating some other vital part of my body. With all the poking, pictures, and Cat scans, I wasn't going to mess with anything. "See you tomorrow," I said. "And thanks for the lotion."

"Don't forget to go see the doc," she reminded me.

Like I could forget.

I unlocked my locker, grabbed my stuff, and made my way to the see Dr. Masterson. Her assistant, Pam caught me in the hallway.

"Let's get you weighed," she said, unloading my arms.

I avoided reading my weight as I stood on the scale.

"Holding steady, that's good." She wrote my weight in my chart. "You've gained a pound, but you still weigh less than when we started. Stress will do that," she said. "Let's go, darlin'," she sang with a smile.

Pam showed me into our usual room.

"We have to stop meeting like this," I teased.

"Soon enough, soon enough. I know you're getting tired of coming here." She scribbled some notes in my chart then examined my chest. "Looks sore. Nice scar. Doctor did a beautiful job on that."

I glanced down, assessing the green, glowing bruise left from the surgery. I wasn't so sure it was beautiful. Maybe over time it would fade, maybe even be hidden at the edge of my areola, maybe even be invisible to someone else inspecting me, but I'd know it was there. "Yeah."

I just wanted to go home. I checked my phone. No messages.

Dressed in her a basketball jersey, shorts and high-tops, Chloe waited for me on the porch steps. By the look on her face, things weren't going well. Even the annoying ice-cream truck riding my bumper didn't spark a smile. I wished the guy's speaker would short out. Christmas tunes, depressing.

"Hey," I called as I came around from the garage.

"Hey," she said in a sulking tone.

"You look pretty glum."

Chloe sighed. "Yeah."

"What gives?" I asked, not sure it was a good idea to ask. Obviously, if I hadn't learned my lesson by now, I never would.

She patted Voodoo's head. "Good kitty." She rubbed his ears with her thumbs as she cradled his face. "Where were you?"

"Oh, so you're going to play it that way, huh? And change the subject." I leaned back on my elbows to catch a few rays of sun on my face. "Ah, that feels good."

"Wanna go to the beach?" she asked. "It sure would feel good to jump in the water."

My eyebrow shot up. "Who's watching you?"

"Funny thing, no one's home," she said.

I perked up, opened my eyes, and bit the inside of my cheek. "What do you mean, 'no one is home?' Where's your mom?"

Chloe shrugged.

"Is your dad off today?" I prodded.

"Nope. He's at work fixing sick kids. Mom was supposed to pick me up from basketball camp, but she didn't show. I walked home." Chloe lifted her bangs. "See the sweat. Man, it's hot out here," she huffed.

"Feels good," I said, basking in the sun.

"Yeah, but you didn't just walk a mile home after doing five million jumping jacks and one hundred layup shots."

"Guess not," I conceded. I dug in my purse for my phone. No messages. I shot John a text thinking he might check his phone. *Where's Brook? Chloe walked home from basketball by herself. Brook isn't home.*

"Who you texting?" Chloe asked, fanning herself. "You got my mom's number?"

"Yup," I said with a snicker, "but I'm sending a message to your dad." I stood up and stretched, my achy skin tightening across my chest. "Come on. Let's go in and get a snack. Something cold for you."

"Can we go to the beach? I want to go to the beach," she said, stretching her legs. "My feet are sweaty."

I unlocked the front door. "Let's see if your dad sent me a message. Maybe your mom will show up." I pushed the door open and Chloe followed me inside. "Come on, let's see what we have in the fridge. When did Bella go home? I liked her." I heard a *clunk*. I turned to see Chloe sitting on the floor peeling off her shoes and socks. I didn't say anything about the pile she left in the middle of the floor. Bradley would be jealous. I could hear his voice in my head. *Why does she get to leave a mess?*

My phone chimed. I read the text aloud to Chloe. *Really swamped. Don't know where Brook is. Maybe she just forgot. Can Chloe hang with you until she gets back?*

"Ask him if we can go to the beach. I know where the spare key is so I can get my stuff," Chloe said, pawing through the fridge. "You got any ice cream?"

"There should be some from the other night."

I replied to John's text. *Chloe can stay with me. She wants to know if we can go to the beach. If we do, how much trouble will I be in with Brook?* I added a worried face.

I helped Chloe scoop Rocky Road ice cream into a parlor dish then I drizzled chocolate sauce on top. Her eyes nearly bugged out of her head.

My phone chimed again. "Let's see what your dad says."

Chloe put a heaping spoonful of ice cream in her mouth then smiled and rubbed her belly. She pretended to give Voodoo a bite.

I read the text. *Go ahead. Leave Brook a note. Chloe knows where the key is. Brook has your number. She'll find you.* There was a winking yellow face followed by a p.s. *I'll take the heat. I owe you.* I smiled as the memory of his lips on mine rushed back.

"What did he say?" Chloe asked around a mouthful, trying not to let her food escape her lips.

"We have to leave a note for your mom at your house. When you're done, we'll get the key," I replied, getting the crackers out.

Chloe finished her ice cream, and I watched her scrape the bowl then lick the edges like a cat. "Done, let's go," she said.

"Let me get my stuff." I shoved a few crackers into my mouth and munched as I trotted upstairs to get my tunic to cover my arms and chest then I grabbed my sunhat and some towels. Halfway down the stairs I remembered the Claire Cook novel on my bedside stand. "I'll be there in a second," I called, heading back upstairs.

The front door was wide open when I came back down to get Chloe. I went over to John's house. She'd left the side door wide open and Voodoo was lying on the ground waiting like an obedient cat should. "Good cat, Voodoo," I praised. I poked my head in and called Chloe's name.

Feeling like an intruder, I waited for Chloe to invite me in. The kitchen counter was littered with mail. "Chloe," I called as I stepped inside. "Chloe." Her silence worried me.

I gave one last shout out. "Chloe!" I stepped into the kitchen, perused the magazine on the counter, and waited.

Heavy thuds overhead redirected my attention. I left the narrow kitchen, padding softly toward the banging overtures, careful enough not to disturb anything, while my eyes wandered over framed pictures inspecting for hints about John, Brook, and Chloe's lives.

Chloe strolled by. "Hey, Maggie, what's going on?"

My instincts bristled with caution. "What do you mean, what's going on?" She was in a green racing suit and flip-flops to match.

"I'm almost ready," she said. "I need a few things then I'll be ready to go."

"What was all the racket?" I asked, searching her face for evidence.

"Nothing," she replied. "It wasn't anything." She forced a quick smile.

"Do we need to clean anything up before we go?"

"Nope. I was just getting my suit out of my duffle. It's warm in California, *all* the time. Mom said to bring *all* my suits. Just unpacking a little to get this one."

"You must be taking a lot of stuff. Do you have a paper and a pen? We need to leave a note."

Chloe scooted around the corner. I heard a drawer open then scrape shut. I waited. She trotted back.

"Here," she said, shoving the pen and paper toward me.

"Thanks." I started to write in my best teacher handwriting. "Okay, I told your mom we're going to the beach, that your dad knows, and we will return around five." Chloe approved. She straightened her bathing suit straps as she slipped her feet into a different pair of yellow polka-dotted sandals. I signed my name. "Want to write anything?" I handed Chloe the pen. She drew a heart and wrote her name with some hugs and kisses. Then she put the pen down. The sparkle in her eye flashed. "Ready?"

"Yup, let's go! Maybe those boys will be there again to make sandcastles."

"Maybe. Want to bring Junie B?" I asked, holding up the book that was lying open on the counter next to an empty milk container. I picked it up and shook it to be sure. "Want to throw this away?"

Chloe shrugged. "Sure." She opened a door, dropped it in a trashcan on some rollers, and shut the cupboard. "Mom can thank me later."

"What?"

"She leaves stuff out all the time. She's not very neat. Drives Dad crazy. I heard him tell her once she wasn't very responsible."

"Oh. Let's go."

We locked the door and headed out.

"Let's get your camera and Bones," Chloe said.

I packed up the car and the three of us were off.

Chapter 34

Bones dug in the sand under the tree. I tied his leash to a bench carved up with lovers' names and teenage graffiti. His collapsible bowl was deep in the beach bag under Chloe's book and the towels. I tugged then yanked. Junie B. popped out of the bag. A piece of paper fell from between the pages. I hadn't noticed it back at the house. I scanned the horizon, checking on Chloe, who had found the Mark Spitz boys from the other day. I unfolded the white paper.

The wind carried Chloe's laughter. I glanced up, wondering if she knew. I wondered if John knew. When things like this happened at school, it usually resulted in bouts of rash behavior, followed by melancholy faces boring sad holes through me.

I patted Bones' head then put the letter in my camera bag. "I'll be right back with your dish."

He wagged his tail then gave a little *woof.* Grains of sand drifted through my toes as I padded toward the fountain. The earth warmed me. Water from the spigot sprayed across my feet as I filled the dog dish. The cold drops soothed the heartache brewing for Chloe. I lifted my skirt up to my thigh, let the water wash over my shins, then moved out of the way for a tall, tan skinny mom in a bikini wanting to wash off her toddler. I smiled, wondering how she kept her shape.

Bones wagged his tail as I returned. I told him to sit just like the dog trainer taught us and he did. A wave of pride came over me and I wondered if anyone was watching. Maybe we would be okay after all. I'd just have to be consistent and patient. Chloe ran up, dug out her goggles, and ran back to the where the boys were splashing. There was a dark curly-haired woman sitting in a low lawn chair, under a red umbrella surrounded by buckets, shovels, and oversized plastic Tonka trucks. Chloe waved for me to come over. I got my camera and headed her way.

The woman in the chair smiled at me.

"Hi," I said. "Those your boys?"

"Yup. Harry and Walter."

A shiver ran down my spine. "Great names," I said, taking the lens cap off the camera.

"They're named after their grandfathers. Harry's the oldest," she said with pride. "Chloe's a riot."

"Oh, I see she's introduced herself." Chloe waded in the lake, bent at the waist, held her nose, and put her face in the water. Her hair skimmed the wet surface.

"The boys are very fond of her. We should exchange numbers so they can have play dates."

"I'd love to, she would love to, but she's not my daughter," I said. The woman's face expressed curiosity wondering what my connection *really* was with Chloe. "She lives next door to me. We are just hanging out today."

"Why don't you sit? I'm Judith, but I prefer Judy," the woman said, inviting me to join her in the empty chair under her umbrella. "It's not wet, yet."

Out of the corner of my eye, I saw Bones gnawing on a bone under the bench. "Thanks." I lifted the camera to my eye, focused the lens, and snapped a picture of Chloe floating on her back with her eyes closed. I turned and held out my hand. "I'm Maggie." The woman's hand was soft and warm. "Walter was my dad's name. Not very common nowadays with all the soap opera names floating around out there." I snapped another picture.

"Are you a photographer?" she asked. "I'm terrible at taking pictures, but a great baker."

I smiled at her. "We should trade services. I'm not much of a baker. I don't mind cooking, but my mom is the baker in the family. I did more when my son was little."

"How old is he now?" Judy asked, rubbing sunscreen on her shins.

"Bradley is twenty-two," I replied. "He's in Boston working as an intern at a law firm. They want to hire him. He's going to take the job." I wanted him to be independent, but I just didn't think it would come so soon.

"Wow, that's great. You don't look old enough to have a son that's twenty-two."

"Thanks," I said. "Would you mind if I snapped some pictures of your boys?"

"Go ahead."

Harry had Walter in a headlock. Both boys laughed. Chloe was digging in the wet sand over to the side.

"If I give you my number or email, would you mind sending some pictures my way?" Judy asked.

"Sure will. After all, they are your boys. I'm just an innocent bystander."

Chloe noticed me sitting there when she stood up to get another bucket of water. She gave me a little wave. Her smile minus one more tooth. She didn't tell me another *fang* fell out. That's what she liked to call them. I put the camera back up to my eye, zoomed in, and snapped another picture. Her belly protruded as she arched her back, round, perfect, like a youngster's belly should. She ran over to me.

"Do you two know each other?" she asked.

Harry and Walter's mom answered before I could, "We do now. Maggie is a very nice neighbor to bring you to the beach."

Chloe pushed damp strands of hair away from her face. "I know. She's always there, even if I'm a pest sometimes."

I felt a small lump in my throat. Emotion built behind my eyes. I smiled at her. A film of wetness covered my eyes, knowing Brook had left without her.

Chloe fixed the shoulder of my tunic. "You better cover up. You know what the doctor said. No sun." She waggled her finger at me with a mocking grin then kissed me on the cheek, and ran back to her hole.

I wiped at the corner of my eye under my sunglasses.

Judy's face drooped. "Not to be nosy, but why do you have to stay out of the sun?" she asked, offering me a bottle of water from her cooler.

I took it and rolled the cool surface across my forehead. "I have cancer. I'm going through radiation, so I'm not really supposed to be in the sun." The plastic cap snapped open as I twisted. Chloe surprised me when I least expected it. Maybe she did know her mother was gone. Then again, maybe she didn't, and she was just being her usual self, that I had grown to love.

"I'm so sorry," Judy said.

Harry kicked sand into the air as he ran by.

"It's okay. I *think* I'm going to be fine." I gulped the water and watched the three children run along the shore. Laughter erupted in the *whoosh* of the lake as it kissed the Michigan shore. "No," I blurted out.

Judy turned. "What?"

I shook my head. "I meant to say, I *will* be fine. I'm going to be a survivor. I refuse to believe otherwise," I stated with conviction, my words strong, fierce. I held her gaze.

Judy held up her water bottle to me. I touched mine to hers. A thin grin crossed her lips. The shoulder strap of her suit flopped to the side as she settled back in her chair. We had matching tattoos. I checked her cleavage. She had a black spot at the top of her breasts. She caught me staring.

"I have two tats on my side and another one here," she said, lifting the side of her suit out of the way. "I'm a survivor, too. It will be two years this August." She smiled. Her eyes followed the football floating past. "Radiation sucks," she grunted. "I had a mastectomy and chemo." She fluffed her short curls. "My eyelashes will never be the same."

"You look great. And you're right. Radiation *does* suck. I am so sick of going." I took a long drag of water. "All I want to do is be at the beach in my suit, not hiding under tunics and hats. I'm sick of peeling chunks of itchy skin. It's ugly and I hate it," I said. "I just want to be done." I wondered if the mystery cane with my father's name scratched in the paint was still in the lost and found.

"I know exactly how you feel." She reached over and patted my hand. "I think we're going to be good friends."

Harry, Walter, and Chloe ran to where we sat. Water dripped from their suits. Harry shook his head like a retriever. We all screeched then laughed.

Bones barked and ran toward the kids. I jumped up, trying to catch him. Chloe ran to the bench to get his leash. He circled the boys begging for attention.

"Bones, come," I said.

His eyes danced with the desire to play.

I held his mischievous stare and pointed in front of me. I cocked my head, giving him *the look*, trying to be serious.

"Come," I said, lowering my voice. I knelt down. My left knee touched the sand. Bones cocked his head. His tail waggled back and forth. He sighed then stepped closer to me and sat down. "Good boy," I praised, patting his head. He rolled over onto his back and let me pat his belly.

"Look, he wiggled out of his collar," Chloe called, as she came running back with the leash, the collar still attached. "He wanted to play with us."

"Can I pet him?" Walter asked, crouching beside me.

"Sure," I answered, rubbing Bones' chest.

"I like his wrinkly face." Walter giggled as he played with his jowls.

Chloe put his collar back on. "Good boy, Bones," she said, patting his rump. Chloe's eyes shone with approval. "You're getting better at this dog stuff, Maggie. You got to remember, this is his day, too."

"You're pretty smart," Judy said with a smirk. She adjusted her bathing suit straps. "Maggie and I are going to exchange phone numbers. If you want to play with the boys sometime, that would be great."

Chloe squinted into the sun, trying to see Judy's face. "I'd like that. My dad can get the number from Maggie."

Chloe shaded her eyes, hurt cut through the rays of sun. Her chin wobbled. She spun around and ran down the beach toward the rock where she and her mother had posed just days ago.

"This is not going to be good," I mumbled to myself. I handed Walter the leash. "Do you think you could watch Bones for a minute?" I asked, checking to see if Judy minded.

"Sure," he answered, consumed by the friendly beast.

"Thanks." I trotted after Chloe. My feet kicked up wet sand. With one eye on Chloe and one eye on horizon, I noticed that the sky was streaked with jet streams. I wondered which one Brook had left behind. Did she really think leaving Chloe a note would suffice? I wondered what other promises she'd made and had broken. It wasn't fair.

Chloe scurried up the rock like a lizard. She stared up to the sky and yelled at the top of her lungs, "Momma! Why didn't you take me with you?" She sat down on the edge of the rock, pulled her legs up to her belly, hugged them, then buried her face in her chest. Her hair fell forward, covering her cheeks.

I caught my breath.

The hitch in my breathing made my chest ache.

I wanted Chloe to stay, but not like this. Poor baby.

Slowly I climbed the rock, stepping carefully to keep my balance then sat next to Chloe. I pulled my legs to my chest and hugged them. Her shoulders quaked. Muffled sobs escaped. I let her grieve. What seemed like a lifetime finally passed. I didn't make eye contact as Chloe surfaced for air. "So you know your mom left?"

She sniffed. "Yeah." Her voice wavered. "She left me a note."

"I saw." I glanced sideways. "It fell out of your Junie B. book."

Chloe tucked her sundried hair behind her ears, the ends still wet from dunking her head in the lake. She wiped her nose with the back of her hand. "How come you didn't say anything?"

"Because I didn't know if you knew and it wasn't my place to tell you. Obviously, your dad doesn't know. When did you find her note?"

"When I got home from basketball," she whimpered. "She always does this and I hate it."

I put my arm around her shoulders. "I'm so sorry, honey," I said, forcing the words over the lump in my throat.

I kept my thoughts of Brook to myself. Chloe didn't need my jaded views. Besides, Brook was her mother, and mommas were sacred. The bond between Chloe and her mother was stronger than our new thread of friendship even if it was marred with worn patches ready to snap. Chloe would have to decide in her own time and on her own terms how to deal with Brook. The best thing I could do, was just be there.

Chloe shook out her legs then nuzzled into my side. She was warm. The damp ends of her hair felt cool against my radiated skin as it soaked through my cotton tunic.

"I should have known," Chloe said. "She's not very good at being a mom. I really wanted to go," she sobbed.

With my arm around her shoulder, I held her close. "I know you did."

Chloe's emerald-green eyes were dark like a summer storm, the rims of her eyes red from the thunder.

"Can we go home?" she asked.

"We sure can."

Chloe traced the bones of my hand resting in my lap with her finger. "You're not going to die from your cancer, are you?"

I pulled my arm from around her shoulder and lifted her chin with my finger. "No one really knows what will happen to you when you get sick, but if I have anything to say about it, then no." I searched her eyes for that usual charge.

Chloe reached up and touched my cheek. "Good."

Chapter 35

Chloe and I had planned on sleeping outside, but the drizzle had turned into a steady rain so John pitched Chloe's pup tent in my living room. Secretly, I was glad for an indoor retreat. I hadn't slept on the ground in ages. Bradley was about eleven and he and Beckett had talked me into going camping up north at the Petoskey State Park. My back ached for a week after the adventure, and the bug bites were miserably itchy.

"There, you two lovely ladies are all set," John said as he poked his head out from the pup tent doorway.

"Thanks, Dad," Chloe crooned as she played with Bones. "This will be great. Hey, Maggie." Chloe rearranged her pink and purple plaid sleeping bag.

"Yes, Chloe." I put the graham crackers, chocolate bars, and marshmallows on the coffee table. Bones waddled over, and I scratched his head.

"Can Bones sleep in my tent?" she asked.

"Sure," I answered. Better him than me. "His new dog bed is in the library."

Chloe scooted out of the living room and through the foyer to the library.

I sat on the sofa with my feet up on the table. "I know it's summer, but building a fire is always a good idea."

John sat down at the other end of the sofa. "Good thing you don't have any furniture in this room. I don't know where else we'd put her tent."

I smirked. "We'd find a place. Are you staying for s'mores?"

"Are you kidding me? Yeah," he replied.

I took a sip of my wine. John's green eyes flickered in the fire's light. I held my glass toward him. He picked up his beer and clinked my glass. "Cheers," I said with a wink.

"Cheers. Here's to good neighbors. Make that fabulous neighbors."

"I don't know about fabulous, but I did help you get rid of Nanny Nora, and I'm not so sure I did so well with Brook. I have a dog in need of tweaking his manners, and then there's my mother." I snickered and John's eyes lit up.

"Thank you," he said, tilting his beer bottle in my direction. "Chloe loves you, and you really didn't have to take her overnight."

I glanced into the fire. Flames licked the logs making hot embers for perfectly browned marshmallows. "I have a confession." I took a shallow breath. My chest rose and fell as I listened to Chloe in the library talking to Bones about staying off the furniture. A grin crossed my lips. "I'm glad Chloe didn't go. I would have missed her too much." I paused. "Truth is, she's helping me get through the summer. Nanny Nora and Brook, well, they were just bonus entertainment." I drained my wineglass and peered over the edge of the crystal into John's eyes.

"I have a confession as well," he said, leaning closer to me. "I am really glad she didn't go, too. I would have missed her even more than you, and with her gone, I wouldn't have an excuse to come over here to hang out."

"Well, as long as we are telling all our secrets." I nudged his shoulder. "You don't need an excuse to come over."

John smiled and patted my hand. His warm fingertips were soft, soothing. That was one drawback of living alone. I craved human touch even in the simplest form. I gave his hand a little squeeze and held on just for a moment. "Have you heard from Brook?"

"She called earlier, but I don't want to get into that now. I'd like to enjoy my evening. Let's just say, some things never change. I think she told Chloe she'd take her to get even with you."

I raised an eyebrow in his direction. "That's silly."

He let out a little chuckle. "Come on, she didn't want to share her with you. Here you are, independent, Chloe's newest friend, she doesn't have those things." He paused. "She saw that you were close to Chloe. I don't know if she'll ever have that."

I patted his hand. "Maybe we should make s'mores now?" I knew it was selfish, but I reveled in his compliment.

"Thanks for being here, Maggie," John whispered.

Chloe ran in dragging Voodoo by his purple string behind her. "Is it time for s'mores yet?" she asked, eyeing the goodies on the table.

"Yup," I answered, handing the marshmallow bag to John. "Can you open these for us with your big muscles?"

John flexed his biceps. Chloe giggled then squeezed his arm with pride. He tore open the plastic, popped one into his mouth, then threaded the white sugary pillows onto the roasting sticks. "Can I burn mine?"

I wrinkled my nose in disgust. "I guess," I said, "whatever floats your boat."

Chloe shrugged at me. "It takes all kinds." She unwrapped the chocolate bars and lined up the individual crackers on the table. While she gave her dad instructions on how brown her marshmallows should be, Bones snuck a cracker then ran into the kitchen.

"Tomorrow, we'll have blueberry pancakes for breakfast," I stated, feeling more hungry than I had in months. "Then we'll whip up a batch of cookies just for fun. How does that sound?"

"Woo-hoo," Chloe cheered. "Mom never bakes with me."

I couldn't fathom a house with children and no baking. Baking was a special kind of love. Brook's priorities were different, though, something I didn't understand. "How come your mom never bakes with you?"

"She doesn't like to measure," she answered.

"Oh," I said quietly.

"That's just her excuse. She wants to stay skinny. Mom said it would ruin her body," Chloe added. "She has a reason for everything."

I squished my gooey marshmallow between the graham crackers and chocolate. I took a big bite, savoring every crumb, thinking I didn't have that problem.

John's marshmallow caught fire and he quickly blew it out. "Perfect," he exclaimed.

Chloe wrinkled her nose. "It's black," she moaned. "Gross."

"To you, my sweet pea, it may be black. To me, it's perfection." John put his s'more together, gobbled it down in three bites, and strung another roasting stick with more marshmallows. "One more, then I have to go. You two ladies, I'm sure, have pressing girl stuff to talk about, plus I'm beat."

Chloe and I shot each other a look. "Girl stuff?" we said in unison. Then we both said, "Jinx, you owe me a Coke," at exactly the same time. It had taken most of the summer, but we were beginning to synchronize. Her jack-o'-lantern smile had more gaps. Her hair was longer and touched her shoulders, and she had more freckles on the bridge of her nose. She wasn't the pesky kid hiding in the bushes anymore. She wasn't the annoying, eavesdropping neighbor. She was Chloe. The girl-next-door who stole my heart.

John smiled at me as I watched Chloe nibble around the edges of her treat. Bones licked up the crumbs she dropped on the floor. "I guess I don't need a vacuum anymore," I said, as I licked the oozing chocolate from the edge of my graham cracker sandwich.

Chloe smirked. "Good thing we have Bones."

"Good thing."

John shoved the last nibble into his mouth then drained his beer. "Sleep tight, don't let the bedbugs bite." He picked Chloe up, hugging her only as a daddy could. She wrapped her legs around his torso. It reminded me of times long gone between Beckett and Bradley, and me and my dad. My dad snuggled better than anyone I knew. Chloe wrapped her arms around John's neck and squeezed tight. "'Night, Daddy," she said, after kissing his bristly face.

John set her down on the sofa next to me. He lifted Chloe's chin with his finger. "Mind your manners, kiddo. Maggie has permission to call me."

"I don't think that will be necessary," I said, catching a twinkle in his eye.

He kissed Chloe on the forehead.

I walked him to the door. "'Night," I said as I brushed crumbs from my shirt. "I'm sure we'll be just fine."

John guided me out the door onto the front porch. "I'm sure you will." He leaned close. "'Night, Maggie," he said, before kissing me on the forehead, too.

Fireflies danced across the yard as I watched him go. He blew me a kiss. I peeked over the side of the porch, and thought for sure I caught sight of a fairy.

By the time I got back inside, Chloe was in her pajamas and curled up on the sofa with her Junie B. book. I listened to her read. "You're getting better," I said, enjoying the way her face beamed with pride. I smiled and rumpled her hair. "That Junie B. cracks me up."

Chloe continued to read.

I cleaned up the crackers, chocolate wrappers, and marshmallows, then brushed the crumbs from the table and tossed them into the fire. "You just about ready for bed?"

"Will you come in the tent with me?" Chloe asked.

"Sure, will I fit?" I asked, poking my head inside.

Bones was sacked out in the corner on his back with his feet up in the air.

"You'll fit. You're small, come on," she urged crawling in ahead of me.

Bones grunted and his eyelids twitched. I crawled inside, too, but my feet stuck out the door. I could see the fire. "This is better than being outside."

"Yeah, no bugs," Chloe added. "Maggie—"

"What?" I curled up on my side while Chloe rearranged her special blanket. She reminded me of Bones in a way as she fixed her spot perfectly before nestling in for a good night's sleep.

"I'm glad you don't find me annoying anymore," she said.

I fingered the ends of her fine hair. I smiled. "Me, too," I said, touching her cheek. "Chloe—"

"What?"

"I think I might be the one who is annoying."

"Maybe, that's why we make such a great pair," she said with a smile. "Will you read to me?"

I took the Junie B. book from her, opened the page where she had her cat-shaped bookmark, and began to read.

Chapter 36

Chloe tore through the kitchen as Bones nipped at her heels. I folded the blueberries into the pancake batter while the griddle warmed on the stove. I held my hand over the pan testing the heat. Chloe took a second trip through the kitchen. This time she stopped at the counter and pulled out a stool. I glanced over my shoulder. She began laying out photos of her mother on the counter that she'd taken from my desk. I decided against getting upset that she invaded my privacy, since it was *her* mother. "I see you found your mom's photos." The batter sizzled as I poured eight round pancakes onto the griddle. Chloe's solemn eyes met mine.

"You gonna send these to her?" she asked, rearranging them.

"I don't know. What do you think I should do with them?" I asked, flipping the pancakes. "You could have them."

She stacked them up. "I like this one the best," she said. "You should send them to her. Might help her get a job."

I took the pancakes off the heat, stacked them on a plate, and poured eight more mounds of bubbling blueberry batter onto the griddle. "I like that one, too. Mostly because it has you in it." Chloe held the photo by the corners and studied her mom's face. Brook's hair was tangled with the wind and Chloe had her arms wrapped around her mom from behind. They were laughing. I flipped the pancakes. "Almost done."

Chloe sighed and cradled her face in her hands. "I fall for it every time," she said, blowing hair out of her eyes.

I turned off the burner then added more pancakes to the stack and set them in front of Chloe. "What do you mean?" I asked.

"This isn't the first time my mom has done this." Chloe plucked some pancakes from the platter and put them on her plate. "She's done this twice before. Says she's taking me and then doesn't. I should be used to it by now."

"Oh." I put some pancakes on my plate, came around the counter, and sat down next to her. "Syrup?" I asked, handing her the bottle.

"Will you pour it? When I do, it always dumps out and then I get soggy pancakes." She sniffed her plate.

"Sure." I drizzled squiggly lines of syrup for her. "Is that enough?"

"Whoa, you're good," she praised. "I know I might look like the kind of kid who loves lots of syrup, but I actually prefer my pancakes a little dry. Don't want to drown the yummy blueberries." She plopped a loose berry into her mouth and smacked her lips.

"Twice before, huh?" I said, taking a bite.

"Yeah, once last Christmas when we lived at our old house and once when I was in kindergarten. I don't know why she does it. I must do something bad," Chloe said, shoving a forkful of pancake into her mouth.

I swallowed. "I don't think that's the reason."

"It's weird how she just leaves. At least this time she left a note."

I took another bite pondering Beckett and his father, Chloe and her mom, thinking how lucky I was to never have experienced that thread of heartache. "I'm going to go out on a limb here." I paused, reminded myself that Brook was Chloe's mother, and to tread lightly. "I think she just knows that your dad can take good care of you while she's working. Maybe that's the way it's supposed to be," I offered.

"I don't know, but I gotta remember this for next time. It stinks." She pouted.

"I have to admit, California would have been fun," I said.

"Maybe." Chloe chewed an oversized bite of pancake, a drip of syrup dribbled down her chin. Her cheeks swelled. "These pancakes are delicious." She dropped a bite down to Bones who was hovering around her like a preying alligator ready to snap. His bottom teeth jutted out. "There you go, boy," she said, glancing down in time to see him gobble up the morsel. "He likes them, too," she chirped. "You should send my mom the pictures. She's going to need them. She needs a lot of things."

"That way she can see you every day," I told her.

"That just sounds like something a grown-up would say just to keep a kid out of *pression*."

"What?" I asked, shoveling in another bite.

"You know, *pression*. When you're sad all the time."

"Oh, you mean depression."

"That's what I said," Chloe said, hitting the palm of her hand against her forehead. "Geez."

I swabbed up the trickle of syrup left on my plate with my last bite. "Okay then, let's send them."

Chloe shrugged. "I can hang one on the wall of my room and put another one in my diary."

"Sounds like a great idea. Besides, what would I do with pictures of your mom?"

"Throw eggs at them," Chloe suggested.

"You wouldn't." I narrowed my eyes and eyed her through my lashes.

"I'm pretty mad at her. You never know," she said with wrinkled brow.

"I'd be mad, too, but I don't think I'd throw eggs at my mom's picture. That's kind of mean."

Chloe ate the last bite of her breakfast. "Do you think she thought about me when she left me here?" Her voice cracked as she pushed her plate away then reached for the stack of photographs.

"Wait, can you please wipe off your hands?" I asked, stopping her. "I'm sure she thinks about you more than you know."

Chloe rubbed her hands on a napkin.

"Thanks for spending the night with me. I really like your pup tent," I said.

"I knew you would."

"We better get dressed. Your dad will be here soon."

Chloe's lips turned down. "Bummer."

John knocked at the door an hour later. "Maggie," he called.

"I'm upstairs. Just a second."

John was dismantling the tent in the living room when I came down.

"Chloe's outside running around with Bones." John pulled the poles out of the sleeves. "Chloe said you are going to send Brook's photos to her. That's awfully nice of you."

"Yeah, I'd like to take credit, but it was Chloe's idea."

His eyes flashed. "Brook's not stable, you know. It's probably better this way anyway."

"Do you think?" I folded up Chloe's sleeping bag. "Would you ever consider getting back together with her?"

He stopped in his tracks and his green eyes flashed. "No. We've talked about this before," he said sternly.

I picked Voodoo up from the floor. "Sorry, I just want to make sure."

"Maggie, Maggie, Maggie," he mumbled, shaking his head.

I knew he thought I was foolish. I squeezed my eyes shut momentarily, tried to compose myself, and hide the heat in my cheeks. He put his hands on my waist. I waited for Chloe's intrusion.

"I will never go back to that. We were never a good match."

"Why?" I said, trying to escape his dark expression.

"Maybe you should let it go. I did." John rubbed

his temples. "You're exasperating," he moaned through clenched teeth.

I smiled just a little bit. "I know. Last night, I told Chloe that I was the annoying one."

John put his hands on my shoulders. A thin smile passed over his lips. "I meant what I said. I think we should give this a try. I know you're scared, but damn, woman, let it go, let it all go."

"I don't know if I can. I don't want to hurt Chloe."

The words barely escaped my lips, and he was out the door.

"Anyone in here?" Mom called through the house.

"Great." I slouched down into the sofa as far as I could go, thinking maybe she'd disappear.

"Apparently, I missed a good time last night." She walked around in front of me. "What's the long face for? Everything okay?"

"What's wrong with me?" I asked. "John's a perfectly nice man and I can't even—" Emotion choked me. I put the throw pillow on my face, letting out a shriek. "I am such a dork."

The couch shifted as Mom sat down. She patted my knee.

"You're not a dork by any means. Maybe a little off, confused, but not a dork, honey, and yes, John's a nice man, and very handsome. And no, I don't know what you're waiting for. Nothing will ever be perfect. You already had that and he turned out to be gay."

I peeked out from behind the pillow covering my eyes. Mom leaned her head back against the sofa.

"Marjorie Jean," she said with a sigh. I'm not getting any younger and neither are you." She squeezed her eyes shut. "What in Lord's name do you have to lose?

I believed she was praying. I covered my face again with the pillow. "Everything," I said.

"You're not going to lose everything. Quit with the theatrics and get on with your life. God didn't put you on this earth to live in this big house alone forever."

"Easy for you to say," I retorted. "You live alone, and you're fine." Warm surges flooded my body. I uncovered my face and intercepted my mother's scowl.

She huffed. "Have it your way," she said as she got up. "Sometimes you just have to take a chance."

Chapter 37

Rain pounded against the roof. The weather forecast hadn't predicted rain, but then again, it was Michigan. Bones huddled under my desk at my feet. Keeping focused proved difficult knowing Chloe was next door mourning the loss of her mother. My phone chimed with a text. I peered over the top of my glasses to read it.

Chloe wants to know if she can still go to dog classes with you now that she is staying home with me. She knows you went again without her.

I typed back my answer. *Yes. Class is tomorrow night at 6:00.* I added a winking smiling face. I put the phone down then picked up my paintbrush. I dipped it in the orange paint. My phone chimed again. I poked at the screen with one finger to read John's next message.

Are you mad at me?

A wild grin crept across my lips contemplating the possibility. I tapped at the letters on the screen. *I thought you were the one who was mad at me.* I pressed the send button.

I waited for a response, as I continued painted my orange Halloween cows. John didn't respond.

The doorbell rang.

Thunderclouds rolled overhead.

I answered the front door.

John stood on the porch with his hands stuffed in his pockets, his shoulders dotted with water spots. "Can I come in?"

I pushed the screen door open. "Sure."

He took his hands out of his pockets and closed the door quietly behind him as he closed the distance between us. I held my ground. Our eyes locked. "Where's Chloe?" I whispered as John leaned into me and put his hands on my waist.

"She's with the Mark Spitz boys, as you call them. There are two new boys on Harry and Walter's block and they're all playing in some fancy treehouse. Chloe said something about hunting for fairies and magic pebbles."

I smiled. "Sounds like fun." The weight of John's body rested on mine. Electricity sparked behind his green eyes. "What's this all about?" Anticipation filled my belly.

"This," he whispered.

His lips grazed mine. I let my hands wander across his chest as I searched his eyes. He held me close. "I can be stubborn, too. You are messing with the wrong man."

His breathy words tickled my ear. "I know," I replied. I swallowed away hesitation before kissing him. When I opened my eyes, John was staring at me.

"Now, we're getting somewhere," he said, brushing back stray curls from my face.

"I just don't want—" I paused, searching his eyes for understanding.

He put his finger on my lips. "Stop worrying, Maggie. If it is meant to be, it will work out."

Focusing on his stare, I tuned the world out around me. "But Chloe—"

"Shush," he whispered. "I know you don't want to hurt Chloe. We will take baby steps."

I closed my eyes. I was always the good girl. I did what I thought was expected. I made sure everyone around me was okay. Now, I teetered on the edge of unconventionality.

John stood before me with blazing green eyes, a horseshoe tattoo on his left shoulder, and words of promise. I was a middle-aged woman with a grown son being chased by a handsome neighbor with a seven-year-old daughter. Mom's voice rang in my head, urging me to let go of my perfect ideals.

John caressed my cheek then kissed my forehead.

In that moment, the past slipped away as my heart beat wildly, and I surrendered.

Maggie's journey continues in: *Maggie's Fork in the Road*

CPSIA information can be obtained at www.ICGtesting.com
Printed in the USA
BVOW06s0756161115

427022BV00007B/82/P